DEAD OF
WINTER

KRESLEY COLE

DEAD OF WINTER

THE ARCANA CHRONICLES

SIMON AND SCHUSTER

First published in Great Britain by Simon & Schuster UK Ltd, 2015
A CBS COMPANY
Originally published in the USA in 2015 by Simon & Schuster Books for Young Readers,
an imprint of Simon & Schuster Children's Division, New York.

1 3 5 7 9 10 8 6 4 2

Simon & Schuster UK Ltd
1st Floor, 222 Gray's Inn Road
London WC1X 8HB
www.simonandschuster.co.uk

Simon & Schuster Australia, Sydney
Simon & Schuster India, New Delhi

A CIP catalogue record for this book
is available from the British Library

Hardback ISBN 978-1-4711-2284-2
Paperback ISBN 978-1-4711-2285-9
Ebook ISBN 978-1-4711-2286-6

Printed a

places and
or are used

DEDICATED WITH MUCH LOVE TO THE
EXTRAORDINARY CHRISTINA LAUREN
(CHRISTINA HOBBS AND LAUREN BILLINGS).
IT ALL BEGAN ON A BUS . . .

ACKNOWLEDGMENTS

My deepest thanks . . .

To my editor, Zareen Jaffery, and the production department at S&S Books for Young Readers, for letting me color outside the lines (lifesavers)!

To Marie L., for your invaluable assistance with Cajun French, and for patiently answering all my questions. ("We'd use *sauve* for a guy?" "Why is there an English word in the translation?" "*Lier* versus *amarrer*. Thoughts?")

To Beth Kendrick and Barbara Ankrum, for all your support and eagle-eyed beta reads!

I couldn't have done this without you all!

— *The Major Arcana* —

0. *The Fool, Gamekeeper of Old (Matthew)*
I. *The Magician, Master of Illusions (Finneas)*
II. *The High Priestess, Ruler of the Deep*
III. *The Empress, Our Lady of Thorns (Evie)*
IV. *The Emperor, Stone Overlord*
~~V. The Hierophant, He of the Dark Rites (Guthrie)~~
VI. *The Lovers, Duke & Duchess Most Perverse (Vincent & Violet)*
VII. *The Chariot, Wicked Champion*
VIII. *Strength, Mistress of Fauna (Lark)*
~~IX. The Hermit, Master of Alchemy (Arthur)~~
X. *Wheel of Fortune, Lady of Fate*
~~XI. Justice, She Who Harrows (Spite)~~
XII. *The Hanged Man, Our Lord Uncanny*
XIII. *Death, The Endless Knight (Aric)*
~~XIV. Temperance, Collectress of Sins (Calanthe)~~
~~XV. The Devil, Foul Desecrator (Ogen)~~
XVI. *The Tower, Lord of Lightning (Joules)*
~~XVII. The Star, Arcane Navigator~~
XVIII. *The Moon, Bringer of Doubt (Selena)*
XIX. *The Sun, Hail the Glorious Illuminator*
XX. *Judgment, The Archangel (Gabriel)*
XXI. *The World, This Unearthly One (Tess)*

THE FIELD OF BATTLE

During the Flash, a global cataclysmic flare, the surface of the earth was scorched to ash, and bodies of water evaporated. All plant life was killed, most animals as well. The vast majority of humans perished, with women hardest hit. After months of total drought, rain falls constantly. The sun has ceased to rise, leaving the world in endless night. Plague spreads.

OBSTACLES

Militias unify, consolidating power. Slavers and cannibals hunt for new victims. All are bent on capturing females. The Bagmen, contagious zombies created by the Flash, roam the dark, thirsting for moisture, especially blood.

FOES

The Arcana. Into every dark age, twenty-two kids are born with supernatural powers and destined to fight in a life-or-death game. Our stories are depicted on the Major Arcana cards of a Tarot deck. I'm the Empress; we play again *now*. In my sights: the Lovers, who hold Jack captive.

ARSENAL

To defeat the Lovers and the others, I'll have to draw on my Empress powers: enhanced healing, the ability to control anything that roots or blooms, thorn tornadoes— and poison. Because I'm the princess of it. . . .

DEAD OF WINTER

1

Inhale exhale inhale exhale

As I raced over the countryside on horseback, I kept hearing deep, ragged breaths.

Rain fell from the black sky, drops pelting my face. Winds whipped my horse's mane and made my poncho hood flap.

But I still heard breaths.

The tiny hairs on my nape rose. My mare snorted, her ears pricked forward. I didn't have Lark's animal keenness or the senses of a huntress like Selena, but I could feel someone—or some*thing*—watching me.

Stalking me?

Inhale exhale

I rode harder, pushing myself, pushing my staggering horse, forcing her to navigate the rocky terrain faster than was safe.

I hadn't slept since fleeing Death's lair days ago—if you could call them "days" in this never-ending darkness. Sheer will kept me in the saddle. Delirium was taking hold.

Maybe nothing stalked me, and my own breaths sounded foreign to my ears. If I could just rest for a few minutes . . .

Focus, Evie! So much was on the line. Jack's *life* was.

I was determined to save him from the Lovers, Vincent and Violet Milovníci.

Sadistic Vincent had captured him; Violet journeyed to meet up with her brother. Once they reunited, those twin serial killers would torture Jack with their *contraptions.*

I raced to beat Violet, taking untold risks. Even now, I couldn't believe what I'd done to escape Aric.

Every other minute, a raindrop would hit one of my eyes directly, the sting blurring my vision. I would blink to clear my eyes, and details of my last encounter with Death would blossom in my mind. . . .

The feel of his sword-roughened palms as he'd seized my waist and laid me in his bed. His rasped words: "If you surrender to me, you will be mine alone. My wife in truth. I will do anything to have that." Even coercing me, promising to save Jack—for a price.

Blink.

His scent—sandalwood, pine, masculine—had weakened my will like a drug, quelling the heat of battle inside me. Still I'd managed to say: "This won't work out as you plan."

Blink.

His head had inched closer, his amber eyes intent, just before his lips had covered mine. His kiss had a way of muddling my thoughts, making me forget all the things I needed to remember.

Blink.

"There. That's better," he'd murmured as he'd removed my clothes. "Just let me see you . . . touch you." With his supernatural strength, he must have taken pains not to rip the lace of my panties.

When I lay naked before him, his amber eyes had glittered like stars. Pinpoints of light had mesmerized me. "So lovely, *sievā.* My gods, you humble me." He'd given me one of his rare unguarded smiles. "This is joy I feel, is it not?" I'd wanted to sob.

Blink. Blink. Blink.

I shook my head hard. I needed to pay attention. I couldn't afford to get lost in memories. To get *lost* at all.

When I'd readied a bug-out bag and my gear in a panic, Matthew had telepathically directed me: —*Follow the rushing water upstream into slaver territory. Find the soot valley, then travel its length. If you reach the mass gravesite, you've gone too far. Ascend the next mountain to the stone forest.—*

Yet since then, he hadn't answered any of my calls.

I reached the end of a soot-filled valley and started the climb. Rain began to pour.

Minutes? hours? days? passed. Despite the threat I'd sensed, I could barely stay awake. My head kept dipping. Maybe I could close my eyes—just for a second. I dropped forward, resting my cheek against the horse's mane, an arm on either side of her neck.

My lids slid shut.

When I opened them, I was at Haven.

The mare was gone. No rain, no winds. The sky was star-strewn black. All around me, that eerie A.F. silence.

Matthew, am I in one of your visions? Every detail felt so real. Bitter ash tinged my tongue. The scent of scorched oaks and sugarcane stung my nose. In the distance, Haven House was a blackened ruin. My mother's funeral pyre.

I'd burned her body and our home.

Jack had secretly helped her die. I understood *why*. I didn't accept *how*. I couldn't reconcile *after*.

How many lies he'd told.

Grief ripped through me, for my mother, for our life before the Flash. My new existence was so brutal and visceral, I wondered if my pre-apocalypse memories were actually a soft and hazy dream.

What was real? *Un*real?

Though Matthew had looked away when my mom had died, he could still access scenes from the past. Was he giving me the memory of her death?

A breeze feathered over the ash on the ground, the sound beautiful— like sighing. I heard my mother's faint voice telling Jack, "Use the pillow. . . ."

No, Matthew! I'm not ready to see this! Not ready—
A wolf's howl pierced the night.

I jolted awake in the saddle. The rain had dwindled to a foggy drizzle. How long had I been out?

I rubbed my gritty eyes. Almost screamed. I was surrounded by shadowy figures.

Wait, not *figures*. All around me were towering stacks of rocks, placed like logs for a bonfire. There were so many stacks the area resembled a forest. The stone forest.

Who would waste calories to assemble these? And why did I find them so chilling?

Matthew, are you there?

At last, I felt his presence in my mind! —*Empress!*—

Has Violet joined her brother yet?

—*The Violet is not there.*—

Oh, thank God.

—*Soon.*—

Shit! *You told me Vincent camped within days of Death's castle. I've ridden for DAYS.*

—*Arcana all around.*—

I heard their calls, as if from a sound-out. . . .

—*Eyes to the skies, lads!*— Joules.

—*Trapped in the palm of my hand.*— Tess.

—*I watch you like a hawk.*— Gabriel.

—*Behold the Bringer of Doubt!*— Selena.

—*Don't look at* this *hand, look at* that *one.*— Finn.

—*Crazy like a fox.*— Matthew.

—*We will love you. In our own way.*— The Lovers.

So many Arcana were close. Which meant *I* was close.

—*Terror from the abyss!*— Huh?

Before I could ask about the new call, my sense of being watched returned. I jerked my head around.

4

—Empress, you're one stone forest and one clearing away. Some . . . obstacles between us.—

Movement. Out of the corner of my eye, I saw a man skulking from one stack of rocks to the next.

Another man loped to join the first. The armed pair wore fatigues and creepy night-vision goggles. Soldiers of the Lovers' army?

The stones were for cover, staged as if for a paint-ball course! How long had those men been lying here in wait?

Matthew, I'm in trouble! I slapped the reins against the mare. She whinnied a protest, but increased her speed. Chest heaving, she wound around the stacks.

I craned my head back. Two soldiers had become ten, all with rifles at the ready. Now they walked in plain view. Because I was already surrounded?

As the ground began to flatten, those stacks grew fewer. I raised my hand above my eyes, straining to see. Ahead—the clearing Matthew had spoken of!

My face fell. With no vegetation, it was a quagmire, water and muck pooling in huge craters.

Past that, a wall towered, must be thirty feet high. What lay behind it?

A shot rang out; a bullet whizzed by my head. My mount fled from the sound. "Go, *GO!*"

In my panic, my nails morphed into thorn claws. The razor-sharp edges sliced through the fingers of my gloves. My glyphs stirred, moving over my skin.

A second gunshot. The near-miss bullet pitted the mud beside the horse's hooves. She shrieked, trotting faster.

The shooters missed on purpose. They would want me—and the horse—alive.

Women and horses were two valuable A.F. commodities.

Desperate for safety, I squinted at the wall. Men guarded a brightly lit gate.

5

—Head there, Empress.—

My mare would have to slog through the clearing. It was like a moat fronting that wall. The soldiers would catch me long before then.

A bright color drew my attention. Attached to a post was a handcrafted sign emblazoned with a red skull and crossbones—along with the warning: DANGER! MINES!

And that explained the craters.

Are you kidding, Matthew? Soldiers trailing me; mines ahead. *How do I get past a minefield?*

An agonized yell sounded behind me.

I dared a glance back. Only nine soldiers followed. They ran toward me at a faster clip. The ones at the edges aimed their guns—off to their sides.

Another horrified yell.

And another.

Open gunfire erupted. Muzzle flashes warred with fog; I couldn't make out anything.

I turned forward. Screamed.

Three soldiers stood before me, rifles trained on my face. The mare reared, punching hooves at them.

The other gunmen had been pushing me toward these!

Yet behind them, a black beast melded with shadow. One brilliant golden eye gleamed like a lantern.

Cyclops! Had Lark sent her one-eyed wolf to protect me?

Baring dagger-size fangs, the massive beast gave a spine-chilling snarl. The men twisted around—

Cyclops launched himself at the panic-stricken soldiers, knocking them to the ground. His mighty jaws clamped down on limbs and rifles, snapping through bone and metal.

Body parts sailed into the air. Blood spurted like a mall fountain. I winced, though I should be used to seeing stuff like this.

The wolf lifted his head from the carnage and growled at the stupefied soldiers positioned behind me. Those bastards had driven me into a trap; Cyclops *ate* the trap.

Faced with the beast's dripping maw, they fled headlong.

For me, Cyclops wagged his scarred tail. "Good damn wolf. Good boy."

Matthew said: —*Ride for the fort! You have to make it to the wall.*—

What's behind the wall? For all I knew, Matthew was sending me into the Milovnícis' camp.

—*RIDE!*—

Into mines? We're going to get blown away! Forget my self-healing powers; I couldn't regenerate from decapitation.

—*Go left.*—

Directing me around the danger?

I turned to Cyclops. "I don't know if you can understand me, or if Lark is steering her familiar. But follow my mount carefully unless you want to regrow limbs." He was still limping from our battle with the Devil Card.

He chuffed, and bubbles of blood formed over his snout. With a swish of his tail, he defiantly snapped up a dismembered arm, carrying it like a chew toy. But he did move behind me.

I'm trusting you, Matthew. I swallowed and guided my horse left.

—*MY left!*—

Quick correction. Cyclops followed.

—*Faster, Empress. Or the Azey will figure out our mine moat maze.*—

Your what? *Who are the Azey?*

—*A.S.E. Army of the Southeast. Go right for three seconds. Then left.*—

Holding my breath, I slapped the reins yet again. One thousand one, one thousand two, one thousand three. I tugged the reins to my right.

—*Faster!*—

Soon I was galloping through a minefield, a telepathic Arcana in my mind and a giant wolf at my heels.

I could hear those same wet breaths. The wolf had been following me! If I lived through this night, I was *so* going to owe Lark.

The gate creaked open ahead. I spurred the mare, racing to reach the fort.

With no idea what awaited me . . .

2

The gates slammed closed behind Cyclops's tail.

Matthew was there to greet us, wearing a vacant smile. When he crossed to me and held up his arms, I fell out of the saddle, legs gone boneless. He caught me against himself, helping me stand.

"What is this place?" I wheezed, taking in details. The wall was made of scrap metal: car hoods, road signs, rebar. Large military-style housing tents were spread out over a sizable area. Covered torches hung on lines above, casting light.

"The hunter was busy while you were away."

"This is Jack's?" Horses dozed in a stable, chickens clucked in a coop, and dozens of people milled about.

All guys, naturally. They stared not only at me—a female—but at my colossal one-eyed bodyguard, currently scarfing down the last of his human chew toy. *Wolves gotta eat.*

Matthew peeled me off him, shoving one of his sleeves up. "Take off your gloves, Empress."

I did, too exhausted to protest. My head spun like I'd just stepped off a playground round-a-bout.

He brandished a knife and sliced his pale arm before I could stop him. Then he used his blood to draw a line over the back of my icon hand. "This is Gamekeeper's blood. There's protection here." Crimson crossed over the two markings of my Arcana kills, as if to cancel them out. "Lots of other Arcana here, but we have trues. No one strikes on hallowed ground."

"Truce?"

"*Trues*. The true-hearted cards," he said, adding darkly, "for a time." Matthew had created a war-free area with a power I hadn't known about.

I gazed up at him. In the last three months, he'd grown even taller. Had his birthday passed? Was he seventeen yet? He wore a water-proof parka, a wool button-down, jeans, and a pair of hiking boots, all newish looking. Had Jack sourced clothes for him?

As Aric had done for me?

Inner shake. "Thank you, Matthew. You got me here safely."

With his brown eyes as adoring as a puppy's, he asked, "The Empress is my friend?" He used to declare this. Now he had to ask.

Was I still pissed that he'd covered up Jack's lies? I'd been furious when he'd taught Aric how to neutralize my powers, but Matthew had probably saved my life by doing that.

Maybe I needed to accept that he did everything for a reason. I'd trusted him to steer me through a minefield (talk about a team-building exercise). I'd relied on his mysterious guidance to escape Death.

But trusting Matthew completely would be like falling backward. A free fall. Was I ready?

Life had been too short for grudges before the Flash. Now . . . "Evie *is* your friend." I wrapped my arms around him, hugging him tight. When I pulled back, I said, "Matthew, where is Jack?"

"The hunter is nigh."

"How do I get to him?"

"Horse."

A nondescript middle-aged man approached. With a wary glance at the wolf, he took the mare's reins, promising to care for her. Oh. Horse.

As the guy led her to the stable, I made a mental note to grow her a treat. "Who are all these people?" Some cleaned weapons beneath a bright tarp—the kind you used to see at raucous tailgate parties. Others were heating water and doing laundry.

"Humans. Jack collects them. I like their soup."

"Do they know what we are?"

"Jack lets them think we're gods. They call this Fort Arcana, established Year 1 A.F."

"What about keeping ourselves secret? You told me Arcana and non-Arcana mix poorly. You told me humans burn what they fear."

A glimmer of something unsettling crossed Matthew's features. "There aren't enough humans left to consider."

I'd have to think about that later. "Matthew, I need to get to—"

"The watchtower!" He stepped onto a narrow board path that ran through the muddy camp like a freeway. A plankway. Off he went.

"The what?" My legs were so tired, I could barely balance as I tried to keep up.

Cyclops padded along beside me, his frizzy black fur shimmying. His scarred snout was just to the right of my head, his filthy whiskers almost brushing my cheek. His enormous paws sloshed mud up my pants.

Was that a finger stuck in the knotted scruff under his chin?

I trailed Matthew to the far side of the fort. "Did you send me a vision of my mother? Or did I dream?"

Over his shoulder, he said, "Our enemies laugh. Smite and mad. Fall and struck."

That was his answer? Sometimes I wanted to grab him and shake him.

"We're here." Along the back wall stood a three-story structure, clad in metal sheeting. Matthew climbed a ladder to the top.

I followed, leaving the wolf to prowl below. At every rung, I wheezed and winced. "Can we . . . please talk about . . . a rescue for Jack?"

At the top level, Matthew tilted up a license plate, revealing a small slot. "Empress." He motioned for me to peer out.

"Okay, what am I looking at? Oh, wow." We were high up on a

blustery vantage with a sheer drop-off. A river that looked as broad as the Mississippi coursed below. An amazing sight. Before the rains, there'd been no bodies of water like this.

"The placement of this fort is genius." That minefield moat bordered three sides of the wall, while this steep bluff and river protected the fourth.

"Jack," he said simply. "Fort Arcana grew from you. The mission . . ."

When he couldn't find me at Death's, Jack had targeted the Lovers for me—and for him. He'd had his own vendetta against the Milovnícis.

I gazed across the water at an opposing bluff. Fires dotted the area. Tents stretched for what seemed like miles. A few rock ridges jutted upward, offering protection from attack.

"Is that the Army of the Southeast?" It was huge. I tried to imagine where Jack was being kept. To be this close to him . . .

"Half of the Azey. Azey South. Azey North's not too far away."

Which meant Violet wasn't too far away either. How to get to Jack before she did? "I don't suppose this wind ever dies down?" I could launch spores from here, putting all the soldiers to sleep. Then I'd take a boat across, stroll into their camp, and drag Jack out.

"The winds go all night. Which is all day."

There went that idea—

Shots erupted from across the river, lots of them at one time. My stomach dropped as the sounds echoed over the water. I whirled around to Matthew. "Not him?"

"No. Daily execution." How the Milovnícis kept the rank and file in line.

I sagged with such relief, I almost felt guilty. Then I wondered how those shots had affected Jack.

"He believes no help is coming," Matthew whispered. "Knows he can't escape. Thinks his friends are dead."

The idea of Jack alone, with no hope, gutted me. "Is he . . . is he scared?"

"Certain he'll die. Surprised by how *un*frightened he is."

"You can tell? You always had trouble reading him."

Nod. "Three months' practice."

"But you can't read his future?"

Matthew's brows drew together. "Never wanted this to happen."

"Can you tell him we're coming for him?"

Without a word, Matthew crossed to the ladder and climbed down. I clumsily followed. Back on the ground, he said, "Your alliance is injured."

Did he mean that my allies were benched, or that my alliance was shaky? "Are you taking me to Finn and Selena?" I hadn't seen them in months.

"Across the courtyard to the barracks." Matthew started away again, heading in a different direction, balancing on the boards.

With Cyclops at my side, I tromped along the mud-caked planks through a central area, like a quad (*courtyard* might be a stretch).

When Matthew stopped in front of a tent, I bade the wolf stay outside. He snuffled indignantly, plunking down in the mud.

Taking a deep breath, I tugged down my poncho hood and entered, Matthew behind me.

Selena and Finn lay on cots. The Archer's arm was in a sling—her bow arm. An arrow stretched over her lap, and she petted the feather fletchings, the sound like riffled cards. She stared, seemingly at nothing.

One of Finn's legs was splinted, elevated on a bug-out bag. A metal crutch leaned beside his cot.

A fire burned in the center of the tent, vented out of the roof. More Arcana sat on benches around it: the Tower, Judgment, and the World Card, an alliance of three.

Joules sized me up. Gabriel tilted one of his black wings in greeting. Tess Quinn waved shyly, her fingernails bitten to the quick. Matthew dropped down to sit beside her.

"Well, if it isn't our fair Empress," Joules said in his thick Irish accent.

Selena shot upright, her silver-blond hair tumbling over her shoulders.

"Evie!" Finn called. "How did you get free of Death?"

This could get tricky. "Uh, I had an opportunity to . . . steal away." Steal Death's horse and saddle, steal a new bug-out bag, steal my hi-tech all-weather gear. "It's not important. I'm here now."

"Yet you didn't accept my offer." Joules's reddish brown hair was disheveled, his gaze cagey.

Selena—who'd called out no greeting—said, "If you got a jump on Death to escape, then you could have brought Joules's payment."

Aric hadn't been the only one to offer a deal to save Jack. Joules had demanded Death's severed head in exchange for a rescue. "It's not that simple," I told them. "Things aren't how we thought them."

"Did you have a chance to kill the Reaper or not?" Whatever Joules read in my expression made him say, "You feckin' did! A shot at the Endless Knight! The one who always bloody wins!"

Selena's lips parted. "Death dies; J.D. lives. What part of that equation are you having problems with?"

"We can hash everything out later." I was nearly choking with worry and exhausted to the point of kicking toes-up. "For now, let's focus on—"

"We were in an alliance to defeat Death," Selena bit out. "One you started. When Matthew told us you'd recovered your powers, we believed you'd do whatever it took to free J.D.—especially from the psychotic Lovers." Selena swiped a hand over her livid face. "Instead, you betrayed all of us. J.D. more than anyone! Do you know what they'll do to him?"

My grandmother had told me they warped and perverted their victims, making them confuse torture and pain for pleasure. "I have an idea!" My glyphs moved over my skin, a sign of high emotion—or aggression. But I grappled for patience. "Which is why we need to stop arguing over things that can't be changed and start planning a rescue!"

Maybe Gabriel had done a flyover for recon on the army; he'd know the lay of the land across the river. We could plot a mission.

"*Start* planning?" Selena sneered. "You don't have a plan? You've got some nerve to show up here with no answers and no payment, sauntering in with your fancy new clothes, looking like you haven't missed a meal."

Exactly the way she'd looked when I'd first met *her*.

"Because of you, J.D. is suffering right now." Voice rising with each word, she said, "You should have paid the Tower!" With her supernatural speed, she leapt from the cot, lunging to attack.

3

Selena's good hand was in the air, poised to backhand me; instinctively my thorn claws shot out—

"Gamekeeper's blood!" Matthew cried.

Selena and I both screamed in pain, matching red lines glowing across our hands.

Cyclops sprang inside the tent, baring his monstrous fangs at her. I used Selena's moment of shock to scramble back.

Tess whimpered and shrank away from the beast; Gabriel flared his wings.

"Th-that wolf was dead!" Finn sputtered from his cot. "The cannibals killed all of Lark's war wolves."

Joules opened his palm upright; a silver baton materialized out of thin air—one of his lightning javelins. In a blur, it extended to its full length. "My bolt once fried that very beast!"

Which was why Cyclops's fur was frizzy. "Lark's familiars are . . . hardy." I withheld the full truth: her three wolves were undying—as long as Lark lived.

"It's protecting you?" Selena looked aghast.

"He won't hurt anyone unless I'm in danger."

"You're allied with Lark now?" Finn's gaze darted from me to

Matthew, as if the Fool should've told them this. "Even after she sold us out?"

Matthew rocked back and forth on the bench.

"Lark didn't know us when she made the pact to hand us over to Death," I explained. "For all she knew, we could've been cannibals like the Hierophant's followers."

Finn peered at Cyclops. "But then she did get to know us," he said to the wolf.

Hoping Lark was listening through her familiar?

"And she still betrayed us. *Me.* For days, we were down there in the pitch dark because of her, and the water kept rising, about to drown us." He visibly shook from the memory, and a soft whine came from the wolf's chest. "When I realized she'd played me, it—laid—me—out."

"If the Empress is allied with Lark, then she's allied with Death," Joules said. " She might be here to open the gates for them while we sleep."

I rubbed my still burning hand. "We don't have time for this!"

"You have no idea what we went through over these months." Selena sank down on her cot, adjusting her arm sling. "And it was all to save you from Death!"

Finn tucked his dirty-blond hair behind his ears. "While you were getting chummy with our enemies, we took a cruise through hell."

They made it sound like I'd waltzed over to the other side without a care. "Enough! You all went through hardships, but so have I."

Selena cast me a *bitch, please* look, goading me to say more.

"A cruise through hell is when a cloven-footed monster tells you he's about to feast on your bones—and you believe him." I let that sink in. "Lark stayed by my side to fight Ogen—even as he grew three stories tall! Because of her loyalty to me, she lies in a bed with broken bones."

Finn winced at that. He wasn't over the girl by a long shot.

"I'd be dead if not for her and those wolves." When I gestured at Cyclops, he lay down, sphinxlike and regal. The effect was offset by the finger he still wore in his scruff.

"We heard when Ogen got capped." Joules used the tail of his coat to polish that lethal spear. Cryptic symbols adorned the already gleaming metal. "Didn't quite believe who did the deed."

"It was Death. To save me and Lark."

Excitement shone in Joules's gaze. "He eliminated one from his own alliance. He'll be weaker now. Unless you really are Ogen's replacement?"

I pinched the bridge of my nose, accepting I'd never get through to these people about Aric. And could I truly vouch for him anyway? "Joules, will you help me rescue Jack?"

"For all we know, you'll go get cozy with Vincent and Violet, just like you did with Death and Lark. My alliance won't touch this. We came here to do a job. Job got canceled. We leave tomorrow."

Though Gabriel and Tess hadn't said a word, I sensed they wanted to help. But Joules was like their all-powerful labor leader.

"If you're a mercenary, then what else can I pay you?" I studied his face, trying to gauge my opponent and gain an advantage—like perceptive Jack often did. "Come on, Joules. Everybody wants something."

Death had desired me in his bed; Selena desired Jack. Lark longed to live past her teens. Ogen had hungered for sacrifices on an altar.

Joules was impossible to read, like a bubbling cauldron. Tess was an open book, but I saw nothing for me to use. Mysterious Gabriel had a poker face.

"All I want is Death's head." Because Aric had killed Joules's girlfriend (in self-defense). "Seems I might get it anyway. He'll be comin' after you. Just like the other games."

The unstoppable Endless Knight. I shivered.

"And we'll be waitin'." Joules rose to leave, twirling that javelin, skirting around Cyclops.

Chewing a fingernail, Tess followed. "Sorry, guys."

Gabriel hesitated at the tent flap. "Farewell." His gaze flicked to Selena and back so fast, I almost missed the yearning in his green eyes.

A few months ago, I'd suspected his attraction to the stunning Archer, but his feelings had grown. How to use this?

He exited, leaving me with Selena, Finn, and Matthew.

In a defeated tone, Selena said, "You don't know what it did to J.D., imagining how Death was hurting you."

"I have a good idea, since I was out of my mind worrying about him taking on the Lovers' army and other Arcana. I can just as easily blame you three for his capture!"

"J.D. wouldn't see reason." She retrieved that arrow, petting the flights as if for comfort. "He was crazed for months; then you just abandoned him."

Finn exhaled a long breath. "Look, Eves, I'm sorry about the rough welcome. If you come up with a rescue plan, I want to hear it. I'll help in any way I can."

"How, Magician?" Selena scoffed. "You can't walk without a crutch. I can't draw my bow. How do we take on an army? Joules and Gabriel were our best option."

"I'll infiltrate the camp," I said. "Finn can disguise me as a soldier before I set out." If his illusion would last that long. "He doesn't have to leave the fort. Once I'm across the river, I'll put the guards to sleep with my spores."

"The camp's enormous," Selena said. "How will we know which tent Jack's in?"

We? "The wolf can track his scent." Cyclops chuffed, his exhalation stoking the fire.

Finn adjusted his splint. "In my condition, I don't know if I can cloak an enormous wolf. People are easier."

"Besides, we can't cross the river by boat." Selena tapped the arrow against her chin. "It's controlled by the High Priestess. If we get anywhere near the water, she'll drag us down to the deep."

Terror from the abyss! "She's here? Is she working with the Lovers?" We all glanced at Matthew for an answer, but he stared at his hand. Which meant the subject was closed for him.

I turned back to Selena. "You keep saying *we*. As you told me, you can't draw a bow."

"I guess I'll use a pistol. Or a sword. Even injured, I still have my superhuman reflexes and strength." Her modesty too!

I vacillated, then nodded. "Okay, we'll have to figure out another way across. Is there a bridge?"

"A few miles away," Selena said. "The one where J.D. got nabbed. The Azey patrols it heavily."

With each of her words, my hopes sank. *How to get to Jack? How to get to . . .*

An idea arose. "If we can't go across the river or around it, then we'll go above it."

4

"I'm getting Gabriel to take us over."

Selena rolled her dark brown eyes. "Jesus, ditz. Pop some Adderall. They just got through saying they wouldn't get involved for anything less than Death."

"Did *they* say it? I have a feeling Gabriel will help me." Because I was going to get Selena to flirt with him. Desperate times . . . "They might have this mercenary thing going, but who says he can't moonlight?"

"He's a decent dude," Finn said. "Can't hurt to ask him one on one."

"I'll just go talk to him." I turned to the Archer. "I'll let you know what happens, when I get a spare minute."

Selena's reaction? Her signature *the hell* expression. "Fine! I'll show you where their tent is." She draped a coat over her shoulders like a cape.

I turned to Cyclops. "You're going to stay here with Finn and Matthew." Talking to the animal always made me feel ridiculous (though he was smarter than most beasts—and I might actually be communicating with Lark).

In CLC, the loony bin I'd been clapped up in, patients had only been allowed to watch classic shows on cable, like *Lassie*. I feared any second I was going to say, "What's that, Cyclops? Timmy fell down a Prepper well?"

Selena and I had barely exited the tent before she started criticizing me. "Talk about a long shot. Joules and Gabe are like"—she raised two twined fingers—"*this*. They've had a whirlwind bromance. I'm giving us a one in a billion chance. Which means you're an idiot."

I glared. "Do you know how climbing ivy clings to brick? It pokes and pokes until it finds a weak spot to burrow into. We can do the same. Unless you've got something better to occupy your time?"

She pursed her lips. But she must've seen I was at my limit, because she said, "I'm here, aren't I?"

"Okay, let's talk Lovers." When Matthew had given me my memories of previous games, he'd said they would come sporadically (in order to guard my sanity—har).

I tried to recall the Lovers from the past, but got nothing. Maybe I'd never faced them.

All I kept seeing was an elusive memory of a picnic with my grandmother. *"What have you got there, Evie?"* I dimly remembered her cutting her thumb on a pecan shell, on purpose, blood welling.

"So talk." Selena bounded like a gazelle from one plank to another, all long limbs and grace.

I trudged behind her, as if my boots were weighted. "Death told me they hunger for pain, but I don't know why."

"Maybe because they're hella evil, like the Hierophant and the Alchemist?"

And Ogen? Possibly the High Priestess? What if all Arcana had the capacity for true evil? What if that was what *made* us Arcana? My alter ego—the red witch—could scare even me. "Tell me what you know about the Lovers' powers."

Selena hesitated.

"This is not the time to hold back information." I stopped in the middle of the courtyard. "We need to be working together. I'm going to give this rescue everything I have. Will you?"

She came back to stand in front of me. "I was trained never to reveal my chroniclers' info. Matthew always says, 'Converge and conserve.' I was taught, 'Convergence, conservation, *concealment*.'"

I crossed my arms over my chest, as unbending as an oak.

At length, she said, "For J.D., I'll go against all my extensive training. Because I always have his six, always will, and unfortunately I need you to help him."

Always will?

"In my Arcana primer, there was a lot of speculation about the Lovers."

She'd gotten a primer? I wanted a primer.

Instead I had my grandmother, a Tarasova, a wisewoman of the Tarot. She'd be a wealth of knowledge—if I could find her, *reach* her.

But so might Selena be—if I could *trust* her.

"Some say that if they whisper in your ears at the same time, they can mesmerize you to confuse pain for pleasure. If they clasp hands and swing their arms, they can tempt you to love bad things, like murder and suicide. Is any of this jibing with what you've heard?"

"Ditto on the mesmerizing. But I can't remember much more."

"Other chroniclers were totally vague about them. The Emperor? Everyone can tell you he moves mountains, creates earthquakes, and uses lava to kill. The High Priestess manipulates water, drowning her enemies. Straightforward stuff. But the Lovers are surrounded by mystery. Could be because they always die early in the game. Could be they're good at hiding power secrets. Like most of us."

"I've told you everything I can do. What are you hiding?"

She waved that away. "I didn't know Lark has bulletproof animals or that Ogen could supersize himself that much. Speaking of which, you talked about what the Devil did to you, but not Death."

Death? He nearly seduced me into falling for him, then broke my heart. "Let's focus on the twins, okay? I'll try to get more details from Matthew."

"Good luck with that. If possible, he's making less sense than before, and he's having fits. Only J.D. can calm him down."

I felt a pang that Jack had been looking out for him. "Joules and his crew don't have any info?"

"Gabe's line was the only one that chronicled, and his books got destroyed centuries ago."

I'd bet Aric knew all about the Lovers. As the three-time, reigning Arcana champion, he'd lived for millennia, gathering knowledge the way he gathered priceless relics. . . .

Two armed sentries passed us. Each wore a hooded camo poncho and carried a rifle. They nodded politely.

Under my breath, I said, "Arcana don't freak them out? Gabriel's wings alone should throw them."

"At first, yeah. But they look to J.D. to see how to act. They hero-worship 'the hunter.'"

Charismatic Jack could be so compelling when he wanted to.

"He uses our help to maintain order," Selena said. "The Azey might have the twins, but J.D.'s got three Arcana himself—a psychic, an exquisite bow-goddess, and an illusionist."

"How did this place come to be?"

"He built a lot of the wall with his own hands, worked himself to exhaustion. It'd stand up against a tank." She couldn't sound prouder. "He's been recruiting skilled Azey dissenters, leaving messages for scouts. With his leadership and Finn's illusions, we've been stealing tons from the army: food, fuel, even the mines J.D. planted in the moat."

"It sounds like you guys are gaining momentum."

Selena nodded. "That's why the Azey sent half their force to set up shop across the river. Their guns are out of range—for now—but we think they're hauling heavier artillery from Azey North. If it reaches here . . ."

Another worry to put on my list. "How did Jack get captured?"

"We were going to blow the bridge I was talking about—while Vincent was on it. We'd taken up position on a cliff overlooking the strike zone, waiting for his convoy to cross. J.D. had his finger hovering over the detonator."

"Matthew told me Vincent surprised him."

"The bastard parked just before the bridge. While we were coming up with a new plan, one of the convoy trucks that had already crossed fired a fifty-cal at us."

I nodded like I knew what that was. It sounded bad. "Go on."

"Bullets chewed the mountain apart. Finn fell, but J.D. and I held on somehow. He climbed up to get a shot at Vincent, so I headed to another rise, drawing fire. Next thing I knew I was falling too."

"How did they know where you'd be?"

She peered around. "I think we've got traitors here, men planted by the Milovnícis."

I rubbed the back of my neck.

"If we can free J.D., we'll smoke them out." She pointed behind me. "Gabe's tent is over there, just past the courtyard. How do we do this with him?"

"You're going to flirt with him."

"Are you mental?"

"He's head over heels for you."

Selena huffed with impatience. "Understandably. But how does this help us? You want me to act like I *like* him? He's completely bizarre."

Yes, he wore an old-timey suit everywhere with a strange tie (a cravat or whatever). And yes, his speech was outdated. But . . . "I was going to say eccentric."

She snorted, then lowered her voice. "Tess told me he was raised on a secluded mountaintop, in some kind of Arcana monastery. His chroniclers were cultish wing-worshippers. They separated themselves from society for generations, waiting for him to be born."

No wonder he was so outdated. "You said his books got destroyed?"

"Villagers tried to burn the cult, à la Frankenstein; the chronicles went up in smoke."

Villagers had tried to burn me in a past life as well. *They burn what they fear.*

"Selena, I'm not asking you to nest with Gabriel. All you have to do is ask him really nice to fly us over." I reached up to brush her silvery-blond hair back, tucking a silken lock behind her ear. "I miss lip gloss, and clearly you do too."

"Shut it. I can't believe I'm going along with this. I hate it when girls use their wiles. Normally, I'd just strangle him until he agreed."

I sighed. "That's plan B. Sometimes climbing ivy does that too."

5

"Yo, Gabe!" Outside their tent, Selena cast me a glare for good measure. "I need to talk to you."

He rushed out, flattening his black wings to duck under the tent flap. His long black hair was tied back in a ponytail. Like Lark, he had claws and a set of fangs. His eyes were leaf green.

He was a striking, if unusual-looking, guy.

"Selena," he breathed, cheeks flushed. "Uh, and the Empress too."

Why was I even here? As Matthew would say, "Nature and course. Love and bloom."

"Greetings to you both." He adjusted his suit coat. Must be a bitch to line up the slits in the back with the bases of his wings. "What is the issue at hand, ladies?"

Selena rolled her eyes. "You mean: *what's up?*"

Wow, way to flirt. She was a regular coquette.

He nodded. "For me, I believe all things are best when pointed *up*."

She and I blinked at him. Gentlemanly Gabriel probably had no idea his words sounded kind of dirty.

"Whatever." Wasting no time, Selena said, "We're going in to rescue J.D., and you're going to help."

He glanced over his shoulder and back. "Joules has already spoken on the subject. Our alliance will not—"

"I'm not asking your alliance," she interrupted. "I'm asking you. All we need is transpo. You don't have to do anything but fly us across the river."

I recalled another of his talents—animal-like senses. "And to track Jack's scent. It'd mean a lot to me, and so much to Selena." I cast her a look.

"Yeah. It'd really mean a lot, Gabe," she added, laying a hand on his muscular arm.

His lips parted, and his wings seemed to flutter uncontrollably. Wait, had he grimaced from the movement? Was something wrong with our transpo?

"Everything all right?" I asked.

He didn't answer, just stared at the hand on his arm.

To her credit, Selena gave it a squeeze. "So we can count on you?"

When he remained undecided—or mind-boggled by her touch—I said, "Help us end the Lovers tonight." Well, at least one of them.

Collecting himself, he said, "I thought you didn't want to play the game, Empress."

"I don't. But I need time to figure out a way to stop it." I pictured the game as a machine with cogs and wheels—that I longed to blow up. "The twins are going to keep coming after all of us."

"What is your plan?"

"Finn disguises us. You fly us over. We march right into the Lovers' camp. I fumigate their tent. Selena and I extract Jack."

Gabriel was quiet for long moments.

With a glare, Selena removed her hand; at once, he said, "I shall assist you with more than transportation, as a full-fledged member of the team. But I have a condition."

Full-fledged said the boy with wings. "Let's hear it."

"We go there to assassinate any Milovníci. Not to ask them to be in an alliance. Not to spare them."

I totally agreed, but hadn't thought he'd be this hard-core.

"We've talked to soldiers here about the general and his spawn. They must be stopped."

"We'll take them out," I assured him.

He offered his claw-tipped hand, and we shook. "Joules will be displeased. I sense an AC/DC moment in my future."

Huh? "Like the band?""

"No, like the currents. But I'll handle him."

"You do that," Selena said. "Bring a bandanna for a spore mask and meet us at the watchtower. Midnight sharp."

I frowned. "That's hours away."

"Their soldiers maintain a regular schedule," she explained. "Like they do here. Reveille in the morning, even though there's no daybreak. At midnight, most of the camp will be asleep." To Gabriel, she said, "Don't let any humans know what we're planning."

"Understood."

I furtively kicked Selena's boot; she straightened and said, "Oh. Thanks, Gabe. I won't forget this."

"It will be my pleasure, Selena. I look forward to it." His eyes widened. "I mean, not that I am pleased about the occasion."

Selena let him off the hook. "I look forward to kicking serial killer ass."

He grinned. "Precisely."

We started back toward Selena and Finn's tent. Halfway there, she murmured, "I can't believe he's going against Joules! I would've bet my bow he'd refuse. My God, we might free J.D. tonight. Evie, if this works . . ." Though Selena was 100 percent, grade-A badass, her eyes glinted, a hairline fracture in her prickly façade. "If we get him back, you and I'll be solid again."

"Were we ever solid?" I was so different from her, and we'd hated each other at first. But we'd muddled along until we'd begun to rely on one another. And now she was lowering her guard a degree.

As soon as the thought occurred to me, her expression hardened.

"In every game, the Archer has an arrow for the Empress."

I exhaled. "Yeah, yeah, I remember."

"In this game, I might have misplaced it." Shoulders squared, she turned from me.

As she strode away, I realized two things:

That's the closest she'll ever come to telling me we're friends.

I'll take it.

6

"Battle comes for the Empress."

Near midnight, Matthew and I had holed up in the top floor of the watchtower. We sat facing each other, the toes of our boots touching. We spoke with hushed voices, as we had in the back of that van with Jack and Selena.

A gas lantern flickered light. Outside, a storm raged. Cyclops stood watch below.

"I'm ready." To take on psychotic mass murderers. To head into the skies with a winged boy. A gust rocked the watchtower, making it shudder. Not exactly the greatest conditions to fly in. . . .

After Selena and I had secured Gabriel's help, I'd checked on the mare (doing much better; still pissed at me), then headed to the tent Jack shared with Matthew.

I'd tried to rest, but as soon as I lay down on Jack's cot, his familiar, pulse-quickening scent had surrounded me. I'd alternated between bouts of missing him and jolts of panic about his imprisonment.

There'd been little sleep.

"Do you want to go tonight?" I asked Matthew.

He shrugged, like I'd asked him to go grab a slice. "Got stuff to do."

"Like what?"

"Stuff," he answered, sounding like such a teenage boy.

"Will you tell me about the Lovers? Anything at all?"

"Duke and Duchess Most Perverse." He lowered his voice even more. "Their card's upside down. Reverse. Perverse."

"But what does that mean?"

He rocked forward and back. "Animus, animal passions, disharmony, conflict, jealousy. When they say *love*, they mean *destroy*. They want retribution because they chronicle and remember."

"What are their powers?"

His rocking slowed. "They don't use them as they have."

"What did you mean about smite, fall, mad, and struck?"

He nodded. "Sometimes the world spins in reverse. Sometimes battles do too. The word *carousel* means little battle."

I nodded back as if that made sense. "Matthew, what will they do to Jack if I fail? Will they mesmerize him? Control his mind?"

"They are vain. They practice their craft. With sharp tools, they remove things, discard them, transform people. You begin as one thing and die as another." A gust punctuated his low words.

Chills skittered over me. Here we sat in a tree-house type structure, telling scary stories by lantern light. As kids used to.

Post-apocalypse, all the stories were real.

"You don't want to know more about their craft." Matthew shivered. "*I* didn't. Power is your burden; knowledge is mine."

"What power?"

"You have more abilities now."

Though I grew weaker overall from lack of sunlight, I had learned a new skill.

When I'd been in the gardens beneath Death's home, preparing for the Devil's attack, I'd unwittingly taken the knowledge of those plants into me—along with all their relatives.

Before, I'd revived and controlled plants and trees, but I'd never *known* them. Now I could recreate them without seed; I could generate differing spores to make one sleep for a time—or forever. The same with the toxin on my lips.

"Phytogenesis," I said.

"Phytogenesis," he echoed solemnly.

"Did you plan for me to fight Ogen? So I'd be among all that green as blood was spilling?" *Trusting him is a free fall.*

"Claimed your crown yet?"

My hundredth frown of the night. "Like on my card?" The Empress tableau and Tarot card depicted her/me with a crown of twelve brilliant stars. "Is that what you meant?"

He stared at his hand. Subject closed.

Okay . . . "Even when I fought Ogen, I spared Death and Lark. I controlled the red witch." Matthew should give me props.

"You can muzzle her, but can you invoke?" Or none at all.

Invoke the witch? "She comes out when I'm under attack." Pain drew her in a hurry. Fury as well. "It's kind of automatic. Why would I invoke her?"

"Jack is missing."

I sighed, resigned to letting him steer our conversation. "Yes, he is."

"Your heart aches again. His does too. Hopes. High. Dashed. Love. He reflects over his life."

"Like what?"

"Crossroads and missed opportunities. He has more regrets than the very old. Wishes he'd never lied to you."

"So do I." He'd lied with as much skill as he read people. I rose and walked over to the lookout slot, scanning as if I could see him.

Even though I feared I could never trust him again, I still loved him.

"He wishes he could have seen you just one last time." Matthew's tone turned sly. "I could show you his reflections."

Trespass in Jack's mind? But then, he had listened to the tape of my life story—without permission. "What he's thinking about right now? Show me."

"From his eyes," Matthew whispered.

A vision began to play, so immersive that the world around me faded away. As Jack's memory became my own, I was transported into the ramshackle cabin he'd shared with his mother. Through an open doorway, I could smell the bayou, could hear frogs and cicadas.

His mother was smiling down at him. She'd had stunning good looks, with her tanned skin, high cheekbones, and long raven hair. Jack had gotten his coloring from her.

But shadows laced her gray eyes as she introduced him to two visitors.

Maman calls me over to meet them: a middle-aged woman and a girl around my age, maybe eight or so. Everyone says Maman and I are dirt poor, but this pair doan look like they're doing much better.

"Jack, this is Eula and her daughter, Clotile. Clotile's your half sister."

She'd been tiny, all skinny legs and big soulful eyes. Sadness filled me because I knew Clotile's ultimate fate.

Less than nine years from that day, she would survive an apocalypse—only to be captured by Vincent and Violet.

Clotile had escaped them, just long enough to shoot herself. Jack still didn't know why. Had she committed suicide to give him a chance to get free? Or because she couldn't live with what the Lovers had done to her?

I tell Maman, "I doan have a sister." I got a younger half brother though. Earlier this summer, Maman had driven us all the way to Sterling to show me my father's mansion. She said it should've been ours. We'd watched Radcliffe and his other son, Brandon, tossing a football in the front yard.

My half brother kind of looked like me. But this girl's scrawny with light brown hair and pale skin.

"You two got the same father. Radcliffe." Maman can barely say his name.

"Maybe, Hélène." Eula snorts. "I'm giving it one in three."

Clotile gazes at the ceiling. I get the sense she's embarrassed that she can't pin down who her père is—but kind of used to it too.

Eula strides toward me and grasps my face in a way I hate. "Oh, ouais, you got his blood, for sure. Not that it matters anyway. You'll never get a dime out of him." She drops her hand. "You and Clotile go play. Your mère and me are goan to have a couple of drinks."

When Maman drinks she turns into a different person. I give her a look that says, Doan do this. *But she gazes away.* What'd I expect, me?

Clotile takes my hand with a wide smile, and we head outside. She's sweet enough, I suppose. And she can't help being my sister.

I take her out onto the floating pier I've pieced together, showing her how to check traps. She watches in amazement, like I'm turning water into wine or something.

Out of the blue, she says, "I think you are *my big brother."*

I doan know how I feel about that. She's not bad company, doan talk a lot. Her stomach's been grumbling, but she woan admit she's hungry. At least I've learned to feed myself, can hunt and fish and cook my take. I could help her out now and again.

"Maybe I am." Then I scowl, kicking a trap back in the water. Just what I need—another mouth to feed!

A loud truck rumbles down our muddy track of a driveway, parking in front of the cabin. Two men stomp inside, hailing greetings, making our mothers laugh.

I can hear a metal opener tinking against beer bottles, can hear the throat of a bourbon fifth against a shot glass. They turn up music on a radio I "found" a couple months back and pair off.

The zydeco doan disguise what's happening inside. For the first time, Clotile looks upset.

I figure I'd do just about anything to keep this scrawny little fille from crying. "We can borrow a pirogue and paddle out farther. I got more traps, me."

She latches on to this like a bass on a line, and we doan get back for hours.

Near sunset, we creep up the cabin steps. "Stay behind me, girl," I whisper. When Maman's beaux get drunk, they always need to swing their fists—usually at her or me.

Inside is all a mess. Eula and a man are naked and passed out on the couch I got to sleep on. Clotile shrugs at that sight like she doan care, but her cheeks are red, her eyes glassy.

Maman's door is open—I hear a man snoring from the bed—but I know better than to glance in that direction.

Beside the couch is my stack of library books; liquor's spilled over them. It makes me so angry, like I need to swing my fists.

Clenching my jaw, I snag a few beers out of the icebox. Clotile doan miss a beat, grabbing the bottle opener. We head back out to the pier. As we watch the sun set between two cypress trees, she pops open beers for us, like she's been doing this for a while.

I never have, but figure, Why not? I sip, not sold on the taste. I suppose it'll grow on me.

By the second one, I feel great, relaxed in my own skin. "Clotile?"

"Hmm?" She looks mellow, buzzed herself.

"Everybody says we got no hope of goan anywhere. You ever think we deserve better than the Basin?"

Without hesitation, she says, "Non."

I ponder it over another sip. "Ouais, me neither."

My eyes blurred with tears.

Yet Jack *had* made plans to get out of the Basin and fight for a better life. He'd intended to fly in the face of everything he'd grown up believing.

That struck me as unimaginably brave.

Did he still feel he didn't deserve better? If Clotile had ever dared to hope for more, she'd been punished with something much, much worse than Basin life.

With me as a lingering witness to his thoughts, Jack's mind turned to another sliver of time.

He and I were walking hand in hand, just after we'd had sex for the first and only time—and right before we'd gone into battle against the cannibals.

'Bout to face shittier odds than I ever have, stone-cold sober, and I never felt so good. Is this what being at peace means? No damn wonder everyone wants to feel this way.

Evie glances up at me with those blue eyes, and she's so fucking beautiful I nearly trip over my feet. Her scent is honeysuckle, which means she's all but purring. Her lips curve, and that smile hits me harder than any punch. She's got no regrets.

Good. 'Cause I'm never letting her go. I might reach too high to have her, but she doan think so. I want to say something, to tell her how I feel about what we just did. Everything I think to say could be taken the wrong way.

So I squeeze her hand and keep it simple. "À moi, Evangeline." Mine.

She promises me: "Always."

And I believe her.

"Hey, blondie!" Finn called from below. "Is this a no-boys-allowed tree house?"

I jerked my head up, my tie with Jack severed.

7

"You're early," I told the Magician as Matthew and I climbed down. We still had twenty minutes.

"Wanted to avoid the midnight-hour traffic."

The three of us hurried into the first floor. Metal sheeting made up the walls. Moldy hay covered the ground. A rough-hewn table and a couple of benches furnished the area.

Finn sat on one, raising his leg along it. Matthew took a seat next to him.

When Cyclops padded over hesitantly, Finn grumbled, "Free fort, sit where you want." But he kind of grinned when the wolf plopped down right beside him.

"We could've come to you," I told him. Maneuvering through this camp must be hell for him.

Sweat beaded his lip, and he was out of breath. "The closer I am to you guys, the better for the illusions."

The watchtower wasn't that far from his tent. How close were we cutting it?

He situated his crutch over his lap. Aged stickers of cats decorated the metal parts. Who had it once belonged to? "So an Empress, a horse, and a wolf walk into a fort. . . ."

"If this is a dirty joke, I'll pass." I'd missed the Magician's humor. Tilting my head at him, I said, "You don't look so good, Finn."

Was there even a spare Advil to be found? Selena's arm had to be hurting her too, but with her extensive training, she probably knew Jedi tricks to limit pain.

"I feel like a bucket of fuck, but I'll be ready," he assured me. "Right, Matto?"

"Ready Magician!"

I sat on the other bench. "I heard you took a header off a ridge."

"II to the Azey. That army blows Baggers. My bear-trap injury never quite healed up. Didn't take much to rebreak my leg. Selena was worse off, though. She broke her arm in two places, cracked her ribs, and fractured her collarbone."

Just a week ago? I'd suspected she had accelerated healing.

"Somehow she dragged me back to the fort."

For Selena to refrain from killing Arcana was one thing. Quite another for her to save another card. She'd shown loyalty to someone other than Jack.

I guessed she and Finn had smoothed over their animosity.

"Good thing I'm dying young," Finn continued in a nonchalant tone, "or I'd be shit out of luck with this bum leg."

"Dying young?" He *wasn't* kidding.

"Made peace with it." He shrugged. "Kind of think we all should."

"Because of the game? We don't know that yet." As I spoke, another gust howled, drilling horizontal rain against the metal walls.

Finn looked up warily. "Not just because of the game."

After three months of near constant downpours, the weather was shifting. Occasionally, we'd get hurricane-force winds—and a fog so thick it bordered on tangible. "Have you guys gotten snow here yet?" I thought I'd spied a single flake the night I'd left Aric.

"Not looking forward to that. SoCal surfer boy here, remember? Just think: if the snow comes down like the rain has . . ."

"Snowmageddon!" Matthew cried, cracking both of them up.

"Yeah, Matto, that groundhog came out to check for nuclear winter. But then a Bagger ate him!"

He almost had me laughing. As soon as I got Jack safe.

Finn's demeanor turned serious again. "Eves . . ." He opened his mouth, closed it, then frowned at the wolf. He probably wanted to talk about Lark—without her overhearing.

I'd help him out. "There's a medic who's taking good care of her."

He nodded, but a question lingered in his gaze. He peeled at a sticker of an orange tabby.

"She felt terrible about how everything went down," I told him. "When she realized you'd survived the mine collapse, her entire face lit up. Her eyes watered. She was as into you as you were into her."

"We're here for a mission, people"—Selena swept inside—"not group therapy."

Gabriel was right behind her, watching the Archer—like a hawk.

She assessed me. "You gonna have enough juice for this? Don't see your glyphs."

My Empress power gauge. "I'll have enough." Since emotions fueled my powers, I feared I'd have too much. "And you?"

Under her jacket, she wore a pistol holster; over it, an arm sling. A sword belt circled her narrow waist. "I got a Glock and a cutlass. Consider my swash buckled."

Joules barged inside, his skin sparking with anger. AC/DC. "You're really goin' to do this?" he demanded of Gabriel. "Infiltrate an enemy camp with a bowless Archer—and an untrustworthy Empress? How do you know she won't lose her shite and claw you to death?"

Dick.

"Selena has weapons," Gabriel pointed out. "And I trust the Empress in this."

Yes, I'd gotten more control of the vicious red witch; didn't mean it was foolproof. If we failed tonight and I didn't return with Jack, would she slip the leash?

Oh, man, I really hoped I didn't murder Gabriel and Selena.

I cleared my throat. "You guys have your bandannas?" The wetted material would serve as a filter against my spores. I hoped.

Gabriel tugged one from his jacket pocket. "And I have Jack's scent from his tent. But I need to lock on it over there before you deploy."

"Just let me know you're ready." I was acting like I had total command over my powers. No matter how stressful, painful, or *lethal* the situation grew.

Joules created a spear in his palm, twirling it. "The other side of the river is out of my range, Gabe. You're goin' to be on your own. No cover, no backup."

"I've already given my word that I will go."

Joules sparked brighter. "And I told you I wouldn't, not without payment."

"Then we part ways here for a time," Gabriel said gravely.

"Enough with the bromance!" Selena snapped. "Joules, this area is reserved for people about to do shit. So kindly remove your Oirish arse."

"One day, Archer . . ." But he did turn to leave, passing Tess on her way in.

"Hey, guys." She pulled off her hood, smoothing her long mousy brown hair back. "Can I go too?"

I shared a look with Selena, then asked, "Uh, why?"

"I can help you carry Jack if he's been injured. Selena can only use one arm, and Gabe might be busy."

When we remained unconvinced, she said, "I let you down before, Evie. I want to make up for it."

Tess had balked when she'd had a chance to stab Death—but what if she hadn't? I never would have known the real Aric.

Yet then, had I truly *known* him? The man behind the armor? "Tess, if you'd gone forward that day, you would've been too late. Death was already getting free. You don't owe me anything."

"I know I'm the laughingstock of the Arcana," she quietly said. "But

I can't stop being that unless I do something meaningful. I'm asking. Please."

Gabriel studied her expression. "She's going," he decided. "She can help. Do you have your bandanna?"

Tess nodded eagerly.

Selena raised her brows at the angel. "Do you know something about her powers that I don't? As in, do they ever work?"

On the day I first met Tess, Matthew had listed some of her mind-blowing abilities. Teleportation, levitation, time manipulation, and more. She was the World Card, the great Quintessence. Unfortunately, she struggled with her gifts.

"She could surprise you, Archer."

"So she goes." Selena hiked her shoulders. "You're in luck, Evie. If we get chased, she'll be even slower than you are." To Tess, she said, "You screw this rescue up, and I'll skewer you with my new sword." She unsheathed a few inches of it with a threatening look.

Gabriel frowned at that, fluttering his silky black wings. Again, he grimaced with the movement.

"Come clean about the injury, Gabriel," I said.

"I was shot during a flyover last week." He stretched out a wing, revealing a bullet wound in that feathery expanse. A hole went straight through the bony part. "I haven't quite healed yet."

From last week? So he had rapid healing, like Death and Selena.

"Unfortunately, wings provide a large target. As Joules says, 'It's like hittin' the broad side of a barn!'" An Arcana weakness. "We can wait a couple of days, ladies, or I can take you one at a time tonight."

"Tonight," I quickly said.

"The problem is that we go one at a time on the return leg as well."

"We need to get to Jack, now—hell or high water, and all that." I turned to Matthew. "Any tips? Anything you'd like to tell me about our mission?"

"I already did." He cast me a look of pure confusion. "Carousel? Struck? Ah! You listen poorly!"

Had he ever been this exasperated with me before? "Of course, sweetheart. I just meant anything in addition to that. Hey, maybe you could tell me how long till Violet closes in?"

"In a way, she's here."

"What does that mean? I thought we had more time before the twins joined up." Had they already begun Jack's torture?

"She's here, in a way." He'd just reversed his words.

My breaths shallowed. "Gabriel, I'll cross with you first—and last on the way back." I turned to Finn. "Get to work."

"On it." He rolled his head on his neck. "You guys will be able to see each other, but to everyone else, you'll look like soldiers." He began to chant in his mysterious magician language, the air blurring at his lips.

By the time he'd finished, the four of us looked like unshaven, middle-aged men armed with machine guns.

Finn had grown even paler. "Just try not to get too stressed. Sweating and increased heart rates affect my illusions. Good luck, guys."

"Thanks, Magician." I hastened outside, the others following.

Gabriel crossed to stand before me. "Empress, are you ready?"

I was putting a ton of trust in him, an Arcana. Though I owed Lark, her betrayal *had* done a number on me. "Uh, ready."

When Gabriel gripped me under my arms, Selena jerked her chin at me. "See you on the other side." She knew I was having doubts.

The trues only worked in this fort. Once we left, Gabriel could drop me in the drink.

For the High Priestess to drag down to the abyss.

I could use my body vine, the one that grew from my skin, to tether myself to him, but that might screw with Finn's illusion. I would risk a dip to save Jack. I would risk anything.

—in our own way, in our own way.—

The Lovers' call. It was loud because of proximity, but sounded staticky. "Let's go, Gabriel!"

Without warning, he shot into the air, making my stomach plunge. I squeezed my eyes tight, fighting not to shriek.

43

"There's nothing to be frightened of," he said. "You can look now."

I cracked open my lids. "Wh-why are we going so high?" We seemed to be a mile above the river. Up here, the winds were gale force. Were we making progress at all? Hovering in place?

"I don't know the Priestess's reach." Another Arcana secret. "Better safe than sorry." His voice sounded strained. From the pain in his wing? What if it gave out?

My heart was thundering. With his acute senses, he could surely hear it.

"For all that you're the Empress, you're still a regular girl, aren't you?"

I'd revealed a fear of heights. Had they thought me fearless before?

I squinted against the wind, gazing back at the fort. Outside the minefield, I could make out lighter dots across black ground. The stone forest. After the Flash, men lacked cover for shootouts; instead of—oh, I don't know—not shooting at each other, they'd built rock trees.

Gabriel followed my gaze. "From up on high, I see things that can't be random—shapes, designs, clues—all the time."

I blinked again. From here, those white stacks kind of looked like stars in an inky sky.

"Empress, I have the senses of both angel and animal, and I recognize the gods' return."

"Um, okay?" *Cult crazy, cult crazy, I'm about to die.*

"No matter what happens, I want you to know that I dearly wish you could end this game."

What *happens*? Did he mean, like, any second now? I should've bound us in vine!

Just when I was sure he was about to drop me, he descended to the edge of the bluff on the other side. "You're the only Arcana fighting for a different future than the one we've been dealt."

As we touched down, I felt guilty for doubting him.

"I go now. For Selena." Eager much? He saluted, then took to the air once more, the backdraft of his wings whipping my poncho.

Long moments later, he flew back with the Archer in his arms, holding her close, reluctant to let her go once they landed.

Oblivious, Selena pushed at him to stand on her own. Gabriel cleared his throat. "I return with Quintessence." He disappeared into the murk once more.

As Selena and I waited, misgivings about my plan arose. "What if something goes wrong?" I tucked the end of my ponytail into my poncho hood. "What do you think the Lovers would hit back with? Would they use guns?" So far, most Arcana had spurned them.

Selena limbered up, stretching one of her long legs. "Some say the Lovers throw poison darts like Cupid himself. And wouldn't that be adorable?" she added in a disgusted tone. "But I'd expect guns, considering their army."

Poison didn't affect me, and a bullet wouldn't kill me. Not so for the others. Was I leading them to their deaths? I'd gotten used to being a leader, telling people what needed to be done. Still hadn't gotten used to the responsibility.

"But check this, Evie—my arrow's already in flight. So I don't give a shit what the Duke and Duchess Most Perverse are packing. If you told me the twins could vaporize archers with their eyes, I'd still try to save J.D."

Oddly, that made me feel better, as if she'd pep-talked me.

When Gabriel returned with a wide-eyed Tess, he said, "Allow me to detect Jack's scent and get a lay of the land. It might take a few moments with these winds."

As we waited, the World Card bit her fingernails and tapped one of her boots. To everyone else, she'd appear to be a two-hundred-pound soldier with a nervous disorder.

Selena slapped the girl's hand. "At ease, Quintessence."

"You could stay here," I told Tess. "Keep watch or something."

"She goes where I go," Gabriel said. "And I've got the scent. Ladies, shall we rescue the hunter?"

8

The camp was like a ghost town. No soldiers roamed the grounds as we navigated our way through a maze of tents and lean-tos.

One large tent had light spilling from it, and male voices carried from within.

A middle-aged woman shuffled around a nearby cooking fire, ladling food into bowls. Her ankles were hobbled, her feet bare on the freezing ground.

A slave. Under General Milovníci's orders, this army abducted females, "involuntary recruits."

My nails lengthened, turning into purple thorn claws.

Selena must've noticed my tension. "Don't even think about it. Stay focused on J.D. Once we free him, we'll worry about these prisoners."

With difficulty, I turned away from the woman.

Gabriel inhaled short bursts of air. "I scent Jack just around the corner of the ridge ahead. He's in a tent that's off by itself, a boon for us."

Selena's gaze swept the area. "Can you tell how many guards?"

"I think about twenty or so."

I shoved up my sleeve to reach the glimmering spore glyph on my forearm. "Pull up your bandannas. It's time."

Once the others were ready, I drew from the glyph, filling my hand with a sleeping toxin. As we rounded the corner, I blew against my palm to spread the spores. Like starting a blaze from kindling.

Dozens of men guarded a gigantic tent. And they all wore . . .

Gas masks.

My invisible onslaught drifted harmlessly over them, carried off on the wind.

Tess gasped, muttering, "You can't put them to sleep."

"Keep it together!" Selena yanked down her bandanna, and the others did too.

Now what were we going to do? There was no reason for us—or the four soldiers we resembled—to be this far from the main camp.

"Gabriel, you'll have to talk to them," I whispered. "Tell them that Vincent sent for us."

He called to the guards, "Greetings!" He might as well have said, "Hail, fellow, well met!"

I inwardly groaned. Tess gasped again.

"Vincent summoned us."

A tall, lanky soldier, the apparent leader, said, "He told us he doesn't want to be disturbed." The man sounded creepy through his gas mask. "Not for any . . ." He trailed off, eyes going wide.

At Tess.

Her illusion flickered like an old TV, going from girl to burly soldier. Girl. Then soldier.

"Enemy in the camp!" one of the guards bellowed.

We whirled around and bolted. With yells, half of the men gave chase.

Gabriel spread his wings, snagging Selena.

"Don't take me first!" She flailed against his grip. "They're dead if we leave them!"

He shot into the air like a reverse bungee, arcing upward and away.

Tess and I kept running. Conjuring my powers on the move like this felt impossible. I needed time to concentrate and seed my arsenal. Or I needed the witch. . . .

If we could just buy time for Gabriel to return! The bluff dropped off at a sheer cliff, so I skirted the edge of it, heading down the mountain. "This way!" I cried, careening along a winding trail.

Down and down we went into a gully of rock, those guards right on our heels. At last, the gully opened up into an inlet, a sandy beach that led to the river's shore. The Priestess's domain.

—Terror from the abyss!—

Between breaths, Tess asked, "D-did you hear her, Evie?"

The guards barreled onto the beach, pinning us back against an Arcana. Would I rather be a captive of the Lovers? Or bet on the Priestess not to kill me if I trespassed into her element?

I'd choose the Lovers. "Stop, Tess. Don't go any closer to the shore—"

A huge splash sounded behind us. We twisted around.

Towering plumes of water burst from the surface. Like tentacles, they snaked across the sand.

To drag Tess and me down.

We ran toward the dumbstruck soldiers, but those tentacles focused on me. Wet pressure coiled around one of my boots! Caught!

Yank. I landed flat on my face, spitting a mouthful of sand, half-blinded by grit.

The thing jerked me toward the river, my body plowing the beach. I scrabbled for purchase, but the tentacle reeled me in like a fish.

Tess lunged forward to grab my hand. I stretched for her. Every time she got close, the tentacle snatched me back.

As if playing with us.

A girl's disembodied voice said, *"Enemies almighty."* Was the *river* speaking? "I thought you'd give me more sport than this, Empress."

Taunting me? On the heels of my failed rescue?

Fury banked inside me, like fuel—or bait—for the red witch. My glyphs stirred, my hair reddening. My claws dug into my palms until blood poured to seed my own soldiers.

I spat more sand. "Get out of the way, Tess!"

She scrambled back.

Vines erupted from the ground, shooting like rockets toward those tentacles. The ropes of green twined around each arm of water, choking them, forcing them to regrow.

Gabriel yelled from above. Returned!

But he couldn't get around the vine and water strikes to reach me and Tess.

Wherever the Priestess launched a water tentacle, my plants were ready to intercept and strangle. My arsenal fed from hers, fattening right before my eyes, seeping water.

When the tentacle around my ankle collapsed into a puddle, I levered myself to my feet. Vines flanked me, helping me stand.

"Come, Priestess, *touch*." I raised my palm, and three barbs appeared. "And pay my price!" I tossed the barbs into the air, and a thorn tornado spun to life.

The Priestess attacked once more, but the tornado sheared her water feelers down like a propeller. They grew slower, regenerating with difficulty. She was weakening!

I laughed at her. "The earth went so long without water, Priestess. You must still be feeling it."

"Only for a time, my sister enemy." Her watery voice carried a melodic accent. "Ah, this rain, it falls without cease, no?"

The weary tentacles dropped, a last splash in the river. A final wave rippled. "We'll meet again, Empress." The surface settled to glass calm as the Priestess retreated.

Gabriel landed just outside my barbs, flaring his fangs, claws, and wings at our next threat.

The soldiers were slack-jawed, but their weapons stayed trained.

The red witch in me was unconcerned: *Nothing that an old-fashioned thorn flaying can't take care of.* I smiled at them, and knew it was a harrowing sight. *Yes, gentlemen, you* are *all about to die.*

"Behind me, Tess." When she crept to my back, I raised a hand to skin them alive—

That tall leader motioned for the others to lower their weapons. To me, he said, "C-can you kill the twins?"

9

"As a matter of fact, I'm on my way to do just that," I promised him. "Right after I descend on you like a scourge." The tornado tightened and vines snapped straight, poised to strike.

To his credit, the leader didn't lose control of his bladder. "I'm . . . my name is Franklin. We don't want to stop you. We want to help you."

Tess whispered, "We should listen to them."

Since my former plan had resulted in zero gain, I'd hear what this Franklin had to say. I inhaled for calm, exhaling. Again.

Bring it back, Eves. Muzzle the witch. "We'll discuss this," I told them, "once you take off your masks."

He nodded to his men, and one by one, they did. Franklin appeared to be in his late twenties, with black hair, wide-set brown eyes, and a gap in his front teeth.

When Gabriel sheathed his claws, I let my tornado slow, a compressed cyclone ringing our feet. "I'm surprised you would turn against your . . . leaders." I had a hard time assigning that word to the Lovers.

"Most of this army hates the Milovnícis, but they've got spies everywhere. Anyone suspected of stepping out of line gets executed, along with family and friends. Or worse, the general gives them to the twins."

If the Hierophant had manipulated his followers through mind control, the Milovnícis did it the old-fashioned way: tyranny.

I canted my head at Franklin. "Have you ever tried to kill the twins yourselves?"

"Yeah. I got this handpicked crew, and we're ready. But each time, weird stuff happens. You might have better luck at it since all of this"—he indicated us—"is, uh, weird."

"Tell me about Vincent and Violet," I said. "What weird stuff?"

"We think they can *teleport*. Like in the comics." Franklin must've expected us to laugh in his face.

We three Arcana listened intently. "Go on," I said with a glance at Tess. She shared that ability. In theory.

"A couple of weeks ago, we'd planned to assassinate Violet. Right before it was time, we got radioed that she was in the other camp. But I'd just seen her in ours."

No wonder Matthew had difficulty getting a bead on her!

How did one fight a teleporter? Of course they couldn't teleport if they were spore-drunk. "I can kill them," I told Franklin. "And I will. But Jack Deveaux is my first concern."

He nodded. "We've got to hurry, then. The twins were raring to go."

"Violet *is* here?"

"I saw her in the tent just before Vincent ordered us to wear gas masks."

My barbs soared, tornadic once more. The soldiers stepped back.

Gabriel cocked his head. "It's true. I can hear the Lovers from here. Jack refuses to torture another prisoner, so they're going to torture him."

I started sprinting back to the camp, Gabriel and Tess behind me, my thorns and vines trailing them. The soldiers followed at a distance.

We reached the bluff where we first landed. Between breaths, I told Gabriel, "We have to get to him before—"

Jack's roar of pain sounded. Two yells joined it in chorus. The twins were mimicking him?

DEAD OF WINTER —+—

I turned to the angel with wide eyes. "What did they do?"

He stutter-stepped, putting the back of his arm against his mouth.

"What, Gabriel?"

He lowered his arm, revealing his pale face. "It's bad." He sounded like a doctor about to deliver a terminal prognosis. "Empress, they used a hot spoon to . . . to take out one of his eyes."

"*WHAT?*" I'd misheard—or Gabriel had. That couldn't have happened.

Another of Jack's bellows carried across the night.

Gabriel flinched. "And again."

The earth seemed to go atilt. No, no, no. *Not* happening. My claws shredded my palms, blood pouring.

"He's blind," Gabriel murmured in a daze. "They laugh. It's done. They've left him for now."

I'd . . . failed.

I'd failed Jack. Rose stalks burst forth all around me. The ground began to move, roots growing, like snakes roiling beneath the surface.

The red witch ached to make her enemies pay! To rain down thorns and poison on the Lovers and every soul in this camp.

But what I really wanted was *not* to have failed Jack.

Why hadn't I moved faster? Fought the Priestess faster? Why had I run from the soldiers instead of taking bullets?

I imagined Jack's pain and shrieked my fury. When the twins were removing his second eye, he would have known he was about to be blinded forever. And he'd been helpless to stop the mutilation.

A hot spoon.

I felt like my heart had stopped. My world had. . . .

Through the chaos of my mind, a memory whispered. Something Matthew had said.

I pushed aside fantasies—of forcing Vincent and Violet to gouge out each other's eyes, to wear each other's scalps—and focused on that one fragile sprout of a memory pushing through to the surface.

A breath left me.

53

I wanted *not* to have failed Jack?

I turned to Tess, my lips curling as vines surrounded the unsuspecting girl. I strode up to her, my thorns enveloping the two of us. "You have work to do, World." I stabbed my claws into her shoulders.

She gave a cry. "Evie?"

From behind me, Gabriel growled, "Unhand her, Empress." But he could never breach the barbs.

Tonight, Matthew had said, "Sometimes the world spins in reverse. Sometimes battles do too." He'd meant the World *Card* could spin in reverse.

She could make time do the same.

"Please d-don't hurt me!"

"You know what you have to do, Tess. I won't inject you with poison, if you let the carousel spin and turn back time."

Her jaw slackened. "I don't have my staff to ground me!"

I'd seen her carrying one months ago. "Oh, I'll ground you."

"Each second I go back drains me of life. I don't know how to prevent that. It c-could destroy me."

Merciless, I tightened my claws in her flesh. "Then we'd better hurry."

10

I stared into Tess's dark blue eyes as her power began to manifest.

Her skin heated beneath my hands, and a dull buzz sounded. A breeze blew in a circle around us. From my thorns? No, the current of air flowed clockwise.

Her power stoked, the heat from her body increasing till it scalded me. But I refused to release my hold. The buzz grew in volume. Louder. *Louder*.

Our hair was dragged straight upward. When her body started levitating, I sank my claws deeper. If I hadn't been here to anchor her, would she have floated away?

The noise had gotten so loud her ears bled. Wet warmth slicked down my neck as well.

Suddenly Tess threw back her head and screamed. I could perceive the earth—or our existence or reality or *something*—stilling for one airless instant . . . before grinding into motion. The wrong way.

We were rotating backward! The World Card, Quintessence herself, was making time flow in reverse.

First rotation. Below us came a splash as the Priestess first attacked. The leftover arsenal I'd used against her began to vanish—but within Tess's circle, I remained the same, wet and bloodied.

Tess met my gaze. Her skin paled, her cheeks thinning.

Second rotation. Previous versions of me and Tess fled from the soldiers through the rock gully.

Beneath my claws, she was shedding weight at an alarming rate. "Please, Empress." The whites of her eyes were red, vessels blown. From pressure?

Jack's own eyes were gone. Brutally stolen. So I clawed her harder.

Third rotation. The soldiers had just begun giving chase.

Tess's breathing grew labored. Her face was haggard, her cheekbones jutting sharply. Patches of her raised mane of hair came out, long sections plucked away into the ether.

Fourth rotation. Four disguised Arcana meandered through the camp, almost at the twins' tent.

Tess's sunken red eyes pleaded. She looked like one of my famine victims from a past game. Brittle. Dying.

Her arms deflated in my grip, my bloody claws scraping over bone. *Scrape, scrape . . .*

Would I kill this girl to save Jack's sight? "Not yet, Tess! Not yet!"

Fifth rotation. Still disguised, Gabriel and an earlier version of Tess landed on this bluff, meeting up with Selena and the earlier version of me. The beginning of our mission.

"No more!" I screamed.

As if at the end of a car wreck, the spinning abruptly . . . stopped. Tess's head lolled, the remains of her hair hanging over her face.

The earth righted itself in fitful movements, seeming to gasp from exertion. With a shudder, the rotation ground forward once more.

Those earlier versions of me and Tess disappeared—leaving *us*, two girls aware of the near future, but physically changed. I'd been drained of power, with no arsenal to show for it.

And Tess . . . I released her arms, catching her as she collapsed, unconscious. Her now baggy clothing swallowed her emaciated body. Her teeth chattered, and she shivered for warmth. Would she survive?

"What the hell, Evie?" Selena cried.

She and Gabriel would have no idea why Tess was in this condition. For them, only an instant had passed.

"She used her power?" Gabriel demanded, his disguise faltering.

"Just take her back! Get her warm, and help her. Make sure she survives."

"I go anon." He cradled her slight weight and took to the sky.

As her illusion faded to nothing, Selena narrowed her gaze. "You and Tess don't have disguises. You're bleeding and soaking wet. Portal to another dimension? Or did you go back in time?"

"Violet is here. We have to save Jack in the next few minutes or he loses his eyes—"

"How many minutes?" Selena was already hastening toward the camp. She fiddled with a hi-tech sports watch on her sling arm.

I scrambled to catch up. "Enough time for Tess and me to run to the water's edge, then fight off the Priestess."

Selena raised her brows at that. Then she returned her concentration to the mission. "We'll say four minutes of running. How long did you and the Priestess tussle?"

Tussle? "I have no idea. Three minutes? Thirty?"

"I'm giving us eleven minutes total." Selena clicked the timer on. "Which tent is J.D. in? Without Gabriel—"

"I know which one."

"We don't have disguises!"

"No soldiers are out." I led Selena into the ghost-town camp.

When we passed the hobbled woman, I pressed my forefinger to my lips. After a heartbeat's hesitation, she nodded.

Selena and I continued on, picking up speed as we turned the corner.

"That's the tent."

She slowed. "The one heavily guarded by guys in gas masks?"

"Just keep running!" I passed her.

"This is suicide!" But she sped up.

"Do you want to save Jack or not?" I asked when we were side by side.

"Damn it, Evie!"

"Take off your sling and go all-out Arcana. Even without your bow, you can still look weird. Like you once told me: sell it, sister, or we are dead." I acted on that advice, calling forth my body vine.

It budded from the shimmering glyph over my nape. No more delicate ivy; this time I made it into a thornless rose stalk. Recalling Matthew's mention of a crown, I let it coil around my head, oversize leaves pointing up like arches. In lieu of a dozen stars, I fashioned twelve blooms to garnish it.

Roses were the red witch's flower.

My flower.

Selena tore off her sling and tossed it away. Her every footfall jostled that arm, but she gritted her teeth and withstood the agony.

For Jack, Selena Lua could do *anything*.

She began to glow, her skin the luminous red of a hunter's moon. Her silvery hair danced all around her head like gossamer moonbeams, an awing sight.

"Okay, Archer, how about hammering these guys with some doubt?" One of her powers as the Moon Card.

"It's not that easy." Her eyes darted. "I can't laser-focus it."

Another power secret? "Oh, that reminds me. I think the twins can teleport."

"Son of a bitch!" She glanced at my face. "Your glyphs are dim. Can you fumigate their tent?"

"I might've blown my wad against the Priestess." So much for conserving.

Selena scowled. "I'm going forward, even against teleporters."

"Like I'm not?"

When the soldiers caught sight of us, they aimed their guns, eyes going wide at Selena's appearance, not to mention mine.

We stopped in front of the detail. Selena had once told me that the Empress of Old was "slithery and creepy and sexy." I took a precious instant to catch my breath. "We're here to deliver you from the twins,"

I said in a throaty voice as petals wafted down from my wild reddened hair. "Step aside, and I'll rip their heads from their bodies. Your army will be freed."

The men gazed from me to Selena. We both wore expressions of otherworldly malice.

"It takes creatures like us—to destroy creatures like them. Let us do our jobs, soldiers. Just walk away."

They remained frozen in shock.

The tent behind them was large enough to house a small circus. Jack was somewhere within! So close . . .

I raised my hideous dripping claws. In a tone that might give even Death chills, I said, "If Jack Deveaux loses his eyes, I will slice your flesh to ribbons and choke your lungs with vine. Am—I—clear, Franklin?"

Finally, one man lost control of his bladder. Franklin startled when I said his name. A risk.

Then, with a swallow, he waved his handpicked men away.

We were on.

Selena checked her watch. "Nine minutes. Smash and grab, and watch for teleporting freaks. Let's bring J.D. home."

11

At the tent flap, Selena pulled her gun and mouthed, *One . . . two . . . three.* We charged in.

The *stench.* The air reeked of smoke—and rot.

Randomly placed gas lanterns cast fluttering light. Moving shadows cloaked most of the space. Large beams supported the canvas roof. Rare sawdust covered the floor. With wood so scarce, this extravagance might as well be silk.

Along the edges of the tent, the twins had sectioned off areas with canvas, like stable stalls. The first stall contained a cage of snarling Bagmen.

Unclothed Bagmen? All of their oozing skin was bare. I'd never encountered one completely naked.

Though the creatures looked well-fed—were those blood troughs in the cage?—they were as hostile as ever. Like post-apocalyptic guard dogs. In a frenzy, they stretched their slimy arms past the bars enclosing them.

Each of those mindless beings had a brand on its chest, some kind of symbol, but I couldn't make it out under all the pus and slime.

Behind that cage stood another just like it. Inside, four young guys curled naked on the floor, bodies covered with bites. They gasped through blistered lips, as if dying of thirst.

Dawning realization. The twins were *making* Bagmen. Those four were in transformation—and they knew it. One wept over a trough of blood.

Selena remained grade-A stoic. "Keep going. Eight minutes."

The next stall housed a piece of equipment that looked like a giant juicer. Gore coated it.

Past another partition was something that resembled a sawhorse with a length of sharpened metal atop it. More blood and gore.

The next stall . . . a stand with bats, canes, whips, and pincers. Other things I couldn't place.

Had these very instruments been used on Clotile?

On Jack?

The Hierophant had slaughtered people for food, and the Alchemist had murdered for his sick pursuit of knowledge. I couldn't comprehend why the Lovers tortured. "Where the hell is Jack?"

"We'll find him."

Faced with more and more blood-curdling contraptions, I felt as disconnected as I'd ever been. A few Halloweens back, I'd gone to a haunted house filled with gruesome displays—for *fun*. None of the ghastly things had been real.

This was *happening*. Right? Even as it felt like I'd stepped into one of Matthew's visions.

What was real? *Un*real?

We came upon another victim, a man kneeling with his wrists bound together, tied above his head to a roof support. He was shirtless, his body gaunt, his shoulders bulging at weird angles. Dislocated?

I thought he was balling his hands into fists, then realized his fingers had been cut off.

Stoic Selena actually gave a shudder. That would be her worst fear, wouldn't it? Never to draw another arrow.

His mouth was open. No teeth. A gash had been carved into his stomach. He had one of those brands below his collarbone, but his was older. The raised scar was about the size of a bookmark and depicted an odd symbol: a pair of overlapping triangles, bisected by two arrows, one pointing up, one down.

In front of him was another contraption that looked like a crank over an old-timey wishing well. A slimy rope of some kind had been wound around the crank.

"They're pulling it out," Selena murmured.

Pulling *what* out? She could see so much better than I could! Yet some part of me must have understood because nausea churned.

They remove things, discard them, transform people.

The man turned his head toward us. His eyes were solid black. No, not eyes. Sockets. The twins planned to do that to Jack.

"Six minutes, Evie. We'll come back for that guy." When we neared the far end of the tent, she whispered, "Behind the partition in the back. Listen."

Moans? Of pain? Selena readied her pistol. I bared my claws. We sidled closer.

Closer. Past the partition, we saw—

The twins.

I dry heaved. They were . . . kissing. Twincest.

When the pair started groping, Selena bit out, "Jesus. Get a womb, freaks."

Vincent and Violet took their time breaking apart, their gazes locked. Their pale blue eyes were just as Jack had once described: vacant, like a dead fish's.

Why weren't they threatened by us? Why weren't they trying to mesmerize us?

Though fraternal twins, they were nearly identical, with their marblelike skin and sharpish features.

Their clothing was all black, neatly pressed. Violet wore a cropped jacket and a skirt as full as a ball gown. A trench coat molded over Vincent's tall muscular form.

Expertly drawn eyeliner highlighted their lifeless eyes. Their nails were painted black, no chipping.

Vain? Oh, yeah. They weren't physically attractive, but they were faultless.

They sported brass knuckles on their left hands, as well as a Goth-looking tattoo. In her right hand, Violet held what resembled a remote control.

The twins finally turned to us. They stared at me with such intensity. As if seeing a ghost . . .

"We were wondering when you would arrive, Empress," Vincent said. His voice carried a trace of some European accent.

The Lovers' tableau appeared over them, but the image differed from other Arcana's. Theirs was upside down—reverse, perverse—and flickered like a bad copy. Because they shared it?

"Where is he?" Selena demanded from behind the gun barrel.

I gazed around, saw trunks, tables, and one bed—because the twins shared it. No Jack.

"You're just in time," Violet told us. "Our knave refused to turn the crank." With a swish of her overblown skirts, she stepped aside, drawing back one last partition to reveal—

"Jack!" He knelt with his hands tied and hung above his head, like the other man. He was shirtless, his torso covered with bruises. He seemed to be in and out of consciousness, trying to raise his lolling head.

His arms were dislocated, the right side of his face bloodied. They'd been hitting him with the brass-knuckles on their left hands.

I choked on a breath. That symbol had been branded into Jack's chest, over his heart.

The twins *had* met up—they'd started his torture. They'd burned the smooth skin that I'd sighed against and kissed.

They'd branded my Jack.

As I imagined that ungodly pain, my glyphs went ablaze, radiating through my clothes. Rage pumped inside me. My rose crown slithered around my head and neck as I grew stronger.

These two Arcana were not just going to die; the red witch would make them die bloody.

Selena was ice cold as she aimed her gun. "We'll be taking him now."

"Notice something?" Violet grabbed Jack's hair with her free hand. He didn't react, now completely out. She yanked his head back, exposing a metal collar around his neck, with wires attached and a railroad spike jutting from the loop. "If anything happens to me and I release this pressure sensor"—she raised that remote control—"the hunter gets the spike. Then it's game over."

Dread overran me, and I fought to rein in the witch, to call back my fury.

"If you want him to live, drop the gun, Archer." Vincent motioned toward her weapon. "And kick it over here."

Outwardly cool, Selena complied. Then she eyed the twins with deadly intent, waiting for her opening.

Vincent swooped up the gun, smiling at his sister. "It never fails. Control the beloved, control the lover."

Violet smiled back, releasing Jack. "We go into a person's heart and see who it aches for. Then we enslave both lovers."

Vincent stowed the gun in his waistband, turning to me and Selena. "Imagine our surprise when we discovered the hunter loves the Empress. Could it be requited? We heard your call nearing and we knew—"

"—you were here to save him," Violet continued seamlessly. "Our soldiers might have failed to seize you in the stone forest, but we forced you to come to us. We can control you utterly, because of how you feel about Deveaux."

They were crazy—and that made them hard to gauge—but I didn't detect true animosity toward Selena. Me? They seemed to *despise* me.

"But I sense something else." Violet's eyes widened. "Your love is diluted! Another makes claim to your heart. And not just anyone!"

Vincent laughed. "It's her old nemesis!"

The twins found this astounding. Which, I guessed, it was.

"Unfortunately, we only have one of the men you love," Vincent said. "For now."

Violet frowned at Selena. "The Archer loves the hunter as well? What's so special about him? All he does is steal." When she slapped Jack's face, my claws ached to plunge into her neck like hypodermic needles. "Oh dear. He's gone under again. The selfish man only wakes for his beatings. Which clearly means those are his favorites!"

"We gave you the choice," Vincent told an unconscious Jack. "Torture or be tortured? You mortals always choose incorrectly, until we introduce you to pain, enlightening you. Then you never choose the same!"

I furtively clawed my palms, dripping blood onto the ground. Vines could sneak beneath Violet, then shoot up to secure that sensor. But the risk . . .

Selena had no such qualms, was inching closer, soundless over the sawdust. With her superhuman reflexes, could she strike before Violet reacted?

"So how should we enlighten him?" Violet tapped her chin with a polished black nail. "The Pear of Anguish, the Scavenger's Daughter, the Heretic's Fork, or the Spanish Spider? Or we could simply maim."

"Excellent idea, Vi. His hunter's eyes have watched us so closely, I'm keen to scoop them out." He crossed to a nearby table, turning on a portable camping burner. A charred tablespoon lay beside it.

A knot tightened in my stomach when he raised the utensil over the flame. While it heated, he cast me a casual, la-di-da smile—as if he waited for a coffeemaker to finish a pot.

But Selena closed in on striking range. I needed to distract the twins. "Why do you do it? Why torture?"

"To practice our craft, exploring the pains and pleasures of the flesh," Vincent said. "We are tools used by The First. The First will learn through us."

"First?" Watching the Archer eerily stalk her prey made me glad she was on my side.

Vincent turned the spoon. "The Hallowed First, whom we serve."

"I don't understand."

65

He exhaled. "What we hear is heard. What we see is seen. What we know is known." *If you say so.* "But we soon developed a taste for torture, because we're Arcana."

Insane twin logic. "That doesn't mean you have to torture."

"Did the Hierophant and the Alchemist die peacefully?" Vincent's expression was superior.

Both had died in agony. "I acted in self-defense—for no other reason." Yet hadn't the red witch gotten a high from the kills?

Violet snapped, "You enjoyed it enough in the last game!" Finally, unconcealed emotion from her. "I doubt *your* tastes have changed."

"What are you talking about?"

When she gazed at Vincent, his pale irises briefly turned black. "Tell her. The First will see her reaction."

"It's you," Violet hissed. "We practice torture—for you."

12

"Didn't you ever wonder why we marched on Haven?'" Vincent asked
me. "We planned to make you a prisoner of our love, getting our
revenge. But this is even better. We know how much harder it is to see
a loved one tormented. You taught us that."

Me?

Violet added, "You once told us, 'Love is the most destructive force
in the universe.' You were right."

I shook my head. "I-I've never seen you before. I don't know what
you're talking about."

"Don't act oblivious!" Spittle flew from Vincent's lips. "Your line
chronicles, just as ours does."

"I've never read my history. I only know fragments."

They studied me, must've decided I was telling the truth.

"Then we'll bring you up to speed." Violet moved beside her
brother. "In the last game, we were in an alliance. Until you betrayed
us. You trapped me in your vines, but you couldn't catch my lover. To
lure him, you tortured me so savagely—"

"—that I surrendered, to spare my beloved," Vincent picked up. "I
made the choice to sacrifice myself. At least in the end you were true to
your word: you dispatched us swiftly enough."

"Everything we do is because of you." Violet reached for Vincent, playing with the hair at his nape. "Every move our family makes, we consider you. My father named me Violet because I'm the only flower you'll never control. Never again."

She talked as if I'd . . . formed them? Like they formed new Bagmen. My nausea churned anew.

Horrifying words leapt to my tongue: *I was just playing the game.* But I remained silent.

If their story had been written, I would have been the villain.

Then I realized it had been written.

Chronicled.

"We are choice, Empress," Vincent and Violet told me in unison. "We are retribution. And we *remember*. Soon you'll see. We will love you ever so much."

I expected them to clasp hands and swing their arms, but Violet kept playing with his hair while holding that sensor. He continued heating the spoon. When would they reveal their powers?

My gaze darted to Selena. What did she think about all this?

She was so close. I needed to give her more time. "I'm different than I was in the last game," I told the twins. "I'm disgusted by what was done to you. But you'll still punish me?"

Vincent flashed a predator's smile. "In unspeakable ways."

Together, they added, "Practice has made perfect."

I stifled a shudder.

"You'll watch us break and kill the man you love," Vincent said. "Then we'll take you and the Archer north, as prisoners of our love. You'll behold the First with your own eyes—before we take them from you, naturally." He glanced at Selena; she'd already gone motionless. "By the time you arrive, Archer, your arm will be healed," he told her. "A blank canvas for the First to transform."

How did he know about her arm? Spies? "Why torture Selena? She didn't do anything to you."

"The Archer's body glows red, the color of bloodletting," Violet mused. "This fascinates the First. The First will personally torment it."

"She satisfies our tastes." Vincent peeled his gaze from Selena. "You are for retribution."

I told him, "That will never happen."

"How are you going to stop us? An Empress in a world of ash?" He scoffed. "We expected more of a challenge from you and the others. We heard all your calls as you gathered. But only two faced us? This isn't fun at all."

Violet's hand descended to rub her brother's back. "We like games and fun. You've given us neither."

"More are coming," I said, bluffing. "The heavy hitters of our alliance. We're just the opening act."

"Alliances force choices," Vincent said. "When to enter into one. When not to honor one. In a pinch, no Arcana will truly be an ally. You just temporarily use each other."

My relationship with Death bore that out. But what about Selena dragging Finn home despite her broken bones? "That's not true. Not anymore. This game is different. *We* are different."

As if I hadn't spoken, Violet released her brother to traipse behind Jack, that sensor in hand. "Prisoners of our love force choices. Now that we have the two of you and the hunter, will the rest of your alliance try to free you?"

"Of course," I lied. Would Gabriel return? All he knew was that I'd gone crazed and clawed Tess, just as Joules had warned.

"Are you ready over there, Vi? It's almost hot enough." To me, Vincent said, "When the spoon singes away the eyelashes before the metal touches flesh, it's the ideal temperature."

Violet snatched Jack's hair and lifted his head again. "Wake up, knave!" She gave him a shake. Nothing. "He'll come to when you're ready, beloved."

I hastily told them, "If you gouge out *my* eyes, they'll grow back." I thought. "A few months ago, I severed my own thumb, and it regenerated. Don't you want to see that? You can cut off my fingers over and over." A sentence I never imagined I would utter.

Vincent gave me a disinterested wave of his hand. "We're getting to that." He inspected the sizzling spoon.

I was boring him. Think! "Where in the north is the First? Is that your dad?"

Selena gripped her sword hilt, muscles tensing—

"Now, now, Archer." With his free hand, Vincent smoothly brandished and cocked the pistol he'd taken from Selena.

She froze.

He definitely knew how to use that gun. "Go stand next to the Empress," he ordered her. "I want you both front row for this."

When Selena turned toward me and I saw her face, I felt like I'd been punched in the gut.

She wore an expression I'd never seen on her before: bewilderment. For the first time since I'd met her, the Archer had no clue what she was going to do next.

13

"Everything we do to him, we'll do to you," Vincent told me as he closed in on Jack.

Violet beamed with anticipation. "I long for his screams." With a giggle, she admitted, "He'll be so handsome when he yells."

Vincent glowered, jealous. "Vi?"

"Not more than when *you* yell, my love."

While they had their Lovers' quarrel, I whispered to Selena, "Use me. As a bullet shield. Get to the sensor."

"Fuckin' A, Evie." She grabbed my shoulder. "Ready?"

I nodded, bracing for bullets—

A shrieking whistle sounded, like an approaching rocket. Loud as an explosion, the tent canvas above us . . . surged upward, disappearing into the night's murk.

Gabriel?

He'd snatched the tent away on a flyby!

Beams collapsed, furniture tumbling. Taking advantage of the twins' confusion, Selena yanked her sword free and lunged for Violet. With blistering speed, she slashed off the girl's arm. Before the limb could hit the floor, Selena snared the sensor.

She slid Violet's thumb off, covering the button with her own. "Got it, you bitch."

Violet smiled even as her blood gushed. "This was unexpected, Archer. Beware the Empress." She fell, her body in a straight line.

Like a card.

Selena lunged to finish Violet; Vincent bellowed, twisting toward Selena with that gun.

A shot rang out. She dodged.

He . . . missed.

The Archer was *pissed*. "I'm gonna shove this sword so far up your ass, Vince." Dripping blade raised, she stormed toward the boy, who took aim once more.

"Eyes to the skies, lads!"

"Incoming, Evie!" Selena yelled, whirling around mid-charge to stiff-arm me.

Sharp pressure on my shoulder; I hurtled through the air, landing in front of Jack.

"Cover J.D.!"

Popping up, I sliced my claws through the line above him. When he collapsed, I threw myself over him.

Never letting go of that sensor, Selena overturned the table in front of us—just as a javelin sank into Vincent's torso.

Thunk.

Vincent stared down, bellowing, *"I return to the FIRST!"*

Bomb blast. Lightning streaked above. The shockwave hit the table, shoving it at us like a car crusher.

"Ahh!" Selena locked her legs against it, resisting the impact. The wood splintered, the tabletop splitting around her boots!

How strong is *she?* She gritted her teeth, protecting us with all her might.

When the scorching heat finally subsided, I rose up from Jack to claw that collar off his neck, exhaling with relief as I tossed it away. I peeked up over the ruins of the table to survey the destruction, scoping out any other threats.

Little remained of Vincent. Violet was a charred pile. Behind us, all the stalls had fallen, revealing the full extent of the Lovers' crazy. Lightning had wiped out the Bagmen and those five victims as well. Freed from pain at last.

Back to Jack. "Can you hear me?" I slashed off the manacles at his blood-encrusted wrists and ankles. "Please say something!" He groaned in pain, but didn't wake.

Selena rose with difficulty. "Check his pulse."

I pressed two fingers against his neck. "I think it's even." Which blunted my immediate panic. "Selena, are you okay?"

Blood ran from a gash on her temple. "I'm all right. You got that collar off him?"

I jerked my chin toward it on the floor.

She glared at the sensor in her fist. When she dropped it, that spike shot into the center of the discarded collar.

I shuddered at how close Jack had come to dying.

"He'll be okay, Evie." She swiped her hand over her temple, shrugging at the blood that came away. "There's a doctor across the river. A podiatrist, but what can you do?"

Jack's skin wept around that brand. "What is this mark?"

"The Lovers' symbol. Their icon is the same."

"Those freaks marked him as their own." A prisoner of their love. "And his shoulders are out of their sockets. What else did they do?"

"They'd only been getting started on him." She gazed down at him, total adoration in her expression. "Whatever they did, he'll come back from it. He's a survivor."

"Is there a blanket? Anything to cover him?" Wait . . . "Where's his rosary? We have to find it for him." It'd been his mother's.

"On it, Empress." Selena only called me that when I'd earned a tiny bit of her respect. She ransacked the Lovers' belongings, scoring a blanket. She wadded it up and lobbed it at me.

I spread it over Jack, drawing his head into my lap. My eyes watered as I smoothed the backs of my fingers over the left side of his face. The right was swollen out of proportion. Bruises mottled his skin.

How much more could he take? I didn't want him to have to be a *survivor*. He'd already been forced into that role well before the apocalypse.

He needed to separate himself from all Arcana. From *me*. My tear struck his cheek.

With a *whoosh*, Gabriel landed beside us, to the amazement of gathering soldiers. Joules strolled over behind him.

The Tower had made the kill, Gabriel there with the assist. As an Arcana, Joules would soon bear the Lovers' icon, a small mark appearing on his hand.

A trophy. And maybe a way to keep score?

"Oi, birds, how about that blast?" Joules gave us a mock bow. "And that was just a one on a scale of a hundred. When the Tower has to come in to save the day, collateral damage happens."

"You could've fried us," Selena told him.

"Serves you two right for nearly killin' Tess. We've never seen her so close to bitin' it."

Ah, God, Tess! "Is she okay?" Now that I wasn't burning with red witch power—and confidence—I flinched to recall my actions.

Gabriel bared his fangs at me. "She will be. In time."

"She's officially no longer the Arcana laughingstock," Selena said. "Because of her, we prevented J.D. from getting his eyeballs scooped out with a hot spoon."

Gabriel's snarl faded.

"No shite?" Joules surveyed the ruins of contraptions, whistling under his breath. "In the next few days, Tess'll plump up right smart. She'll be glad she helped. Lass likes to help."

I asked Gabriel, "Will you please fly Jack to the doc?" I didn't want to part from him, but he needed medical attention.

With a nod, Gabriel easily lifted Jack's big body in a fireman's carry. *Note: superhuman strength for Gabriel.* With a grimace of pain, the angel swooped his damaged wings.

I watched him and Jack until they disappeared into the night sky.

Selena rifled through an overturned trunk. "Why'd you come, Tower? You went from *hell no* to *feck it*."

"I started a tab for the Empress. She owes me now. Plus Gabe said he'd do whatever it took to save you, even if it meant using his wing till he crippled it." Joules faced me. "What happened, anyway?"

I told him the highlights, ending with: "Thank you for the save. For whatever reason you did it. You're a hero." I studied his reddening cheeks. "And I think you like it."

His voice went gruff. "Piss off." He ambled away.

Selena returned. "Got J.D.'s stuff." She wore his crossbow strapped over her back and his bug-out bag slung over a shoulder. His rosary dangled from her free hand.

"You found the rosary!" *Rose*-ary. "Can I see it? And Jack's bag?"

With a grudging look, she handed them over. I stowed the beads in my pocket, hugging the bag to my chest.

She slumped down beside me.

There Selena and I sat in the drizzle, shoulder to shoulder, as if nothing had come between us over these months. As if we were still on the same page.

As if we didn't love the same man.

She said, "I couldn't find the Lovers' chronicles, though."

"Their father must have them." The battle had been close for me and the Archer, but the Lovers were now dead. So why wouldn't my uneasiness fade? Yes, we still had the general to contend with, but how tough could a mortal be? "After tonight, will Milovníci continue terrorizing people?"

"Who can tell? All I know is he's about to meet up with his kids real soon."

When more soldiers closed in to gawk—at us, at the bodies, at the contraptions—that guy Franklin approached us. He'd ditched the gas mask, but it had left him with hat head. Gas mask head? "Is Deveaux going to be okay?"

"I think so. Thank you for asking."

He toed a bloody clump of sawdust. "Are you his girlfriend?"

Selena raised her brows, as if she couldn't wait to hear my answer.

"Jack and I went to school together." For five days. "We met up after the Flash. I'm Evie. This is Selena. Sorry for the abrupt entrance before. We were on a clock." When he nodded, I asked, "Do you know Jack?"

"I knew of him from the Louisiana reservist unit, before the Azey took it over. Made a real name for himself as a bow hunter. He destroyed hundreds of Bagmen and never wasted a bullet."

The man that monsters should fear.

Selena told me, "We came across some guys from Canada who'd all heard of J.D. from different sources. But they said the number of Baggers was in the thousands."

Was Jack growing into a folk hero?

Selena turned to Franklin. With her typical diplomacy, she asked, "The crank—who was attached to it?"

"A few months back, a couple of guys helped Deveaux escape the general's firing squad." Franklin looked away. "The twins tortured them since then. The last one alive was having his intestines pulled out inch by inch."

That was what I'd seen. The slimy rope. Oh, dear God. The Lovers had tried to force Jack to turn the crank, to torment someone who'd saved his life.

"You never thought to help those men?" Selena demanded. "Or the four guys getting cooked into Baggers?"

Franklin's shame was palpable. "I wanted to! But I've got a little brother in Azey North. He's only twelve. Every time I stepped out of line, I risked my life—and his. There are spies everywhere." He exhaled a long breath. "Or, there were. They bugged out, running north."

"What will happen to the women here?" I searched the crowd for that hobbled lady.

"Per Deveaux's orders, I've already seen to their release, protection, and provisioning."

76

I frowned at him. "What orders?"

"He's in charge now. In his messages, Deveaux promised to lead the white hats among us, the good guys who protect people in need."

"Thanks, Franklin. I'll tell him you asked after him." When the man strode off, I turned to Selena. "In charge? Why would Jack entangle himself in all this? To help total strangers?" He'd protested whenever I'd done the same, insisting that we could only worry about ourselves and our own survival.

"When he assumes command here, we can liberate the other half."

"That sounds like a ton of responsibility."

Selena nodded. "He's different now."

I wanted her to unpack that comment, but other looky-loo soldiers clustered around us. When they stared at me and Selena, Joules wandered back our way, producing another javelin.

He paced, twirling it menacingly. Guarding us? "Oi! You wanna ride the lightning, my friend?" His electrified skin sparked in the drizzle.

"These soldiers can't get enough Arcana," Selena said. "Guys who handle lightning and girls who grow vines. Flying angels."

"No one here saw me grow vines. Well, they did. But only before we went back in time." Again, a sentence I never thought I'd say. "What a night." My brain felt like mush. Like it was limping along. "Did you know any of the stuff about me and the Lovers? Were they telling the truth about the last game?"

"They weren't lying."

"That might've been good to know before I went in there to face them." Why hadn't Death told me?

She shrugged. "I considered telling you, but I didn't want you to chicken out just because some army-backed serial killers planned to mutilate and murder you."

Right. "How can you know for sure what I did back then?"

"It's in my chronicles. In past games, the Archer would travel with an entire contingent, like war correspondents. They saw the Lovers' remains. Definitely had the Empress's stamp."

The red witch's stamp.

Selena examined her swollen arm. "Matthew should've told you this stuff. He should've warned J.D. about getting captured. How about a heads-up about the Priestess?"

"You can't blame him. He's doing the best he can. And maybe he tells us everything we need to know, but we fail at understanding." Like I had when he'd told me about Tess manipulating time.

"How'd you fight the Priestess, anyway?"

"She sent water tentacles, so I choked them with my vines."

"Tentacles? Evie, she could've swept you into the river like a guppy. Or crushed you with a tsunami. She was playing with you."

Every time I identified the very last card we'd ever have to kill, another one popped up.

As if reading my mind, Selena asked, "You still think we can end all this?"

In a hushed voice, I said, "There isn't a *trues* over here, and we're worth four icons between us. But neither Joules nor Gabriel targeted us."

"I can't tell who's crazier—you, for continuing to believe we can end the game, or me, for starting to believe you," she said. "I never imagined someone like you would be a leader, other than a cheer*leader*."

"Post-apocalypse, doesn't everyone need to evolve?"

She raised her face to the intermittent rain. "Jesus, Evie, what if it catches on? What if we could all live in peace? Use these powers for good?"

I'd had the same thought! "We could repurpose ourselves." Fight freaking crime, anything.

"If evil Arcana don't get in our way." Selena faced me. "Speaking of which, what's going on between you and Death?"

Between us? My escape and his sword. According to the twins: burgeoning love.

Since I'd left him, Death hadn't telepathically contacted me, hadn't overtaken me on the road. What if he . . . couldn't? "I learned more about my history with him. This won't be news to you, but Aric had reason to hate me."

"You call Death *Aric*?" she spat. "So that murderer has a human name?"

"It's not all black and white," I insisted. "I came to care for him."

She looked more disgusted by me than she had by the Lovers' making out. "If I see him, I *will* put an arrow in his heart."

"Good luck with that. Last time, your arrows disintegrated against his armor."

"You actually give a damn about him? Up is down and down is up. What about J.D.?"

"I haven't been able to think past a rescue. Now I'll take some time and sort things out in my head." Once I got some rest. I'd had only a few hours over days.

"J.D. wasn't the only one who's changed in the last three months. Things between us are different."

After Jack had thought I was lost for good, had he given Selena what she wanted most in this world?

Himself?

Something like grief swamped me. I'd wanted him far away from this sick game. If he'd then gotten with another card . . . ?

It had never, never occurred to me that Jack might not want me back, might not be clamoring to tell me his side of the story. "Wh-what changed then?"

Before she could answer, the angel landed once more. "Jack is with the physician."

"Thank you, Gabriel."

He gave me a solemn nod. Maybe he should see the doc next. After his dive-bomb, that bullet hole was now the size of a salad plate.

He offered his claw-tipped hand to Selena. "Your carriage awaits."

I thought that was cute, but she just gave him a *really?* look and stood on her own.

She had no way of knowing that he'd evacuated her first—at least, before time reversed itself. "Shouldn't we take the bridge back?" I nodded at his wing.

"We'll wait till the bridge is one hundred percent secured." He caught my eye. "It's too dangerous yet, for you and *Selena*."

Oh, right. He'd take the pain just to hold her.

She frowned when he pulled her into his arms, cradling her against him. "We'll talk later, Evie."

I gave her a thumbs-up; she flipped me off as he took to the air once more.

"Oi, flower girl!" Joules called to me. "How long does it take for the icon to show on my hand?" I guessed he wanted his trophy.

I hated that I knew the answer to his question twice over. "It's pretty much instant."

"Then who the feck stole my icon?"

14

As Jack slept, I sat on the edge of his cot, replaying the doc's prognosis.

The man's examination of Jack's skull had revealed two bad knots; most likely concussed. He'd fixed Jack's dislocated arms, cleaned his wounds, and bandaged the angry burn on his chest.

He predicted a full recovery—*if* Jack took it easy for a couple of weeks. But the doc had also told me how long Jack would carry the Lovers' mark, that reminder of his torture.

For the rest of his life.

Which made me need to poison something.

I retracted my budding claws, whispering to Jack, "Brand or not, you'll always be breathtaking to me." I tenderly tucked the cover around him, staggered by the love I felt for him.

I'd tried so hard to get over him. Never could. In fact, I'd celebrated when I could go an hour without thinking about him.

But we had so much standing between us. Too little trust, too much danger.

I needed to let him go, to steer him away from all this. Yet all I wanted to do was curl up next to his battered body. . . .

I heard Joules out in the fort, stomping up and down the plankway, making a stink about his missing icon. He'd already insisted on a mandatory hand check for all Arcana.

Had the transfer gone wacky because Selena struck first, starting the attack?

Matthew's answers to Joules's heated questions—and mine—hadn't been in the realm of coherent. The boy had looked done in.

I gazed over at his half of the tent. My chest squeezed when I realized his only belongings in the world were his bug-out bag, a model of some sci-fi alien, and a Mad Libs book.

Beside Jack's cot? Magazines for different trades: electricians, mechanics, contractors. Under his cot, he'd stored fifths of whiskey, making me wonder if he was still on the wagon. Atop a small desk were maps of this region. He'd been redrawing them to reflect the new landscape.

My gaze fell on Jack's bug-out bag. I unzipped it and peeked inside. Among all his survival gear, he still had that copy of *Robinson Crusoe* I'd given him.

And there was the cell phone that had belonged to Brandon, my onetime boyfriend, and Jack's half brother. Not that it could make a call. Jack had told me he'd constantly sourced power for it—just so he could look at the videos and pictures of me.

I even found the Alchemist's recording of my life story in a small player.

Surely Jack wouldn't keep these things with him at all times if he'd moved on from me.

I fished out his envelope of photos. The first night I'd been on the road with him, he'd shown me the contents of his bag, but he hadn't wanted me to see these.

Turnabout, Jack. I glanced through them, finding nothing bad, just photos of his friends and his mom.

Jack stirred. Was he waking? I stuffed everything back in his pack.

His gray eyes opened. Bloodshot, weary, but so familiar. "Evangeline?" He blinked, as if he couldn't believe I was with him. "You real? Another dream?" He sounded half-dead.

He and I had been separated for three months. Felt like three years.

"I'm here with you." I took his hand in mine. "You're safe now."

With his brows drawn, he rubbed his callused fingers over my skin, like he was testing my *realness*. "Never thought I'd get free from the twins. Much less see you again."

"The resident doc patched you up. Everything's going to be okay."

"And you're watching over me? *Ma belle infirmière*." My pretty nurse. He'd always loved when I'd fussed over him.

"Before I forget . . ." I drew his rosary from my pocket.

He spared it a brief glance, gaze returning to me. With a hint of his heartbreaking grin, he said, "My prayers already got answered, *non*?"

I didn't address that. "Selena found it." I leaned over and clasped it around his neck.

"*Merci*." He peered up at me. "Christ, I missed those blue eyes of yours. *Ma fille aux yeux bleus*." My blue-eyed girl. "Didn't think I'd ever see them again."

You almost didn't.

Then he stared at some point past me. "What the hell?"

Cyclops had nosed his head inside the tent flap. "Oh. One of Lark's wolves is protecting me. Long story. He won't hurt you."

Jack looked even more confused.

To distract him, I said, "Hey, when you get back on your feet, you can show me all around this place. Not many guys have their own forts."

"You can't leave from here." His muscles tensed, making him wince. "Promise me you woan leave."

I had nowhere to go. No home whatsoever. I wanted one though. Fresh from viewing Haven's ruins, I felt the agonizing lack. "I won't leave."

As if that one burst of energy had sapped his remaining strength, his lids grew heavy. "I know . . . what they did . . . to Clotile."

Curiosity preyed on me. "What, Jack? And what did they do to you?"

He seemed to struggle against sleep with everything in him—"Doan want to take my eyes off you"—but he lost in the end.

Selena had entered the tent and heard the last. I couldn't read her reaction. Despite Jack's words, something could've happened between him and Selena. I might be the interloper here.

She set Jack's trusty crossbow on his desk. Since I'd last seen it, he'd modified the weapon, adding a flashlight and painting the auto-loading arrow cartridge.

"Has Joules calmed down yet?" I asked her. "Did he find the culprit?"

"The Tower's latest farfetched theory? Nanoseconds before his lightning hit, the Priestess somehow swooped in and 'insta-drowned' the twins, shoving water into their lungs. He's furious and plans to go 'spearfishing' for her." Selena frowned. "I wonder if she can be electrocuted." We could hope. "Matthew's outside, said he needs to talk to you."

"Will you stay?"

"Duh."

Though exhausted, I forced myself to stand, then shrugged into my poncho. Maybe Matthew would reveal what Jack had been through. Clotile . . .

Or how about a rundown of my history with the Lovers?

While I was out, I'd make some fruit for Tess. Nothing said "sorry I became a witch from nightmares and almost killed you" like a gift basket of fruit.

I stepped out into the biting air and drizzle. Cyclops loped beside me, barking a couple of times, as if to tell me something. *Slaver's got Timmy!*

"Empress." Matthew looked as bad as I felt—his face wan, his shoulders slumped with fatigue.

"What's happened?" Did he feel guilty because of how things had gone down?

He gazed at me with those woebegone brown eyes. "Tredici nears."

"I don't know what that is, sweetheart. Hey, aren't you happy that we rescued Jack?"

"I couldn't see." He hugged his arms around his torso, batting his fists against his parka. "The Lovers!" The lowest hum came from him.

I reached forward to pry his arms away. "We won the day. We lived through it."

He stared down at me. "The twins—inseparable. Never parted."

"I get that now." In life—and in death—they were together. "Matthew, I need to know what they did to Jack."

"A path. You won't like where it leads."

I'd gone months without decoder-ring talk. Now I was back in the thick of it. Though I was about to pass out, I asked, "What does that mean?"

"I can't steer, can't change. Before there were waves or eddies; now stone. Our enemies laugh."

"Honey, you're scaring me. And I'm so tired. Can we do this later?" He raised his palm. "Hold, please."

"Are you talking to someone else?" Matthew was the Arcana switchboard, a medium. "To . . . Aric? Is he in your eyes?" Watching me through Matthew?

Now that Jack was safe, my traitorous mind turned to Death. I *missed* Aric—or, at least, the man I'd thought he was. I missed his dry wit. I missed reading with him and dancing before his rapt gaze.

Some part of me had been on the verge of loving him. Even the twins had seen that. Yet that time with him had been canceled out by his actions. "Will he come for me?" I gazed at the walls of the fort. Would the minefield be enough to keep him out? I couldn't hide here forever.

"Meeting!" Matthew took my hand, leading me away from the tent.

"I need to grow some food and then get back to Jack."

He pulled with more insistence. He'd gotten even stronger, was almost as broad-shouldered as Jack.

At the front of the fort, Matthew gave a nod, and soldiers opened the gates. Before Cyclops could follow, they closed behind us.

"I told Jack I wouldn't leave. Matthew?"

He didn't answer, just continued leading me down a rocky trail, lower and lower as the mist thickened.

"Um, we're getting close to the shore."

"Still surface."

The trail had opened up into a beach area, similar to the one across the river. "Is it safe here?" Wary, I gazed around. I'd bet kids had once come here, drinking beer and swimming on hot, sunny days.

I missed those days so bitterly I could weep.

—*TERROR FROM THE ABYSS!*—

The call boomed in my head. "What is this, Matthew?" I wrested my hand from his.

At the beach's edge, a section of water rose.

"I'm introducing you to . . . the High Priestess."

15

When the Priestess had said we'd meet again, I thought she'd meant far in the future—some distant clash.

Not later the same night!

That rising water morphed, taking on shape. The details grew finer and finer until the outline of a girl emerged.

"Farewell, Fool," the water girl said.

I turned to Matthew.

Gone.

Damn it! I turned back to the Priestess. Though she wouldn't remember our skirmish, the feel of her tentacles was fresh in my mind. "Are you going to attack me out of the blue?" Again.

"Not at present. Though every attack of mine must be out of the *blue*, no?" How could water sound amused? "Have we peace between us for this meeting?"

I recalled Selena's guppy comment. The Priestess hadn't killed me, was instead calling a meeting. Maybe she could become an ally. "We have peace."

The water morphed again, taking the shape of an oval, like a mirror. As the ripples stilled, a firelit temple came into view. The oval had become a window for me to see through!

Sitting upon a coral throne was a girl about my age with luminous fawn-colored eyes, flawless ebony skin, and long black hair braided over her shoulder. She wore frothy white robes (sea-foam?), iridescent blue opera-length gloves, and a glittering crown of water. A golden trident stretched over her lap.

She was spellbinding.

"Hail Tar Ro, Empress."

Huh? "Hail Tar Ro to you too?"

"What is your given name for this game?" Her words were warmly accented, the rhythms calling to mind balmy breezes and faraway places.

"I'm Evie Greene."

Something unseen skittered around her throne. A real tentacle? "I'm Circe Rémire." Water sluiced down stone walls behind her. Was her temple underwater?

Until I learned her location, I couldn't fight her even if I wanted to. "You're here, but you're not here."

"I can inhabit certain bodies of water. For instance, if the Empress followed a stream from Death's lair, I could follow her."

She'd been watching me. "How's that possible?"

"How is any of this possible?" She waved a sparkly blue arm at her temple.

My eyes widened. She wasn't wearing gloves. Dazzling scales ran up her forearms, ending with a dainty blue fin at each elbow.

If I'd deemed Lark cool to have a bird of prey with a little leather helmet, Circe's scales were right up there.

"The game makes the impossible possible."

Witches and angels and devils and time travel. My head spun. I needed to get back to Jack. To feed Tess.

"I understand you had an eventful night." Circe literally didn't know the half of it. "A grand clash amid that mortal army." She seemed to be settling in for a big fat chat.

Was the Priestess lonely? As Death had been?

"Eventful," I agreed, peering at her hand. No markings. "Do

you know what happened to the Lovers' icon?" More of that creepy skittering sounded. I couldn't see what was at her feet—and maybe that was a good thing?

"Their icon is right where it should be. As are the two you wear."

Odd way to answer. "I never want another. I plan to stop this game."

She tilted her head, giving me what might have been a sad smile. "You always had a high regard for yourself."

"How would you know that? I thought no one but the Fool had memories of past lives."

"My previous incarnation cast a spell, allowing me to relive my memories through trances. Who needs a chronicler when you have firsthand information?"

A spell? "Are you a witch?"

"It depends who you ask," she said wryly. "Did the Fool give you your memories? In visions and dreams?"

"He did. I've been accessing them slowly."

"Wise. I view mine for ten minutes a day, every day without fail."

She came across as so disciplined and with-it. Unlike me. I could go weeks without a vision, then binge-watch. No wonder my brain felt like jelly.

"With each memory, I better appreciate how epic this game is," she continued. "It shapes the history of gods and man, yet the Empress doesn't want to play anymore? There's no stopping it, Evie Greene."

"Because it's impossible? You just said the game makes the impossible possible. When the alternative is murdering kids, I've got to try."

"Did you try?" She gave my hand a knowing look.

"I did." I'd wanted to appear strong, but fatigue washed over me. "I tried so hard, Circe. It's not murder if done in self-defense, or to defend the people you love."

"The Empress speaks of love—and not with derision. Now I see why Death is so taken with you this game. *You* are not *you*."

"Thanks?" I felt so out of it, the coyote to her roadrunner. "So why did you want to meet?"

"You're a mystery. I concern myself with mysteries. With esoteric lore. With things that must be brought to light."

"Like the mysteries of the deep?"

"Just so." More skittering. "Another time, another place, I might have liked to know this incarnation of you."

"Why not now? We can ally."

"We are enemies almighty, Evie Greene."

"Were we ever allies?"

"Sworn allies. Oh, the games we played! I remember the forest we claimed. I had a river, and you had your green killers. How we used to laugh together! No card could challenge us—until the Emperor arrived with his ember eyes full of fire, his hands bleeding lava. He's the one you should be targeting. Put the Lovers and your mortal male behind you."

Check-check on the Lovers. Leaning toward never on my mortal male. "You know about Jack?"

"I hear whispers. They flow down to me like water seeking its own level. Yet I can't figure out what you did with Death."

Had I been eating the lotus with Aric, uncaring that my real life was outside his castle? Before he'd captured me, I'd been a friend, a girlfriend, a granddaughter. My human life had come first.

Did it still?

Moving on . . . "The Emperor's not close. I haven't heard his call." I couldn't remember what it was.

"By the time you hear him, it's already too late." Circe shook her head ruefully, and on either side of the water window, whirlpools began to twirl in the river. The blanket of mist turned into thousands of soft cyclones. "He'll be coming. With so many Arcana converging, we'll all be attracted, pulled as if by tides."

"And you'll be waiting to drag them to their deaths?"

"As ever." In a quieter tone, she said, "Sometimes they ask me to take them to the abyss. Sometimes that's the only place they can see to go."

Her words gave me chills.

"But not the Emperor. That no-necked tyrant craves cataclysm.

This game, he calls himself Richter. As in *scale*." With a grin, she said, "We should thrash him just for that."

I found my lips curling. "We were friends, weren't we? Not just allies."

She fidgeted with the trident on her lap, jutting her chin. "As close as sisters, if you must know."

"Until I betrayed you?"

Glare.

Show of hands: who didn't *I betray in past games?* "I'm so sorry. I wish I hadn't."

Circe's glare changed to an expression of bafflement. "*You* are not *you*," she repeated. "Until next time, hail Tar Ro, Empress."

The water window disintegrated, as if melting.

The Priestess was gone.

Jack was still out when I returned to his tent.

Selena sat in a chair beside his cot. "Took you long enough." As if she'd minded.

She and I might be solid again, but Selena would always be a superhuman pain in the ass. "Matthew hasn't come back?" I'd been gone awhile.

After my confusing meeting with the Priestess, Cyclops and I had found a secluded patch of ground for me to grow fruit. My phylogenesis had been a sluggish process, taking tons of blood.

By the end, I'd been so woozy I'd blundered my way to Tess's tent. But I'd delivered a bumper crop, a poncho full of treats, more than she could ever eat by herself.

With the archangel watching over her, she'd slept, her body so small under the blankets. But she'd already looked better.

Selena stood. "Matto's probably wandering around the fort. As usual." She gazed past me. "You're letting that butt-ugly wolf inside?"

"The majestic wolf—that keeps saving my life—is an indoor pet." I'd had a night like no other, just wanted to pass out.

"Whatever. You look like shit. Go to sleep, but plan on a talk when you get up."

"About what?"

"Things." With a lingering look at Jack, she ducked out of the tent.

Sleep. Yes. I took Matthew's cot, figuring he'd wake me if he wanted it back.

I lay on my side, so I could watch Jack. Despite my exhaustion and recent blood loss, I remained awake, as if my gaze refused to be parted from him.

At what should been dawn, roosters crowed. They did at Death's home as well, undaunted by the lack of sun. Lark had once told me they crowed to their own rhythms.

Though the camp would be waking, maybe I could get an hour of sleep.

As I drifted away, I wondered what today would bring. . . .

16

Earthquake?!

I shot awake in my shuddering cot, swaying with dizziness. Why was no one screaming?

Where was Jack? Matthew?

I rubbed my eyes. Oh. False alarm. Cyclops slept along the length of the cot, shaking it as he twitched in dreams.

I reached over and stroked his frizzy fur. "The things I put up with for you." He woke, stretching his scarred limbs.

Wait, why was I in Jack's cot? And not wearing pants? My jeans hung over the chair. Had he undressed me?

Matthew ducked inside. "Empress." He looked even worse than yesterday.

"Sweetheart, are you okay?" Cyclops rose and padded past him, heading outside. I really hoped the wolf was fort-trained.

"I'm not feeling well." Matthew moved to his cot, sitting stiffly.

"What hurts?"

His pale skin was stark against his black coat. "My brain."

"Have you slept?"

"Yes. Days ago." Who *wasn't* strung out on zero sleep?

"You'll feel better once you get some rest." Which might be a lie. I'd awakened just as tired as before, only now I had a headache.

He nodded. "A respite's necessary." Anticipating my next question, he gestured toward the river. "Jack rode over to the army with the Tower and Judgment. Order! Discipline!" Joules and Gabriel were getting involved?

"Shouldn't Jack be in bed—instead of riding through the dark and rain?" So much for not wanting to let me out of his sight.

"Once he sets his mind . . ."

I sighed. "Don't I know it." It'd taken me so long to be near him, and he was out of reach again. "What time is it?"

Shrug. "Dark."

"Thanks." I pivoted my legs over the side of the cot. The nearby fire crackled, but it did little to ward away the damp cold. I found myself missing my luxurious room at Death's, then felt a ripple of guilt.

Matthew studied the ceiling so I could fetch my jeans.

I buttoned them, finding them looser. Only a few days away from Aric's, and I'd already lost weight. Speaking of which . . . "How is Tess?"

"She's okay. Like a reactor. She needed to regenerate."

"Regenerate like me?"

He rolled his eyes. "Nooo. Like a reactor."

"So when will she be up and about?"

"She's up. About." Just when I felt relief, he added, "Mostly bald."

I winced. "I'm going to have to make that up to her." I hunted for my boots, found them at the foot of the cot. "Can we please talk about last night? About what the twins did to Jack?" I'd planned on airing out everything between me and him, but how could I after he'd suffered so much?

"His story to tell."

"That's all you'll give me?"

His damp hair flopped over his forehead, and he shoved it back. He needed a haircut. "The Army grinds on, a windmill spins." He'd told me this often in the past.

The Azey had once marched on Haven because the farm had been equipped with ready sources of water: windmill water pumps. In his own way, Matthew had been warning me of the Lovers' approach.

Yet then I frowned, remembering what Vincent had told me. "The Milovnícis never cared about Haven's water. They came only for me."

"True."

"So why did you mention windmills?"

"They spin to the scent of roses."

Stifling my irritation, I sat on a trunk to pull on my boots. "Do you want to tell me about my history with the twins?" I'd once feared that much of Death's ruthlessness had been shaped by past versions of me. I'd shaped the Lovers as well?

"I gave you the history. Up to you now."

"To access those memories? You can't just tell me? They said they practiced torture for me."

He stared at his hand. Subject closed.

"Okay, then, what about the Priestess? Can we get her into our alliance?"

"Snow falls on graves." He wrapped his arms around himself.

"What graves, sweetheart? Are you cold?" Though the fire was crackling along, I looked around for another log. Didn't see one.

Of course not. The resources here were limited. How much precious wood had Jack spent on this fire, to warm me alone while he was gone?

Matthew said, "Tredici nears."

"What is Tredici?" It was too early in the morning, or the afternoon, or whenever, for this kind of confusion. "Will you explain?"

He blinked, as if I'd asked him a ridiculous question.

Inhaling for patience, I said, "So. Today's a big day for me. Do you have any advice that won't make my head hurt worse?"

"Everything from me makes you hurt. Power is your burden. Knowledge is mine. But I gave you everything before I lose my head."

"What are you talking about?" I crossed to him, pressing the backs of my fingers against one of his sallow cheeks. No fever. "Can you try to rest now?"

"Too much to do."

He'd said that before. "Like what? Do you want me to help you with any—"

He stood, turned toward the exit, then left me.

"Good talk, buddy," I said to myself. Grabbing my bug-out bag, I went searching for a place to get cleaned up.

In a communal bathroom facility, I washed with cold water, brushed my teeth, and changed into clean clothes—jeans, halter, hoodie. I felt better, but I couldn't shake that nagging headache.

I checked on Tess, who was taking a nap—*reactoring*, I suppose. About a third of the fruit I'd made for her was gone, and she steadily gained weight. Someone had left a baseball cap to cover her patchy hair.

As I headed back to the tent, chafing my hands against the chill, the gates creaked open.

Jack.

He rode into the courtyard astride a striking gray horse. I stood off in the shadows, not drawing attention to myself, just watching him.

His face was less swollen. The bandage on his chest peeked up from the collar of his flannel shirt and camo jacket. His crossbow was strapped over his other shoulder.

Joules rode in, Gabriel landing nearby. All the people in the fort cheered for the returning heroes.

When a wagon loaded with supplies rolled in, Jack called orders to soldiers. A few offloaded pallets of cans. Another group went around to lift a large gun off the back.

Jack dismounted, moving stiffly. He unstrapped a bulky camo duffel bag from his saddle, hauling it over his body. Men gathered around him, asking questions. Despite his younger age, they hung on his every word.

His unforgiving life had honed him, giving him hard-earned skills, but he'd never had a chance to utilize them to this degree.

It'd taken an apocalypse for Jack to come into his own as a leader.

He paused midsentence, then turned in my direction, as if he sensed me there.

I stepped from the shadows, and our eyes met, his so vivid and gray. His gaze roamed over my face and figure the way it had on our first day of school together, like he hadn't seen a girl in years.

Never taking his focus off me, he said something that made the other men nod and set off; then he crossed the distance between us.

Without a word, he clasped my hand, leading me to his tent. How would I approach this talk? I needed to tell him about Aric, but now wasn't the right time.

The tent seemed so much smaller with him in it, because Jack was larger than life. He pulled off that duffel bag, setting aside his bow.

We stood staring at each other in silence. At length, he moved to stand before me. "Didn't think you could get prettier." Curling his finger under my chin, he leaned down to kiss me.

I was stunned, motionless. I'd pictured our reunion, but I'd never imagined him just walking up and kissing me. A thrill cascaded through me.

God, I'd missed the feel of his lips. I gasped with pleasure.

But right when my hands decided to reach for him, my feet stepped me back. "Um, how are you feeling?"

He was clearly disappointed by my reaction. What else had he expected? The problems between us hadn't magically fixed themselves. "You know me: *tête dure.*" Hard head. "I was more worried about you."

"I'm fine. You know me: regeneration."

By the way he removed his coat, you'd never know the extent of his injuries. But that muscle ticked in his jaw. His tell. He wore a shoulder holster with two pistols, unstrapping that as well.

"When did you start carrying guns?"

"When I started goan up against firepower." He dragged his flask out of a pocket and took a pull.

I sat on Matthew's cot, as stiffly as he had before. "So you, Joules, and Gabriel took over the army?"

"*Ouais.* I wanted you and Selena there to give you credit, but she's off somewhere, and you shooed me away when I tried to wake you

97

earlier." I had? "Didn't want to leave you, but I needed to make sure those *filles* were being treated right."

Of course he would. I'd never known any man who hated violence against women so much.

"When folks see Arcana like Joules and Gabriel, they tend to step in line." He stoked the fire. "I'm not above using that to achieve some order around here."

He sat across from me, elbows on his knees, flask at the ready. His thick black hair tumbled over his forehead, and tousles jutted above his ears.

I'd once threaded my fingers through his hair, drawing him down to me. "When did you decide to go public with our kind?" He now had seven of us here, an Arcana Justice League.

He took another swig. "I remembered that in the Basin everybody told themselves stories. We'd tell ourselves we could tolerate living there because we had our friends and family with us. Or that we were tied to those lands by our history. I started thinking folks needed new stories, and I just happened to have a kid with me who can make illusions and a girl whose skin glows." He shrugged, then seemed to regret the movement. "We've been giving people a new story to tell."

Though the sentiment was heartening, I was still surprised by his involvement. "In the past you didn't concern yourself with others. You called serving your fellow man bullshit. You said *live* people were the worst kind."

"I hadn't met many solid characters then. Over these months, I have."

"You never went looking for trouble. Sound familiar? This is a heaping ton of trouble."

"Dis-moi quelque chose que j'connaîs pas." Tell me something I don't know. "But I've realized some things."

"Like what?"

"We might be goan extinct, Evie. As in, our species is goan to lose this one. And yet Milovníci is the only one mobilizing folks? Somebody's got to stand up to him. For some reason, it's fallen to me." Another swig.

"You're drinking again. I thought you quit." He'd started so young.

"Had to be sharp to get back to you. To fight your enemies." A shadow crossed his expression. "But after a while, you didn't want me to."

I couldn't deny that. "And now?"

In a low tone, he said, "Drinking helps with the pain." I knew he meant *anguish*. His tolerance for physical pain was off the charts. "I didn't expect you to come, Evie."

"Of course I would." In a softer voice, I said, "Will you please tell me what happened to you? To Clotile?"

He faced me with such a tormented look that I shivered. "I'll *never* tell you. *Jamais*."

"Jack, I have to know."

"I felt the same way. Now? I wish to Christ I didn't know." His flask shook in his hand. "I wish I could've killed those two myself—making it last."

"Your friend was with you. I'm so sorry."

Brows drawn tight, he said, "You ever order yourself not to think about something? With my podna . . ." Jack's breaths whistled like a weight pressed down on his chest. "I'm hanging on by a thread here, Evangeline."

Oh, Jack. My gaze dipped to the edge of his bandage. There was no way I could tell him about Aric. Not right now. I refused to snip that thread.

Jack pulled up his shirt to conceal the bandage. Embarrassed? In front of me? "I'll have this forever, *non*?" He lifted his chin. "That's what the doc said."

"You survived Vincent and Violet. Which is all that matters."

"You nearly didn't. Selena told me you fought off the High Priestess too."

I nodded.

"And that you almost killed Tess for me. Made the girl . . . take you back in time, to save my sight. What the hell happened? Joules and Gabe woan say much about it."

Deciding on total honesty, I said, "The twins took out your eyes with a hot spoon."

"Doan know how to react to that." So he took a drink. "I saw Tess this morning. *Maigre, non?*" Skinny, no? "But she wasn't mad. Couldn't say enough good about you."

Then she must not remember what happened. "I heard you yell. I lost it."

Hope flared in those gray eyes. "If you care that much, did you come here to be with me? Like we were? Or like we could be in time?"

"Things are different now." I didn't want him to expect something I wasn't sure I could give. "They just are."

"Maybe you came running out of guilt. Because Arcana had me?"

"I'd already planned to find you—before you were taken."

"Death was goan to let you go?"

"Not exactly." Never. "It doesn't matter. I'm here now."

"It does matter. How did you get away?"

"Matthew helped me." True, but evasive.

"But you didn't take down the Reaper?" Again, I felt Jack's disappointment in me. "Even after what he did to us? Even after he left me and *coo-yôn*, Finn and Selena to die?" He pointed to my hands, to the icons. "You killed two. Why not Death?"

"I learned more about the history of the games, about why he hated me. I wasn't exactly Miss Congeniality in the past. I betrayed him in ways you can't imagine."

Jack swiped his hand over his bruised face. "Try me."

"It's complicated. Earlier I didn't press for answers from you, and now I want to drop this subject."

He looked like he was just getting started. "Joules told me about the offer he made you. You had a chance to get me freed days ago, but you didn't take it!" "There's a lot about Death that you don't know. That *I* didn't."

"He's goan to be coming for you."

I wasn't convinced. "I have no idea what to expect."

"Did you know you were the only one he could touch?"

I shook my head. "Not before I was taken."

"I didn't figure much could shock me anymore. Then I found out the bastard wanted you for himself. Not to kill—but to keep. That true?"

"It was." Once.

"*Coo-yôn* told me all about him. A rich noble knight. Speaks eight languages or some shit. Gave you a warm room in a castle and protection from this entire fucking world." I'd ordered Matthew to tell Jack I was safe; he might have spread it on a little heavy. "Maybe you were stupid to leave."

Stupid? "You've got a lot of nerve coming at me like this! You were the one who lied to me." I grappled with my temper, reminding myself of all he'd been through.

"Death told you those things just to drive a wedge between us."

"If you'd been honest with me, the truth wouldn't have been such a blow."

"How the hell was I supposed to tell you about your mother?" He finished his flask. "A thousand times I imagined your reaction. There was nothing I could say that didn't equal me losing you."

"For so long, I was trapped at Death's, with no friends or family to turn to. Then I learned that you'd done this thing. That you'd lied about it. Easily." My words appeared to hurt him worse than his recent torture. "Do you remember when we promised each other there'd be no more secrets between us? I do. I remember your eyes darted." Like it was yesterday . . .

"Are you lying to me? Jack, nothing is more important than trust right now. Considering this game, this whole world, we have to be able to depend on each other."

"I'm not lying. You can trust me alone, Evie. I got no secrets, peekôn. Except for how bad I want you."

"I was such an idiot to believe you," I said. "I bought everything you told me, against my better judgment. You heaped so much shit on me for keeping things from you—when you hid plenty from me!"

He shoved his fingers through his hair. "I sensed things were off with you. I sensed you were in danger. I needed to know more, because I wanted to protect you. But my secrets would do nothing but tear us apart."

"Then try me now. Tell me what happened that night with my mother."

"You got to hear this, doan you? To get past it? Then I will. I'll tell you." In preparation, he dragged out a bottle from under his cot, refilling his flask.

Suddenly I wasn't sure I wanted to hear this at all.

17

"Your *mère* got the idea in her head when you were knocked out from that shotgun blast."

My one and only time to fire a weapon.

"She couldn't make it down the stairs, much less out on the road—so she wanted me to take you away, to save you from the Azey. When I pointed out that you'd never leave her, she goes, 'Not unless I'm dead.'"

As I waited breathlessly, he took his seat once more, flask in hand. "Karen told me, 'You're going to help me, son; you just don't know it yet.'"

Though I'd refused to see the vision of her death, Matthew must've given this memory to me. With each of Jack's words, details of the scene seeped into my consciousness.

I could smell the faint traces of gardenia in my mother's room, and Jack's scent: leather, and Castile soap from when he'd washed up that day.

I heard the wheeze in each of Mom's breaths. Her face was twisted from pain, which she'd hidden from me. I could see the pulse point in Jack's neck beating as he scrambled away from my mother, telling her he couldn't help her die. . . .

"No way I'd do that." His gaze went distant. "No fucking way. But she got this look on her face—like she had steel in her eyes. She promised me she'd slit her own throat with a shard of glass if she had to. And damn, Evie, I *believed* her."

My fierce mother would have. "How did you do it?" The words came out as a whisper.

"Between Karen and me, we knew just enough about pills to be dangerous. There used to be a dealer down in the bayou. Before you woke, I rode out and fetched his stash."

"So during that dinner, both of you knew what was going to happen when I went to bed. I never suspected a thing from your behavior." Dee-vee-oh.

"I tried to make it nice for her."

"So she . . . OD'd? There wasn't"—I swallowed—"you didn't use a pillow?"

Jack blanched under his bruises. "She asked me to. Dawn was coming, the army with it. And she was afraid you'd wake up before the dose took hold. I asked her to give it time, distracting her with questions about you."

While I'd slept soundly.

"Christ, I wanted those pills to work, couldn't imagine hurting her like that. But so much was at stake, I suspect . . . I think I would have. She believed I could, told me so." He tipped that flask up. "I doan know what that says about her—or me."

Eyes watering, I surveyed Jack's face. How haunted he was! My mom had sacrificed everything to save me, but at what cost? She'd used a teenage boy to help her die.

I couldn't hate him. Just the opposite.

He'd saved my life and ended my mother's suffering, when I'd been stupidly holding out hope. He'd spared her the horror of a violent passing and stayed with her to the very end.

Matthew's words: "Whenever he helps, he hurts."

Jack had helped and been hurt.

I'd so long associated him with grief because of his involvement in her death.

That association faded to nothing.

"In the end, I think the pills took her by surprise. She was looking at that picture of you, her, and your *grand-mère*. She was half-smiling, half-crying—like she was happy for sixteen years with you, but terrified about your future. No room for her to be afraid for herself, no. I told her I'd take care of you for as long as I could. Then her eyes just . . . slid shut."

Now I knew. Now I had closure. As Jack had once told me, my mother "died in grace."

"Evie, what will it take to get you to forgive me?"

I swiped a sleeve over my eyes. "I forgive you. I have no doubt that my mother would've done it anyway. Because of you, she went peacefully." My voice broke. "Because of you, she wasn't alone."

"But . . ."

"But I don't know how I can trust you. You're really *skilled* at lying. It's like an Arcana talent of yours or something." When Jack had first come to Haven after the Flash, I'd distrusted him fiercely. I felt the same way now.

He shot to his feet, started pacing. "I didn't want to lie!"

"There's a pattern. You wanted to look in my journal, so you stole it. You wanted to know about the Arcana, so you listened to my story on that tape. You demand honesty and disclosure from me, but give me neither in return."

He pinned my gaze with his frenzied one. "I will never lie to you again!"

"How can I believe that?" I cried, standing as well. "Already we have a new unknown between us—what the Lovers did to you. "

"I'll tell you right now: I got more secrets, me. A whole mess of 'em. And some are goan to the grave with me. You're just goan to have to accept that."

If we kept his secrets buried, then couldn't I bury my own?

No. Not telling him about Aric would be as good as lying. Eventually, I'd have to.

He drew closer, until he was staring down at me. "All my life I've dug at mysteries, solved puzzles. If the twins taught me anything, I learned that some things doan need to be known. That they're even uglier when brought to light."

The Priestess's words filtered into my brain. *Mysteries brought to light.* In a way, she and Jack were similar—

"Do you love me?" His blunt question took me off guard.

Total honesty? I swallowed. "Yes."

His eyes briefly slid shut. I thought some of his tension would fade, but it redoubled. "Good. Then you're goan to accept my secrets—and me. Because I can't keep doing this without you."

"This?" We were toe to toe, breathing heavily.

"*This*, Evie. Life after the Flash. Fighting for something better." He tangled one hand through my hair, cupping my head. "It's you for me. Or it's nothing." Holding me tightly, he slanted his mouth over mine.

A hint of whiskey met my tongue—like a match to dry kindling. Lust slammed into me, as if we'd trained my body to react to that sense memory.

He pulled me even closer against him, coaxing me to kiss back. I'd missed him so much! With a moan I did, wrapping my arms around his neck.

He groaned with pleasure—and relief?

I melted from the heat of his body against mine, trying to breathe him into me. We'd only been together once. We deserved another time like our first. He deserved to feel at peace afterward.

What was to stop us . . . ?

Death. What I'd done with Aric. To Aric.

Somehow I managed to draw back. "I have to talk to you." I would explain, make him understand.

He leaned in, pressing kisses to my neck in his toe-curling way. "I missed you, Evangeline. So goddamned much. When you wanted nothing to do with me . . ." He gave a shuddering exhalation against my damp skin. "Thought I'd go mad, me."

More kisses, more heat, more confusion.

This time with him felt momentous, as if I were about to step onto a path I could never leave.

Path?

"Ah, honeysuckle." He loosened his grip from my hair. "You missed me too, *peekôn*." He laid his hands on either side of my neck, tilting my head up with his thumbs so our gazes met. "I'd do it all over to have you back."

He would allow himself to be tortured and branded just to be with me? "Jack . . ."

He took my lips again. Before I knew it, we'd gone tripping to his cot, and his body felt so right covering mine, his lean hips between my thighs.

Between kisses, he murmured, *"Douce comme du miel."* Sweet like honey. His voice was smoldering.

"I . . . I . . ." Couldn't grasp what I'd been about to say. Too busy helping him remove my shirt?

My glyphs shimmered wildly, lighting the tent more than the fire. His big rough hands covered my breasts, squeezing, heating my flesh through my silk bra. I cried out, bowing my back for more. When I rubbed against his palms, he gave a husky groan that sent shivers all over me.

He leaned down, kissing my neck to my chest, following the movements of my glyphs. Between my breasts. Across them. "You belong to me, Evangeline." Kiss. *"With* me." Flick of his tongue. "And I belong to you." He took one of my hands, entwining his fingers with mine, gazing up at my face. "Think about you so damned much, about this. *Je t'aime.* I love you. Always will."

I glanced away from his heartbreaking face. "But I have to tell you . . ." I trailed off.

A weird alertness spiked inside me. My heart had been racing before. Now it pounded because something was wrong. Something was coming.

Some*one*.

I pressed Jack away, rising to my feet.

"What is it?" he asked. "I was moving too fast? We can go slower."

"It isn't you." I pulled my shirt back on. "I've got to see about something."

"Where you goan? I'm coming with you."

"No!" I whirled around with my hand up. "Will you just wait here? Please, for once." I left him sitting with a confounded look on his face.

Outside, a dense fog bank had rolled in, the night like a chamber with all the air sucked out of it. As I walked from the tent, I felt out of body, floating toward an inevitable drop-off.

I peered through the fog. Matthew awaited near the gates. They were already open?

My stomach lurched. What had he done?

Through the murk, an outline of a rider emerged, dressed in black armor.

Death was *here*. He'd gotten past the minefield, inside the wall!

And I had no idea what he would do.

My glyphs shimmered for a completely different reason, reflecting off the mist. I clawed my palms and seeded protection, vines slowly rising up to flank me. *Too* slowly. With no sun, I hadn't recharged from my last battle!

As he neared, the details of his appearance grew clearer. His close-fitting armor outlined his broad shoulders, his muscular legs and arms. He rode tall and proud—so noble astride his ghostly red-eyed stallion.

When my vines twined toward the sky, Death's gaze landed on me.

His eyes began to glow. Like my glyphs, his glowing eyes indicated high emotion—or aggression.

Light was *spilling* through the grille of his menacing helmet.

Fog embraced us as that last night with him washed over me....

When we reached the edge of his bed, I tried once more to talk him out of this. "Please, think about what you're doing! You're coercing me to sleep with you. How can you be right with that?"

He gripped my waist and lifted me with ease, laying me on his bed. Though his palms were sword-roughened, his fingers were elegant, reverent. "It's more than merely bedding you. If you surrender to me, you will be mine alone. My wife in truth. I will do anything to have that. Anything to have you."

When he followed me down, my hands pressed against his bare, tattooed chest. Those black slashing marks told our story, a constant reminder for him never to trust me. But I'd earned his trust.

Was I about to break it again? "Just let me go, Aric. Let me leave this place. I vow I'll come back."

"Never, little wife. I'll never let you go."

My lids grew heavy when his muscles moved beneath my palms. His scent—sandalwood, pine, masculine—weakened my will like a drug, quelling the heat of battle inside me. Still I managed to say: "This won't work out as you plan."

"Won't it?" He smoothed my hair behind my ear. "I believe any outcome will be better than losing the sole woman on earth I can be with. The one that I now love. That's a fairly steep downside."

Love. "I won't necessarily be lost. But if you do this, I will be."

His lips curled. So sensual, so gorgeous. He knew how much he was affecting me. "With enough time, I can coax you from your anger. I did once before."

His head inched closer, amber eyes intent.

Resist him, resist . . .

He took my mouth with his, muddling my thoughts, making me forget all the things I needed to remember. He deepened the contact until our tongues met. With each of his wicked flicks, my body arched to his, as if he were in control of it.

Though he didn't speak, he was still communicating with me through his kiss. He was reminding me that he'd never free me. He was telling me to accept him.

To surrender.

I could so easily get lost in this man, in what he offered. When I moaned, *he drew back, his lids hooded. "There. That's better." He began removing my clothes with his supernatural speed. "Just let me see you . . . touch you."*

Once he'd stripped me of everything but my panties, he stared at my body, eagerness stamped in every tense line of his. "Empress . . ." he groaned, leaning down to lavish kisses all over my breasts, those elegant fingers kneading me.

His lips closed over a hardened peak; my eyes nearly rolled back in my head. When he moved to my other breast, my cry was so sharp, the sound startled me out of this haze.

Resist, Evie! If I lost control, I could lose . . . myself.

The thought sliced through my desire, triggering the toxin on my lips. If he wouldn't release me, I'd take my freedom.

So I grasped Aric's face, pulling him in to kiss me, which he eagerly did. Over and over.

At length, he drew back to tug my panties down. "I want to taste you again. I think about it constantly." With his strength, he must be taking pains not to rip the lace. "Ah, and you need me too."

When I lay naked before him, his amber eyes glittered like stars. Pinpoints of light mesmerized me. "So lovely, sievā. My gods, you humble me." He gave me one of his rare unguarded smiles. "This is joy I feel, is it not?"

I wanted to sob.

His fingers descended, seeking, touching me with reverence. "Tonight you'll take me into you," he rasped. "You'll belong to me alone."

Yet then his eyes narrowed. "Roses?" He released me.

My scent had changed. Sleep now, Death.

"What have you done, creature?"

I scrambled away from him, snatching my shirt over my head. "I came to you for help. You offered me coercion."

He shot back from me, but his movements were clumsy, my toxin already working. He made it to his knees, reaching toward the side of the bed, struggling to get to something.

Surely he wasn't grasping for one of the swords in a nearby stand?

Before he could reach it, his limbs failed him, and he collapsed on the mattress. He managed to turn his head toward me, his hands balling into fists. "And still . . . I should have expected this. Your poison kiss. Again." *His expression was devastated.* "You'd kill me before you ever accepted me."

"Kill you? You're just going to sleep!" *I stood, squaring my shoulders.* "After all we've been through, murder is your first conclusion? And your first reaction is to stab me?" *I waved at his sword, my heart breaking.*

Clearly things hadn't changed between us as much as I'd thought. "I vowed I would never hurt you, Aric. Other Arcana promised to save Jack if I took your life, but I refused."

Once more he tried to reach for his weapon, seeming to will his muscles to move. Would he even now take my head if he had the chance? He'd done it twice before.

"So help me gods, sievā, you . . . will . . . pay. . . ." *His lids slid shut, concealing his anguished eyes. His spellbinding face was free of tension, his body defenseless.*

Fresh from his bed, I disbelieved my own sight. He couldn't *have been reaching for his sword. He'd never hurt me. But if I left him when he was so vulnerable and someone else got to him, I'd be responsible. His guard dog was dead. The wolves remained with Lark. Anyone could steal into the castle.*

A sense of protectiveness surged inside me. I dressed, then started to barricade his bedroom door, planning to climb from his second-story window.

I rationalized with each of my actions. He's always a target for other Arcana. *I dragged over practice swords.* He wouldn't hurt me. He wouldn't! *I lugged over armor.* He was reaching for something else. *I wedged a shield under the door handle.* He loves me.

So why had he tried to coerce me? Why had he vowed to make me pay?

My protectiveness faded, the red witch rising. So much for your soul-deep connection, *she whispered.* He's worth FIVE icons.

Rule of thumb: if a man has beheaded you on more than one occasion and he reaches for his sword . . .

Now he'd come for me, to make me pay. A knighted grim reaper.

I stared in awe, marveling that I'd had the strength to leave him, to poison him. When I hadn't heard from him in days, I'd worried that I'd given him too much, had hurt him. Worry for nothing.

Soldiers stopped and gaped. In the last two hours, both Aric and Jack had ridden through those gates. Where Jack had commanded respect, Death elicited pure fear.

I spied the outline of a giant wolf beside Death's armored warhorse. Cyclops padded along, his maw filled with body parts from the stone forest.

That beast had led Death through the minefield! Or Lark had. She hadn't sent me extra protection because she cared about me. She'd dispatched a spy.

Still gazing at me, Death drew one of his swords. *No!*

The scent of roses flooded the air as my vines tensed and grew. My claws dripped poison, my barbs at the ready.

But he could cut through my vines, and his armor repelled most of my other powers. If he wanted me dead, I was about to be. Unless . . .

Three other Arcana hastened into the foggy courtyard.

"The bloody Reaper!" Joules cried, just as Jack bellowed from behind me, *"Evie!"*

Then all hell broke loose.

18

"I'll fry you!" Joules yelled.

Gabriel sped past me toward some target? Jack?

Cyclops sprang in front of Aric, crouching at the ready.

Ashen and shaking, Matthew muttered *Tredici* over and over. Tess ducked behind him and began to cry. Soldiers scurried from the fray.

Joules's skin sparked in the mist as he hefted one of his javelins.

My gaze darted back to Death. The knight's armored shoulders rose and fell, a weary exhalation. For him, this was just another day, another icon to harvest from an Arcana. Or from several of us.

When the Tower hurled his spear, Aric turned his helmeted head from me. Faster than lightning his sword flashed out. Metal on metal clanged, and the javelin sailed over the fort's walls. Lightning forked out and an explosion sounded in the distance.

Joules howled with frustration.

"Who the fuck let him in?" Jack yelled. Gabriel had intercepted him, holding him back from certain *death*. "Evie, get the hell away from him!"

"Why have you come, Aric?"

Again, Death turned to me. "To do what I always end up doing with you."

He always ended up . . . killing me.

He reached up and removed that menacing helmet. As ever, the Endless Knight was hypnotically beautiful, with his collar-length blond hair framing chiseled features and radiant amber eyes.

In his deep raspy voice, he said, "I always end up *forgiving you.*"

My lips parted. *What?*

"Choke on this, Reaper!" Joules hurled another spear.

Aric deflected it, this time without gazing away from me—as if his starry eyes were greedy for the sight of me.

"Forgive?" I finally managed to say. "You promised to make me pay!"

"I intend to, Empress, but not in the way you're thinking." His accented words were loaded with innuendo.

"How can I believe that? Right before I knocked you out, you went for your sword!"

His blond brows drew together. "I was reaching for a vial of anti-toxin. I'd had it formulated before the Flash, in the hope of neutralizing your poisons. I've always wondered if it would work."

Antitoxin? Confusion rocked me. "B-but we've fought each other so many times. And you . . . you always win."

Another javelin; another sword parry.

"Evie, you get away from him!" Jack bellowed.

"You know well that I would never be able to harm you," Aric chided, "even should I have wanted to. Just as you refuse to hurt me. Twice now you could've killed me. This last time, you took pains to *protect* me."

"But you . . . and then . . . your sword?"

He gazed at me with infinite patience. "Never again, *sievā.*"

I stared into his eyes, that soul-deep sense of connection sweeping over me. Oh, dear gods, I . . . believed him.

I had to defuse this situation before anyone got hurt. The trues! But Matthew couldn't paint his blood on Death's lethal skin. Could I use the Gamekeeper's blood? I ran to Matthew.

He was already slashing his arm. "True-hearted," he whispered. "For now."

I drew my forefinger across his wound, then hurried to Aric.

"Don't you feckin' do it, Empress!" Before I could reach Death, Joules fired again.

Aric deflected, his voice booming in the night: "I begin to tire of this, Tower."

"Aric, let me paint your hand!"

He sheathed his sword and dismounted with that eerie grace. Spurs ringing, he strode to me and removed one spiked gauntlet.

"*Nooo!*" Joules yelled.

I drew a red line across Aric's icons.

At the touch, he shuddered with bliss, lids gone heavy, eyes ablaze.

"Get away!" Jack had broken free from Gabriel, was fearlessly charging for Aric. Jack's bravery was like a living thing inside him— always wanting to be freed.

"Stop!" I rushed to head him off, but he shoved me behind his back, standing up to Aric. The two were about the same height, gazes locked.

"You can't fight Death," I cried. "He's part of the trues."

"I'm not Arcana," Jack bit out.

"Drunk and no sword?" Aric sneered. "This isn't even sporting."

Jack tensed, all his muscles swelling. Because he was about to attack. He smiled a chilling smile. I'd seen it before. *An animal baring its teeth.* He was about to launch himself at Death, his anvil-like fists swinging.

"Jack, you can't hit him! You can't touch his skin and survive! The only reason he's facing you with no helmet is to bait you." I turned to Aric. "If you hurt him, *you* will pay!"

He donned his gauntlet. "I have no intention of aggressing anyone here, love. I arrive on a simple errand, now that you've completed yours."

"Errand?"

In a casual tone, he said, "I've come to take my wife home."

19

Jack's head jerked back as if he'd been struck with a sledgehammer.

A guttural bellow erupted from his chest. He swung for Death.

I screamed, but Aric blocked the hit with his armored wrist.

The knight stared into Jack's eyes. "I always recognize a death wish. Do you want to die, mortal? I can oblige you."

Death wish? "Stop this!" I tried to get between them. "You can't touch him!"

Jack's bruised face was red with rage. "Might be worth it just to knock that snide look off your face!"

"The Empress is right. One touch is all it takes. Well, at least for everyone but her." He gazed down at me. "As was meant to be, *sievā*." He seemed amused by all this, as if he'd just arrived at festivities.

In a blur, Jack's hand shot up, a pistol pointed at Aric's head.

My chest contracted, lungs robbed of air.

Aric had accelerated healing, but even he wouldn't survive a bullet to the brain. If anything happened to him ... Now that I knew he hadn't come here to hurt me, confusing feelings overwhelmed me.

Panic, that sense of protectiveness, an ache in my heart—

Jack cocked the weapon, pressing the barrel against Aric's forehead. "One reason."

While I struggled to breathe, Aric's gaze reluctantly moved from me to Jack. And still, Death looked amused. "Because she'll never forgive you for it."

"Take him out, hunter!" Joules yelled. "Pull the bloody trigger!"

I laid my hand on Jack's arm. "Put down the gun." Nothing. "If you do this, we can never come back from it."

On the razor's edge, he turned to me. "What the hell is he talking about? Wife? *WIFE?*"

"It's complicated," I repeated.

That muscle ticked in his jaw. "I can goddamn keep up, Evangeline!"

"I will explain everything to you, if you come with me back to the tent." If Jack shot Aric, they would both be dead to me. Tears pricked my eyes. "P-please, I'm asking you to do this for me."

"You expect me to let him loose in my camp? Do you give a damn that he wants to kill me?"

"He won't."

"How can you be so sure?"

I gazed at Aric as I said, "If he hurts you in any way, he knows I will *never* stop hating him." Back to Jack. "Please. Talk to me—away from here."

He must've heard the dread in my voice. Finally, he uncocked the gun, lowering it. He cast Aric a murderous look, then stormed away. I followed, glaring at the knight over my shoulder.

He gave me a gallant bow, self-satisfied smile in place. He knew his strike had already found its target.

"What the fuck?" Jack paced the tent, hitting that flask like nobody's business. He could barely look at me, hadn't managed more than cursing.

"I told you that Death and I had a history." With shaking hands, I pulled the tent flap aside, peeking out.

Aric was cooling down Thanatos, his creepy white stallion. The red-eyed beast looked like a cross between an Arabian—and a tank. It even had its own black armor.

Cyclops snacked nearby. *Crunch. Crunch.*

From a distance, the other Arcana gawked at Death—Tess especially seemed entranced by his divine good looks—but their attention didn't appear to disturb him in the least.

I tensed when Matthew wandered over to Aric. The last I'd heard, Matthew had broken ranks, reneging on some deal the two had made.

But he and Death talked calmly. What could they be discussing?

"Christ, Evie, you can't take your eyes off him?"

I closed the flap, then headed for Matthew's cot.

"How much history can you and the Reaper have? You never met him before three months ago."

I sat with my hands folded. They wouldn't stop shaking. The fear I'd felt for Aric bewildered me. "We were together in a past life."

"Dis-moi la vérité!" Tell me the truth!

"I am. Arcana are reincarnated."

His mouth opened, then closed.

"Whoever wins gets to live as an immortal. The rest of us reincarnate for each game. Death has won the last three, so he's lived all this time. But I have memories of being with him."

Pacing, pacing. "That bastard ain't acting like this is a past thing! You sleep with him?"

"You have to understand: I thought you and I were over."

Jack's eyes grew *crazed.* "Did you—sleep—with him?"

"No, but I was . . . with him." The night he'd saved me from Ogen, I'd decided to have sex with Aric. But I hadn't gone through with it.

"I ain't hearing this!" Jack heaved in breaths, like he couldn't get enough air.

"I believed I'd never see you again. But then I couldn't stop thinking about my promise to you, to give you a chance to reach me. So I didn't go any further with him. I told him I was going to get your side of the story about everything."

Jack tipped that flask up, swiping his sleeve over his mouth. "I'm out here, nearly dying every day trying to find you or make it safer for you. And you were almost screwing the man who nearly killed me!"

"I can't explain what it was like when I found out about your lies. It was like something broke in me." I thumped my chest. "*Died* in me. I felt so betrayed by you. By Matthew too. Then I learned that in a past game, I married Death. I tried to poison him—on our wedding night. In another game, I got him to trust me again, then struck once more."

Jack slowed his pacing. "Then you were with him this time out of guilt?"

At one point with Aric, I'd thought of it as *penance*. At another point, I'd been rocked by our connection. "I don't know."

"You came back here—for me. You told me you loved me! Was that just bullshit?"

"No!" I pinched my temples. My nagging headache had turned into a pounding migraine.

"You love that bastard?"

"I care about him. If not for you, I probably would." And if not for his *deal*.

"You always liked the rich ones." Jack's pacing and drinking resumed at full speed. "The blue bloods. Figures you'd go for a knight."

"That's not fair!"

"I can't even wrap my mind around this! He abducted you. You think he's not here to do it again? Maybe you want him to?"

"He can't force me away. I have my powers back."

"That's right—he stole your powers for months, and you reward him. He tried to kill me and your friends, and you reward him. Damn, Evie, where's your loyalty?"

"What about Selena? Have you forgotten that she planned to take me down the night we met her? If you hadn't been there, I would be dead. Beheaded."

I guessed all that had been swept under the rug. "Things change, Jack. This game makes us all villains at some time or another. And besides that, Aric didn't *try* to kill any of you. Ogen demolished the mountain. Death could have ambushed us earlier."

"Why didn't he?"

"I think deep down he hoped I wouldn't be evil. He knew I would never forgive him if any of you died. He considered taking you out in the mine, but didn't."

"You believe he could've? You got a lot of confidence in him."

"He's *Death*—killing is second nature to him." Some would say first nature. "I used my arsenal against him, fighting with everything in me. And I couldn't defeat him."

"But you still let him kiss you? Touch you?" His voice was whiskey roughened, his accent thicker. "Even when I thought you were lost to me, I never turned to another!"

Another. Selena. Jack was telling me he'd never gotten with her. Yet Selena had admitted, "Things between us are different."

"I've had cause to hate in my life; I never hated like I do Death." Aric had said the same about him. "How can I not kill him?" Jack had hit his limit.

I was nearing mine as well. Just over a week ago, the Devil had strangled me. "Pretty meat," he'd sneered as his drool had coated my face. I put my head in my hands. "I need to slow down, just long enough to think." I wished Tess could make time stand still.

"We doan get that luxury. Not since that bastard showed up here. We got a grenade in our camp, with the pin pulled."

On the road, Jack had taught me about grenades: *Once you pull the pin, a grenade is not your friend.*

"What do you want from me, Evie?"

"I want you two not to fight each other. To give me time to sort through things." I met his eyes. "I'm asking you not to hurt him."

"I can't . . . I can't do this now, no. You're fucking gutting me." He rubbed that bandage. "I'd had this hope of being with you again, only thing keeping me goan." He gazed past me. "But now, can't even look at you."

"Please try to see this from—"

A yell sounded across the camp.

Great. What had Death done now?

20

When Jack and I ran outside, we found Aric standing by his horse. Matthew was no longer with him.

Jack eyed the knight with a withering hatred; steady and still, Aric kept his gaze locked on me—

"She's gone! She's been taken!"

"Was that Finn?" I asked.

Jack made for the Magician's tent, while I tried to keep up.

Inside, Finn sat on his cot, Matthew beside him. By the light of the low fire, I couldn't tell which boy looked worse.

Gabriel, Joules, and Tess rushed in right after us.

"What happened here, podna?" Jack asked Finn. "Tell me nice and slow."

"Selena was taken! Two soldiers did it. I walked in on one of them giving her an injection. His partner sneaked up behind me and shot me up. I just came to."

Gabriel's wings snapped open. "How did they get her out of the fort?"

"You tell me," Finn said, baffled.

"We suspected we had traitors planted in this camp." Jack bit out a vile curse in French. "How long ago was this?"

"Five or six hours?" Finn turned to me. "Right when I was going under, one of them was bitching about the wolf guarding you. I think you were also a target."

"*Whose* target?" Jack said.

I feared I knew. "It might be General Milovníci. The Lovers told us they wanted to take me and Selena north to someone they called 'the First.' Maybe they meant their father?" The thought nauseated me as much as it had last night.

"I can catch them by air," Gabriel said, "before they reach the other half of the army."

Jack shook his head. "They'll be spotlighting the skies for you. They've got truck-mounted rifles that can cut you in two."

Gabriel turned on Matthew. "You had to have seen this, Fool!"

Finn raised his crutch to defend Matthew, but Jack blocked the archangel. "Just back off, Gabe! We're goan to get Selena back."

Right at that moment, a staticky call sounded in my head. —*We will love you. In our own way.*—

Every Arcana stilled in shock.

"W-wasn't that the Lovers' call?" Tess adjusted her baseball cap, her still thin body trembling.

"That can't be," I muttered, though I'd heard it.

"Are you sure you guys ganked them?" Finn glanced from one of us to the next. "Yeah?' Then I guess their Arcana power is resur-freaking-rection."

Matthew gave a low cry. "They're *calling*." He stiffened and his voice changed, seeming to vibrate as he vocalized a message: "Empress, we'd planned to make you a prisoner of our love, but it didn't work out. Luckily we'll have Selena to keep us company. Will you let her suffer for you, for the crimes you committed?"

"What crimes?" Joules asked, but everyone shushed him.

Matthew continued: "If you're truly as different as you say, you'll come for your ally. We'll release her in exchange for you—and the hunter. We camp outside the Dolor Salt Mines; be here within four days. No Arcana can travel with you. If we sense another's call—like the archangel's—we'll give Selena to our army. It's your choice, a test of your 'alliance.' When to enter, when not to honor . . . Four days, Empress. We will love you ever so much."

Matthew slumped, the message delivered.

"Vincent and Violet are alive? They have her!" Gabriel started for the exit.

I headed him off. "Just wait! You can't jeopardize her. We'll plan another rescue. Maybe Matthew can block our calls." I turned to him— sucked in a gasp at the blood pouring from his nose. "Sweetheart, what is this?" I reached for him.

Jack was right beside me. *"Coo-yôn?"*

Matthew rocked forward and back, blood soaking his shirt. "Beware the lures . . . strike first . . . or be first struck."

I yanked a bandanna from my pocket and held it against his nose. His eyes pleaded; for me to do what? Why couldn't I figure out how to help him? When Matthew's blood saturated the material, I didn't think, just cried, "Aric!"

"Why you call for him?" Jack sounded like he was about to do murder. "I'm the one who's been looking out for *coo-yôn* for three months. *Me.*"

I sat beside Matthew. "Aric knows things. Arcana things."

An instant later, Death silently entered.

Joules went bug-eyed, producing a javelin. Gabriel's wings flared anew. Tess floated to the back of the tent.

Finn's recent illusions glimmered over him. "Wh-what the hell, people?" He'd been unconscious, didn't know Aric was here. Up went the Magician's crutch again.

"Death is in the trues," I said.

Jack's jaw clenched until I thought he'd grind his molars to dust. "You like to go where you're not welcome, Reaper."

"Often." Aric's pale blond hair shone in the firelight, his breathtaking face highlighted.

"This is actually happenin'," Joules sputtered. "We're in a tent with this rotten, bloody bastard." Speaking to everyone else, he said, "You realize he's killed us all at some point in past games."

Death's lips curled. "Some of you more than once."

Like me.

"Bugger this, I canna be in here." Joules cast Aric a look of scalding animosity. "That demon killed my lass, my Calanthe."

Death's amber eyes narrowed. "*Your* alliance attacked *mine.*"

Gabriel reached for Joules's shoulder, saying under his breath, "Stay. Know thy enemy." He jerked his hand away when the Tower's skin sparked.

"Feckin' Reaper." But Joules did remain, directing his fury toward Jack. "You should have plugged his skull when you had a chance!"

"You think I doan regret that?"

I gazed up at Aric. "Do you know what's happening to Matthew?"

"In past games, the Fool occasionally did this—when someone was about to die. Someone he'd much rather *not.*"

All eyes turned to me. Was I on the chopping block? Or Selena?

"Plus, he must be overloaded," Aric said. "I've seen this before midgame. His mind is simply *full.*"

"What does that mean?" I smoothed Matthew's hair from his damp forehead.

"It's unusual for so many Arcana to converge for extended periods. Our calls would blare like constant megaphones in his head."

The Arcana switchboard.

"Not to mention that he's been seeing all of our futures, deciphering and acting on constantly updating information."

Matthew had tried to tell me he needed a respite. He'd known his mind would be hurt like this?

"Mad and struck." Saliva dripped from his mouth. "System the game. Eddy. Eddy. Now I go over the edge, the dog at my heels."

Jack clasped his shoulder, holding him steady. "*Coo-yôn*, you got to rest now. *Prend-lé aisé. Comprends?*" Take it easy. Understood? "And press this against your nose," he added, handing Matthew another bandanna.

The boy stilled at once. *"Comprends."*

I'd seen Jack calm him before, but not like this. Matthew behaved like a soldier taking an officer's order.

"How is this possible with the Lovers?" Joules demanded of no one in particular. "I tossed their remains into the river!"

Death gave a laugh.

"What's so bleeding funny?"

"Just because you destroyed that pair doesn't mean they're dead."

Now he had everybody's attention.

It must be occurring to each of the Arcana that a source of information—a living, breathing, two-thousand-year-old champion— was talking to them. They would all have questions. He might have the answers.

And Aric could read us so well. "Aww, did I just become the most popular person in this tent?" He shouldn't be this amused. His typical *I-have-power-over-all-I-survey* vibe was in full force.

I got the feeling that he was making moves on a chessboard, and we were all luckless pawns. "Will you please explain how they can be destroyed but still be alive?" I guided Matthew to adjust the bandanna against his nose. Was the blood flow slowing?

"Have none of you truly looked at their card?" Aric gazed from person to person. "How it evokes the many-sided Gemini? How it resembles the Devil's card?"

Blank stares.

"Ah, I see. And why would I reveal their esoteric power? Because of our abiding friendships?" Death was practicing his own concealment. "The Lovers will probably defeat some of you. Aiding you against them would be unwise."

"Do you trust me when I tell you we won't fight you?" I asked him.

Joules snapped, "Speak for yerself, Empress," just as Jack said,

"Doan count on it." Had his hand wandered toward his pistol holster?

Ignoring them, Aric told me, "Twenty centuries of experience is difficult to disregard."

"Your past with me is what got you into trouble in the first place." I'd told him that if he'd come to Haven in the beginning as a friend—instead of tormenting me for months—I would have fallen in love with him, before Jack had ever arrived.

"Perhaps I could share some details." Aric had once accused me of having a conniving glint in my eyes; well, I recognized the calculating gleam in his.

He turned to the others. "I will tell you about the Lovers, for a boon. I want each Arcana's vow never to engage the Empress in combat. A *trues* forever."

Protecting me? Of all the things Death could've demanded . . .

Even Jack appeared a shade less likely to shoot Aric.

"Far cry from a few months ago, Reaper," Joules pointed out, "when you were tellin' us we couldn't kill her because *you* were goin' to do the deed!"

"It is a remarkable turnaround," Death conceded with his customary frankness.

"My alliance already vowed never to hunt hers," Joules said.

"Obliging enough, but you won't have to *hunt* them. The game will make sure you encounter each other."

"I'd never hurt blondie," Finn told Death, apparently over his earlier shock. "But you got my vow."

Tess piped up, "I-I promise it too."

"A vow. To the Reaper?" Gabriel looked torn between his loyalty to the Tower and his desire to *know his enemy*. "Joules, we need this information to save Selena." He faced Aric. "I vow it."

"Oh, for feck's sake!" Joules's skin sparked again. "Fine, I'll vow it, but only because I wasn't plannin' to anyway."

"Very well." After a dramatic pause, Aric said, "The Lovers can clone themselves."

"Oh, my God." The memory of my picnic with Gran surfaced in full. I'd been about seven years old. We'd spread a blanket under an oak. While she'd shelled pecans, I'd played with paper and scissors, cutting out a girl and a boy.

"Evie, what do you have there?"

"Twins," I proudly told her. "Or more." I pulled the paper apart like an accordion. Identical girls and boys stretched out, all holding hands.

"Very good." She picked up a sharp fragment of shell to slice her thumb.

"Gran!"

"Shh." Narrowing her gaze, she swiped blood on the front girl and boy. "They need to mix their blood to duplicate themselves."

I frowned. Sometimes Gran said weird stuff.

"What if you wanted to kill them all? How would you do it?"

I bit my lip, thinking about it for a few moments. I folded the paper back to the original pair. "Kill these two?"

Gran was pleased, her dark eyes sparkling. "Such a clever girl."

She'd been teaching me about Arcana without even mentioning the cards! How many other disguised lessons had I forgotten?

"The source twins are the 'First' or the 'heart,'" Aric said. "Their clones make up the 'body.' They're called *carnates*. You destroyed a pair of them."

Puzzle pieces were fitting into place. "The Vincent clone told me, 'What we hear is heard. What we see is seen. What we know is known.' The source twins see and hear through the carnates." As Lark did with her animals.

Questions erupted from the other Arcana: "If we take one out, can they just create another?" "How long does it take them to duplicate themselves?" "Do they have a hidden replicant army?"

Was Selena on her way to be tortured by the *First* right now?

"The Lovers make clones with their combined blood. They blood-let like some"—Aric indicated me—"but they don't possess accelerated healing. So the number of carnates is limited."

"What about their other rumored powers?" I asked. "Like mesmerizing? Holding hands and swinging their arms or whispering together in a victim's ears?" Had they done that to Jack? I glanced at him with a question in my eyes. Curt shake of his head.

"Swinging their arms?" Finn peeled another cat sticker from his crutch. "Like an Arcana version of the Wonder Twins?"

Aric raised his blond brows. *If you say so.* "The First possess those powers, but the carnates don't." He turned to me. "In any case, you'd be immune, since you broke the Hierophant's mind control over you."

Only because Aric had helped me.

"Then I'm ready for them." Once I got to the source twins in Dolor, I could take them out. Issue number one: where the hell was Dolor?

"Have you fought the Lovers before?" Gabriel asked me. "What were the crimes they spoke of?"

Gazing around, I parted my lips to confess about the alliance I'd betrayed—

"She managed to take them unawares in the last game," Aric quickly said, "then destroyed them." Of course, he knew what I'd done. His gaze warned me to keep quiet.

Show of hands, anyone I didn't betray.

"Alas, they've learned from the past. They'll be ready to counteract the Empress's powers."

"Who defeated them before that?" Gabriel glanced from me to Aric.

"The Hierophant," Aric said. "He mesmerized the carnates, ordering them to slay their own source."

Shit. I glared at his icon on my hand. "There went that option."

"Before that, the Emperor executed the Lovers with a firestorm, burning them and all their duplicates to ash." Aric's icon hand clenched. One of his tells.

What was Death's history with that card?

"Maybe Eves can wrangle that dude into our alliance?" Finn asked. "Emperor and Empress. Sounds like a bond to me."

Aric's irises darkened until they looked like cold amber. "The two earned their titles because they ruled over men—in warring empires."

I had? Okay, sure. "When the Emperor set upon the Lovers, he spared no mortal bystanders."

Then Richter was as despicable as the Priestess had said. Wait a minute . . . She'd told me the Lovers' icon was "right where it should be." She'd known we hadn't killed the true twins! Gee, Circe, thanks for the heads-up.

"Destroy the root," Matthew murmured. "The Moon sets. Moon rises."

"We can't dispatch the Empress and Jack to them alone," Gabriel said. "What can we do? What can *I* do?"

"The Lovers are right," I said. "I'm not going to let Selena pay for what I did in the past. I can take the wolf with me and plan a sneak attack of some kind."

"I'm goan for Selena." Before I could protest, Jack strode toward the exit, jamming his shoulder against Aric's armored one.

He'd done that to Brandon in school. Because Jack refused to deviate from his path in the face of *anyone*.

I shot to my feet to follow him. "Finn, look after Matthew."

"Ten-four, blondie."

Before I left, Matthew gazed up at me. A single tear tracked down his bloody face.

21

"Jack, just wait!"

By the time I caught up with him, he'd already collected his bug-out bag, crossbow, and that mysterious camo duffel.

"Where are you going?"

"Setting off to end the twins." He stopped a passing soldier, grating some orders about a chain of command or something. Then he headed toward the stable.

I jogged to keep up with his long-legged strides. "You think you can waltz in alone and take the twins out?"

"You mean, as a mortal? The Milovnícis infiltrated my fort. I can do the same to their encampment. I got friends in the rank and file, me. I'll have help."

"It's too risky! And the doctor said you're supposed to be resting from your injuries—your concussion. This is for me to do. They want me more than anyone."

"For months, Selena's had my back. Last night, she did. You think I'm goan to leave her hanging in the wind? I'm riding—now."

"Riding? Across the river to take one of their trucks, right?"

He shook his head. "Azey North controls all the cleared roads to Dolor. They'd just be waiting for me. I'm taking the slaver route."

"What is that?"

"It's how black hats move their merchandise for auction."

In the stable, he crossed to the large gray he'd ridden earlier, walking him to a saddling area. "And you? You're goan to sit your ass right here."

Ignoring that, I led my own mare out. She seemed to scowl at me. I wished I could give her more of a rest, but even recovering, she'd be stronger than any of the other horses here.

"Damn it, Evie, you ain't goan! Do you understand how dangerous that route is? It's all off-road tracks snaking through steep ravines. Full of chokepoints, traps, and tolls—where you're expected to pay in people. If you manage to dodge those, you'll thread the needle between more cannibal mines and skirt past a plague colony. Bagmen are everywhere. It's a concentration of all the bad."

"Then why on earth would you go that way?"

Jack turned to me with flinty gray eyes. "Because they'll never expect me to."

"You're not going alone. You know I can look out for myself."

"You'll just slow me down."

"I ride as fast as anyone here." Except Death. My gaze widened. "Aric! He can control his call." If he even had one. "They would never hear him."

"The hell that'll happen! Even if I wasn't about to put a bullet in his skull, it ain't like he's goan to ride out to help Selena. He left her to die. Remember that, you?"

Jack was right. I was attributing traits to Aric that simply weren't there. Why would the ruthless winner of three games risk himself to save another card, much less one outside his alliance?

As if on cue, Aric entered the stable. "Empress, your friends are delightful. Abysmally ignorant about the games, but that's how I usually prefer other Arcana."

Jack's entire body tensed up. "I doan even have time to think about you. But you'll get what's coming to you. I swear it."

"I've been hearing that for two thousand years, mortal." Aric turned to me with glowing eyes. "Yet never have I received what should be coming to me."

Flustered, I gazed away.

He leaned his armored shoulder against a roof support. *—I've missed your company these long days.—*

I jolted to feel his words in my head after such a long absence. If Matthew was the switchboard, Death was king of the airwaves, had learned over his lifetimes how to mentally communicate with any Arcana.

—The human can barely look at you. You must have told him that I had you in my bed.—

I bit my cheek as I answered, *Speaking like this reminds me of all your telepathic threats. I remember you telling me that I'd be under your sword in a week.*

—Had you been the same as before, I would have made good on that promise.—

Sometimes, his honesty shocked me. *What are you even doing here? You stayed away so long, I thought you weren't coming.*

—You missed me, and now are piqued. Know that I was obtaining something that guarantees my success with you.—

More coercion?

—A gift for you. That's why I've allowed the mortal leeway and refrained from a slaying. Because you're about to be mine.—

His confidence unsettled me. *Good to know you were worried about your* wife *alone out on the road. You let me make the journey by myself. And face the twins! Though you knew how much they would hate me.*

—I felt confident that you and six other Arcana, one of the largest alliances yet, could take out a pair of insignificant carnates. To guard you on your way, I bade Lark to dispatch the wolf.—

And spy on me. Cyclops led you past the minefield.

Aloud, Aric said, "Lark sends her regards, wants to know when you're coming home. She's feeling better, by the way."

"I would've asked, but my mind's a little *occupied*. Who knows what could be happening to Selena right now?" Who knew what could be going through Jack's head?

"You're determined to go after her?" Aric said.

"Absolutely. She's my friend."

"You won't ask if I'm willing to assist you?"

I didn't pause, just hefted my appropriated saddle onto my appropriated mare. "Would it make a difference?"

In a contemplative tone, he said, "Perhaps I miscalculated with you earlier this week." He was calculating even now! "Perhaps you would be moved by sacrifice."

"Instead of a *deal*?"

"Just so. I underestimated the depth of your affection for me, Empress. When I was unconscious from your *kiss*"—smirk at Jack—"you took pains to ensure my safety. Your barricade of our bedroom door was as charming as it was heartening. Armor, swords, and shields, like a bird building a nest."

Jack stiffened, clenching his jaw until the muscles bulged.

"He's needling you, Jack. He'll do this until you want to"—I turned to Aric—"strangle him in vine!"

Unfazed, Aric merely raised his brows at me. "Well?"

I struggled with my temper. We did need him. If there was the slightest chance he'd agree . . . "Will you help us?"

—On two conditions. For the duration of this rescue, you make no decisions about your future, concerning me or the mortal. And you resist his advances.—

Borderline close to coercion there, Aric.

—Those are my terms.—

Fine. But I've got a condition of my own. You don't hurt Jack, or put him in a position to get hurt.

Aric inclined his head, saying aloud, "For you, I'll pledge my sword. My standard has a rose on it for a reason." He sounded like a knight speaking to his queen.

Or his empress.

Jack finished saddling the gray. "No way in hell I'm riding with him."

"Excellent," Death said. "You set off alone, and I'll accompany her."

I told Jack, "All things considered, more is better. Especially when the route is as dangerous as you say."

"You can't trust him, no! Out there, you got to trust the people you ride with."

Aric hiked his shoulders. "I've given her my word that I won't hurt you."

Between gritted teeth, Jack said, "Try. To."

"Jack . . ."

"And what about you, Evangeline? You seeded your vines when he arrived—because you didn't know if you'd have to defend yourself from him!"

Death waved that away. "Old habits die hard. But deep down she knows I will never again harm her." He tilted his head at Jack. "Curious that you would decline an extra sword to protect the Empress, the woman you profess to love?"

"I woan ride with you, Reaper. And neither will Evie."

"That would effectively doom the Archer. Shame. From what I heard, you now know how rough the Lovers play. The physical's just a fraction of the damage they can do. Or so I'm told. Would you want that for our poor, dear Selena?"

Joules rushed into the stable. With a scathing look at Death, he told us, "Matthew was sayin' some things that actually made sense, in between the droolin' and crazy eyes and all. Said the three of you will ride out together, or she's dead by week's end."

"Then we have no choice." I told Jack and Aric, "You two are going with me, and we *will* save her."

Joules quietly said, "No, lass. The three of you ride from here—or *you* die."

22

As I followed Jack through the minefield, I chanced a look back at the fort.

Matthew had provided no more information about how I might have died there by week's end. "Fate marked you," he'd whispered, rocking on his cot. "Far from out of the woods, Empress. Fate demands her due."

After that pronouncement, Aric and Jack had shut up and readied for the trip. I currently rode between them. Fitting.

I'd had time to grab bandages for Jack's burn, and for a quick apology to Tess. I'd promised Gabriel that we would return with Selena. In a spur of optimism, I'd snagged her bow for the trip back. I'd hugged an unresponsive Matthew until I thought I'd break him.

Finn had sworn he'd take care of Matthew, and we'd left the wolf to protect them. Who knew if any other traitors had been planted?

Jack figured we could make it to Dolor in three days. Seventy-two hours to reach Selena. Would the twins truly wait until her arm had healed to begin torturing her?

The carnates had inflicted so much damage on Jack in such a short time. Shadows tinged his eyes that had never been there before. New secrets festered inside him that would never see the light. What had they done to him? I asked myself that over and over.

My thoughts were in turmoil, my mind overloaded by all the things happening to us. I'd freaking time-traveled hours ago.

Was this a hint of what it was like for Matthew?

Aric's arrival just added to the chaos. As we'd exited the gates, he'd told me, — *All I wanted was to return you to our home, yet now I find myself aiding my most hated enemy to save another card. You lead me on a merry chase, little wife.* —

I peeked over my shoulder. His eyes were locked on me.

I faced forward, determined to ignore him. He might not have had malicious intent toward me; didn't mean I'd forgiven him.

By the time the three of us had navigated the mines and the stone forest, rain began pouring. Jack pulled up the hood of his jacket. Without a glance back at me, he spurred his horse, setting a punishing pace.

As I followed, I wondered what we would encounter out on the road? Or when we faced the twins?

And how was I going to keep Aric and Jack from killing each other?

Jack was my boyfriend—maybe. If he hadn't washed his hands of me for being hitched to Death, and if I could figure out how to trust him.

Aric was my lethal "husband"—a master manipulator, one who clearly had a trick up his sleeve.

Me, Jack, and Death on a mission.

What could possibly go wrong?

23

Our journey's first stumbling block on the slaver route was like a macabre brainteaser.

One: a narrow dirt road is carpeted with layers of bloated corpses. Two: they died from drowning. Three: there are no rivers or lakes nearby.

After several hours of hauling ass, we'd stopped at the edge of the bodies. The rain had eased to a drizzle, the temperature dropping. That bizarre A.F. fog enveloped us, distorting ambient sounds and cloaking our way. "What happened here?" I'd thought I would welcome any chance to take a break. My migraine worsened with every mile, and I'd lost sensation in my limbs.

"Dam went out," Jack said, without a glance in my direction. "Carried the dead down the ravine for miles and miles."

Most of the victims were older men. Apparently, they'd managed to avoid slavers and the plague, then got wiped out by something they'd never seen coming—and couldn't fight against.

We might be goan extinct.

Aric lifted his visor, revealing his glorious face. "I've seen this in other places. Catastrophic dam failure. The drought cracked the dams, and now we have nonstop rains. No one's manning the plants, no one's discharging overflows."

"So this will keep happening." A new post-apocalypse reality. "Why are the bodies laid out like this?" They formed a nearly level rise a couple of feet high and a hundred feet long, spanning the sides of the ravine.

"They're probably lining much of this section of road." Aric ran his gloved hand over Thanatos's neck. "I suspect they've been here for weeks, entombed in silt, gradually uncovered by rain. We could be riding over others beneath this very layer of soil."

Chilling. "We have to go across the exposed ones?" I didn't see any way around it.

He nodded. "And it's trickier than one would think. Corpses can roll unpredictably. Their skin is slippery and rotted. Sometimes the dead clutch things to them, like packs and weapons. Just follow me, and Thanatos will establish a track." His massive warhorse had sharpened hooves. This ought to be interesting. And by *interesting*, I meant *vomit-inducing*.

Jack looked annoyed, no doubt thinking I should have stayed at the fort. He'd once told me that he kept his eye on me to monitor how I was doing because I never complained. But Aric was right; Jack could scarcely glance my way.

In contrast, I found Aric's eyes on me again and again. And as much as he'd been watching me, he'd been studying Jack.

Earlier, when we'd been forced to slow on a washed-out mountain pass, Jack had finally snapped, "What the hell are you looking at?"

"Something about you is not right."

"You got a lot of nerve to be saying that about me, Grim Reaper."

There'd been a couple of other tense exchanges between the two. But for the most part, they'd behaved.

Jack spurred his mount forward over the corpses at a brisk pace. His horse's hooves ruptured carcasses, sending slushy remains squelching into the air. Bones cracked.

Crack, squelch, crack.

"Just follow my lead, Empress." Aric started across. Thanatos's immense weight compacted bodies. Chest cavities and skulls disintegrated under its hooves.

Crack, squelch, crack.

Driving a car over a corpse was one thing, but this . . .

I rolled my head on my neck, then urged my mare forward to pick her way through Thanatos's gory wake. I really needed to give this poor horse a name. She high-stepped, as if saying "ick, ick" with every hoof fall.

Ahead of me, Death suddenly gripped a sword hilt. Thanatos grew agitated, braided tail flicking.

"What is it?" I called. "Did you hear something?" Over the sounds of our headway?

Jack reined around. *Crack, squelch, crack.* "Why you slowing down, Reaper?"

"There's a threat nearby."

"What direction?" Jack swept his gaze, crossbow ready.

"Even with my uncanny senses, I can't pinpoint it." Death surveyed the area with a cool glance. "I doubt anyone could in this fog."

"Probably just Baggers." Jack slung his bow back over his shoulder. "Hell, maybe nothing's out there, and you're stalling us on purpose."

"Again, feel free to move on."

"For all I know, you could be allied with the Lovers, you. All the other Arcana worked together against them. But you showed up a day after." Jack started forward.

Aric rode up beside him. *Crack, squelch, crack.* Our gruesome soundtrack seemed to be ratcheting up their tempers. "Perhaps I am merely vigilant when taking the Empress over corpses cloaked in preternatural fog. Do you not have any combat sense?"

"We're on a clock."

"Ah. So to rescue the girl you presently favor, you would risk the one you used to favor. You might have a spare female, but I'm intent on keeping the one I have."

"You stirring up shit? It woan work."

"To save your precious Archer, you're leading the Empress of all Arcana on a treacherous journey directly to the Lovers—despite the fact that fate marked her. Still you press onward."

"It was *coo-yôn* who told us to ride out together—in order to save *Evie!*"

"The Fool didn't say to do it recklessly. He didn't say to sacrifice one female for the other. I value the Empress above all things. Just as you do the Archer."

Crack, squelch, crack.

"You doan know what you're talking about."

I muttered, "Back here, guys. Falling farther behind you." I'd only made it about halfway through. Wait . . . Had the bodies beneath me just moved?

No, no. Of course not.

Aric kept at Jack. "You've made a life with Selena. Sharing meals, missions, victory celebrations. The king and queen of Fort Arcana, the hunter and his huntress."

"Is this the kind of underhanded bullshit you been feeding Evangeline for months? You got into her head, sowing doubt about me?" Just past the line of exposed bodies, he slowed to a stop.

Aric intoned, "I've told her a great many truths." He stopped as well, both turning to wait for me.

"So after you mentally tortured her for the better part of a year, you abducted her. Then I'll bet you tortured her some more."

Over the last couple of months, I'd blocked out how traumatic my capture had been. My gloved hands tightened on the reins. Or they would have—right now, they were numb. Yes, I'd wronged Aric. But that wasn't me anymore. Which meant I hadn't deserved to be tormented.

Jack gazed from Aric to me and back. "On the heels of all that, you fill her head with your *truths*?" His eyes met mine and lingered. His brows drew together—as if with realization. "Now I understand what's goan on, me. Couldn't figure it out before." I thought a flash of *pity* crossed his expression—then came a hint of raw, blistering emotion.

"Thrall us, mortal."

Ignoring him, Jack addressed me, "I'll be scouting for a shelter to stop at for a spell, *bébé*. We'll ease our pace. Just hang in there a while longer."

Huh? Jack's attitude had done a one-eighty. If I weren't so exhausted and freezing, I could make sense of this situation.

The bodies roiled. No mistaking it now. "Uh, things might be shifting under me," I called. "And it feels—I don't know—kind of deeper in this spot." Like I was on a *pile* of them.

"You're likely over a clogged culvert of some sort," Aric said. "Where the corpses circled a drain. Continue forward, Empress."

"Yeah. Got it."

The pile heaved upward, lifting me and my horse! "What's happening??"

A more forceful heave. The spooked mare reared; my numb legs, hands . . . I couldn't keep my seat!

I tumbled out of the saddle. Landed on my back. Atop gunky corpses. Oh God, oh God.

The mare trotted a retreat, abandoning me in the carnage. *No name for you!*

The mat of bodies kept roiling like a bounce house.

"I've determined where the threat lies," Aric called. "Empress, it's beneath you."

"What?"

A hand shot up, snatching my ponytail.

Just past my boots, two Bagger heads popped up.

24

"Bagmen!" I screamed.

In a carefree tone, Aric answered, "Use your powers."

I still hadn't recharged them! I gripped my ponytail and jerked back from the clenched hand. Caught fast. "Any time you two feel like helping me!"

"The fuck you doing, Reaper?"

Aric had intercepted Jack, riding in front of him. "As soon as she needs assistance, I'll be first into the fray."

The pair of Baggers struggled to the surface, wedging their arms upward for leverage, their seeping, cream-colored eyes locked on my throat. They wriggled their slime-covered bodies free to their waists, like worms from a rotted apple.

How much longer before more emerged?

The skies chose that moment to open up, dumping buckets of rain. Blinking against water, spitting it, I cried, "Are you shitting me?"

The trapped Baggers lunged for me with so much force, their torsos shot back in recoil. Another lunge freed them to their upper thighs, extending their reach—just as the pile heaved, sending my body rolling toward the pair.

One caught my boot!

"Your powers," Aric called.

"I can't . . . seed anything in corpses!" I kicked against the creature's hold. "And poison doesn't . . . work on Bagmen!"

But my claws were as sharp as razors.

I twisted back and sliced the end of my ponytail off. The hand clutched the length like a prize.

Free to move, I dove toward the Bagger holding my boot, aiming my claws for his throat. He tucked his chin, chomping down, narrowly missing my fingers.

"Shit!"

"Come now, *sievā*, that is *not* how you're meant to use your claws."

"Ugh—you are such a dick!"

"Vines would work better."

Suddenly an arrow jutted from one Bagger's skull. Then the other. They slumped over. Jack must've fired right past Death's head!

I scrambled to stand, tripping forward as the pile shuddered. A boil about to burst.

Aric finally moved out of the way, allowing Jack to ride toward me.

"Move your ass, *bébé*!" He offered his hand. When I managed to grab it, he hauled me into the saddle, spurring his horse. At my ear, he said, "A gem of a guy you got there, Evie."

Once we'd made it to safety, Aric cast me a disappointed look. I was sick of guys giving me that expression!

To Jack, he said, "Whereas you view her as merely a girl, I've been on the receiving end of her powers. I've seen her shake the earth with fury, decimating populations. I know her for the goddess she is." To me, he said, "I'll go clean up the mess you made."

"Wh-what mess?"

The boil burst.

Baggers wailed as they rose, shucking body parts out of their way. They turned toward us, snarling for our blood, creamy eyes unblinking in the rain.

Riding hands-free into the mob, Death drew both swords and attacked.

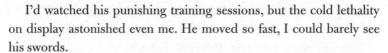

I'd watched his punishing training sessions, but the cold lethality on display astonished even me. He moved so fast, I could barely see his swords.

Just the results. In the rain, heads flew, bodies collapsed over each other, bone fragments and entrails spattered the air. Thanatos trampled some that hadn't completely risen.

The clash lasted only minutes.

When Death returned, magnificent in his rain-slicked armor, he lifted his visor to narrow his eyes at Jack. The grueling tension between them only mounted. "It felt good to ride in and save her, didn't it? Imagine how good she feels whenever she vanquishes her enemies—*on her own.*"

"Like a shadow, Evie," Jack muttered as we approached our potential pit stop. The rain had turned to fog, painting the small cinder-block house in an eerie light.

He was tense, bow ready—because this might be a slavers' den.

After three hours of passing one burned-out structure after another, I was so done in I'd rather face slavers than keep riding. The downpour earlier had soaked me through, and my teeth had chattered for miles.

At least it'd rinsed Bagger funk and corpse gore off me, like a car wash.

Jack had invited me to ride with him, but I'd said no. I doubted Death would approve. And Jack had confused me anyway. Why had his attitude toward me boomeranged?

We climbed the front stairs, Aric trailing us. "I'm surprised you're amenable to stopping, mortal. With the clock and such. The Empress can ride with me, and we'll continue toward Selena."

"Even if there was a snowball's chance in hell of Evie riding with you on that thing you call a horse," Jack said, "we're coming up on serious black-hat territory—which means our mounts need to be fresh."

We'd pushed them all day. Not that Thanatos needed rest. Thanatos bench pressed three eighty and ate bricks for fun.

"This place has been occupied recently." Aric drew one of his swords. "What makes you think the residents won't return?"

"Wagon-wheel ruts lead away from the house. Deep ruts. The slavers took their wagon full of captives north to sell—to the serious black hats I just mentioned." Jack certainly knew his way around this part of the world. "They set out after the last rain. But if they return, we'll kill them. Unless the Reaper is afraid of mortal slavers?"

"In my lifetimes, they've come in many different manifestations. Not once have I feared them."

Jack tried the door. Locked. He kicked it in, and we crossed the threshold into a front sitting room. The interior reeked, like some- one had forgotten to take the trash out (for a garbage truck that would never come again). Most of the furniture had been destroyed, likely for firewood.

A line of shackles was bolted to studs in the wall. Definitely a den.

"Fuckin' hate slavers," Jack grated. "Worse than Baggers."

I stared at those cuffs. "When there was no water, slaves dug wells. So what's the appeal now?"

"Salvage crews." Gaze alert, Jack checked a closet. "There are food stores if you know where to look—Prepper bunkers, government shelters, cargo ships that got beached, silos, rail cars. And sometimes bosses trade slaves for other goods."

We entered a living room that smelled cleaner. There were a couple of lawn chairs, a plastic table, a stone fireplace.

Jack faced Aric with a mean glint in his eyes. "Maybe Evie should be asking you about slavers, since you're the one who kidnapped her. Pretty much the same difference, *non*? I wonder how you kept her bound. You shackle her? A sixteen-year-old girl?"

Instead of denying it or downplaying it, Aric said, "Absolutely." There was that startling honesty again. "And once she cut off her own thumb to free herself from her bonds, she called up an army of green and nearly destroyed us all."

The mere memory of that day drained me. "Can we just not talk right now?"

"Come on, Evie." With me in tow, Jack cleared two back bedrooms and a bathroom, ushering me into the latter. "Why doan you change?" he said, setting up his spare flashlight. "I'll find some dry wood and get a fire goan. Stay in here, and take your time." He obviously didn't want me to be alone with Aric.

Dry wood? Was there such a thing anymore? "I can help."

"*Non*, I got this."

Guilt weighed on me. "You're the one who was injured."

"I ain't *un*used to getting my clock cleaned, *bébé*." Because his mother's *beaux* had introduced him to violence early.

When he helped me take off my bug-out bag and poncho, I asked, "Why are you being so nice to me?"

He turned to go, but hesitated at the door. "See things clearer than before."

I felt just the opposite.

Once he left, I gripped the counter, fighting a wave of dizziness. Could I keep riding at this pace? My headache throbbed, my legs and arms trembling. I stared into the mirror. My skin was so pale, my eyes seeming too big for my face.

In the reflection, I spied one of those shower squeegees behind me and felt a pang for the previous owners.

What a waste of your limited time.

Things could be worse. I could be dead like them. Though waterlogged and chilled, I remained free. No shackles circled my wrists, no Bagger bites marked my skin.

I stripped and hung up today's clothes, then unzipped my bug-out bag. Inside, I had an ultra-small sleeping bag, energy bars, a canteen, bandages for Jack, and more clothes. I dug for another change.

Banging sounded from somewhere else in the house. What was Jack doing?

I'd just finished dressing when I heard him return to the living room. "So you're two thousand years older than she is?" he said to Aric. "There's robbing the cradle—and then there's *this*. She's a teenager, you *fils de putain*."

"When I married her, I was *younger* than she was," Aric pointed out. "I can't control that I've endured this long. In any case, counting her various incarnations, she's lived on this earth for well over a century. She has memories of games when she was older, a woman grown."

"The unwed girl in there is named *Evie Greene*. She went to Sterling High, and she grew up in cane country like me. And even if you had married her, you never consummated it, no." He could be just as snide as Aric. "Not like Evie and me did." *Low blow, Jack.*

"I'm going to make you pay for that. In time."

"Now I know why you tried to stop us that night. How'd that work out for you? All my life, folks been telling me I cheat death. Guess they were right."

"The honor doesn't belong to the one she chose first for her bed," Aric bit out. "It belongs to the one she chooses to keep there."

"And you think that's goan to be you? You're delusional in your old age, you."

Hostility continued to seethe between them, along with a cutthroat rivalry.

Now I was about to have to wade right into the middle of it. In a daze, I turned toward the door, nearly leaving my bag behind. Accustomed to the security at Aric's, I'd forgotten the first rule of survival out on the road.

Jack had tried so hard to teach me. I'd thought he was just being cruel.

And now I knew why he'd gotten angry whenever I'd been hungry. I would never forget the image of him as a little boy kicking that trap in frustration. . . .

Back in the living room, a fire was going. Clever Jack had harvested boards from the building's walls.

He sat at the hearth cleaning that crossbow, his own bug-out bag at his feet, his jacket drying nearby.

Helmet in hand, Aric paced along a line of dirt-caked windows, casting glances outside. Tonight, he moved soundlessly in that armor. Sometimes his spurs clinked as he entered a room; other times silent. Maybe he adjusted his stride. "The mortal's handy, Empress. Your very own squire."

Jack didn't rise to the bait, asking me, "You eat anything?"

I sat beside the fire, dropping my bag. "Not yet." I stretched my hands to the warmth.

Once my fingers thawed, I retrieved my canteen and dinner, a nutritious energy bar. Those bars gave me enough calories for an entire day, but the taste was so foul, I earned every one of them. I peeled the wrapper, knowing I'd need the energy to keep up with these two.

Jack polished his bow's arrow cartridge with the tail of his shirt. "It's goan to get worse and worse on this route. I brought an extra bulletproof vest for you." Like the one he wore. "When we head out, I want you to try it."

That vest would swallow me.

Death scoffed, "She can take a hundred bullets to the heart and survive."

"I bet you know just what can kill her—since you've offed her so many times in past lives."

"I wouldn't say *many*. And she's tried for me just as often." Aric made a last round along the windows, then took a seat against the wall near the door. One arm rested over a bent knee.

"How'd you murder a girl who can regenerate, you? Decapitate her?" *If a guy has beheaded you on more than one occasion . . .* "Did you do to her what you did to those Baggers earlier? Sounds like a match made in hell to me."

Aric's fists clenched, the metal of his spiked gauntlets grinding. No doubt he wanted to drive those spikes into Jack's face. "Unlike you and the Archer, who have everything in common?" To me, Aric said,

"I would advise you to ask the mortal if he's been with her in all these months, but then, he'd simply lie to you."

Aric's words cut right to the heart of my problems with Jack: trust. Despite Jack's denial, I wondered again if something had transpired between him and Selena. She wanted him so much. . . .

The bar tasted like cardboard. I struggled to chew it. If Jack had lied to me about her, I could never accept him.

"You stirring the pot again, Reaper? Evie's the one I want. It'll always be that way."

I glanced over at him with a question in my eyes. In a matter of hours, we'd gone from *I can't look at you* to this. Why the turnaround?

"You had many women before the Empress." Aric took a whetstone from a pouch on his swordbelt. "You'll have them after her as well." He slid one sword free.

That muscle ticked in Jack's jaw. "I found the one I'm goan to be with. It's her for me. Period. I'll protect her with my life."

Aric ran that stone along his sword blade. *Graaaate.* "As will I."

"Like you did with those Baggers? I wrote the book on toughening Evie up, but that was too much risk."

Graaaate. "Arcana are superhuman—should our lessons be merely human in intensity? Or even *humane* for that matter? Those Bagmen had been washed away with those victims, buried alive among them for weeks, perhaps months. They chose to rise today—because they finally had *motivation*. They tapped into the depths of their blood-thirsty natures for more strength. In battle, the Empress should do no less."

"She can't do that if she's dead, no."

"I'm right here," I cried. "Right—here. If you two are going to fight, then do it over something other than me." I folded up the remains of the bar, stowing it and the canteen. Dinner had officially concluded.

Aric raised his brows. "Aside from you, I have no quarrel with the mortal. He's an uncouth drunkard who slaughters the English language every time he attempts it, but I probably wouldn't kill him just for that."

"You keep talking about slaying me, Reaper. Let's go outside and see if you can."

My impatience boiled over. "Just stop it—both of you! Get your heads in the game. We're out here to save someone's life."

After a hesitation, Jack returned his attention to his bow, Aric to his sword.

I asked Aric, "Can you call to Selena without the Lovers hearing?"

"Of course."

"Will you tell her we're coming for her? And ask her for any information that can help us?"

"What makes you think she'll respond to Death?" *Graaaate.* "But for you, I'll try—because it seems I can deny you nothing." He paused, his gaze going distant for long moments. "She's ignoring me, letting my words drift over her thoughts. A feat not easily done. Someone taught her a great deal about focus."

That extensive Archer training. Looking from Aric to Jack, I asked, "What's our plan?"

"I'm curious as well." Aric turned to Jack. "How far are you willing to risk the Empress in this endeavor?"

"If not for *coo-yôn's* prediction, she'd still be back at the outpost."

I shook my head. "I need to help. Jack, the Lovers want revenge against me. I was in an alliance with them in the last game, but I betrayed them. Horribly. Their line chronicles, so they know every detail."

"Why didn't you tell me?"

"I didn't know until they said something."

He jerked his chin at Aric. "I bet he knew that history. Guess he couldn't find time in three months to warn you about a pair of psycho killers who're out for your blood."

I had wondered the same.

Graaaate. "After she earned my trust, I had only scant hours with her—because of your foolhardy capture. And actually that insults the Fool."

I rubbed my temples. "Can we just talk about the plan, please?"

Jack cast a last scowl at Aric, then shifted his attention to me. "I'm meeting some dissenters from Azey North tomorrow on the road. I'll work with whatever I learn, see if I can trust them. At worst, they can give me intel on Selena. At best, they'll help me take the twins and the general off guard. I'll kill those three, free Selena, and seize command."

Aric raised his sword, eyeing the edge. "So our 'plan' rests on how well the mortal can read his co-conspirators' trustworthiness?"

"You got a better idea, Reaper? I'm all ears."

"You assume the source twins and the Archer will be in Dolor?"

"*Ouais.* Until I hear different. It's the only waypoint I got."

I asked, "If anything goes wrong, will the Lovers retaliate against Selena? Or if they find out another Arcana is riding with me?"

"Empress, they're *already* torturing her."

I flinched and thought Jack had too. No doubt reliving his own torment, the ordeal he would never tell me about. "Will they kill her?"

Aric shook his head. "Not for a while. She's the most valuable thing they possess. Consider the lengths they went to in order to acquire her. If they were going to murder her outright, it would already be done."

Death had gone to lengths to acquire—and keep—me. He'd had a suite prepared in his apocalypse-proof castle. I could understand how Aric had accrued so much power through the ages, to prepare for and weather the end of the world.

But how had the Milovnícis gotten the upper hand—over everyone? "How did the general amass an army?"

"He owned a private security firm in Virginia," Jack said, "with a mini-army of mercenaries—the kind of paramilitary that rescued kidnapped CEOs and stuff. The Milovnícis and those mercs must've holed up during the Flash. Afterward, his men overran smaller militias in the Southeast, one after another. He built the Azey like a snowball."

A bloody, murderous snowball—

Suddenly both Jack and Aric tensed. Outside, Thanatos gave a low nicker.

"What is it?" I asked.

Aric rose with that lethal grace. "I'm going to stand watch."

Jack was on his feet as well. "If there's something out there, I'm ready to fight."

"The day I need your help . . ." Aric trailed off. "I will *never* need your help, mortal." To me, he said, "Get some sleep. You can rest secure, *sievā*."

"What's that word mean?" Jack demanded.

Aric delighted in telling him, "*Sievā* means *wife*."

25

I gazed at the door long after Aric had gone, disbelieving he'd left me alone with Jack, threat or no.

I suspected he was testing me, testing my promise.

"You're staring after Death," Jack said, drawing my attention. Anger warred with confusion in his expression. "You worried about him?"

My protectiveness toward Aric hadn't waned. "Yes." Worry filled me—for him and Jack. For Selena and Matthew.

"Because you think we need him? Or because you think you care about him?"

"Both." I did care about Aric, maybe even more than *cared*.

I'd told Jack and Aric to get their heads in the game. I was one to talk. I couldn't stop comparing the two.

Jack's passion and drive versus Death's intensity and Arcana connection. God help me, I could see myself with either.

Or...neither? They'd both hurt me. The red witch in me whispered, *That's what dust is for: to leave them in it.*

I wished I could get objective advice. Damn, I missed my best friend Mel. She probably would've told me to keep both guys, collecting men like handbags.

Jack set his bow down and began to pace in front of the hearth, his eyes so vivid in the firelight. His black hair had dried, reflecting the flames like a raven's wing. "Death hurt you in all these ways, but you still give a damn about him." Out came his flask. "I was dishonest with you over one thing, and you can't tell me if you'll stay with me?"

"Put yourself in his shoes, Jack. I tried to murder him after convincing him that I was madly in love with him. I did this to him not once, but twice."

"*You* didn't do anything to him, no! Some long-ago Empress did. You ever heard of Stockholm syndrome? That's what's goan on."

My lips parted. "That's why you looked at me with pity earlier! That's why your entire attitude changed? You no longer hate me for getting with him, because you're putting all the blame on him."

Jack stopped pacing to face me. "A two-thousand-year-old man stole a vulnerable girl and broke her down."

He made me sound like Persephone, the daughter of Demeter, forced into the underworld by Hades. But Jack didn't understand: attitude-wise, I skewed more toward wrathful Demeter than I ever had toward vulnerable Persephone.

"I'm not a girl anymore. I *have* lived over a hundred years; I feel those previous lives. But even if I didn't, A.F. years are like dog years. Since the Flash, I cared for my mother as if I were the adult, I've killed, I've planned and executed coups. I've had to grow up fast."

He swigged his flask. "Why doan you tell me what it was like with Death in the beginning?"

Hell. If I gave Jack the details, he'd stride right out those doors and shoot Aric—who wore impenetrable armor. A bullet would simply bounce off. "I don't want to talk about it."

"He messed with your mind," Jack insisted. "That's why you think you feel something for him. No other reason could explain this turnaround."

"You really believe I've been brainwashed?"

"Evie"—Jack held my gaze—"it happened to you once before." At CLC. "I saw your drawing of Death in your journal, even before the Flash. You depicted a monster. *Un scélérat.*" A villain.

"Aric has done a lot to me. But he's also helped me. At the Hierophant's, I was about to eat . . . human flesh. It was an inch from my lips. I would've been lost forever." Like the filmy-eyed survivors who would hunt me till I died. "Aric stalled Guthrie long enough for my poison to work. And then he saved me from drowning and from Ogen."

"You wouldn't have been in any of those situations if not for that bastard! He needs to die. By my hand."

"You're not listening to me! Every time you say you're going to kill him, what you're really saying is 'I know better than you.'"

"When we're together again, you'll see."

"You're so certain we will be?"

A stark look crossed his face. "Of course I am! I told you we could get through anything, and I meant it."

"I do think you meant it—at the time."

"At the time? I'm the one constant here. Me! I never gave up on us, never got with another, even when the opportunity presented itself."

"With Selena?" Had things happened? Or did Jack keep mentioning this because he *regretted* not taking her up on it?

"It doan matter who with. Death can insinuate it as much as he likes, but nothing went on between me and her."

I wished I could believe every word that came out of his mouth; I wished my mistrust would fade.

But I couldn't; and it didn't. "At any rate, I still think it's wrong to involve you with Arcana."

"This is all bigger than you and other cards. The Lovers are connected to the largest fighting force in the South. Maybe even in the world."

The Flash itself could have been a tribute to the Sun Card, gone wrong.

"The stakes are higher than just this game." He crossed to me. "They're the highest they've ever been. We're on the brink." Our eyes met. "*Bébé*, you can deny me for other reasons, but not because you're Arcana."

"What about because I can't trust you?"

He knelt before me, putting his forehead to mine, his warm hands covering my shoulders. "I'm goan to earn your trust. You give me the time, and it will happen. Evangeline, what we got together"—his gaze was slate gray—"*ça vaut la peine.*" It's worth the trouble.

Jack was rugged and rough around the edges, filled with fierce passions and needs that called to my own. My hard-living Cajun. His hands began to move, rubbing my shoulders, my arms.

He was going to kiss me. Though I craved for him to, I drew back. "This isn't a good idea."

Jack studied my face. "You worried Death'll come back in and fight me?"

Yes! "We can talk, or I can go to sleep. Those are your options."

With clear reluctance, he let me go. "Talk about what?"

"Uh, what else has been happening in your life?" Lame.

"Something big." He sat beside me on the hearth. "*Coo-yôn* hinted that I need to head home, that I could do some good there. Once we get Selena back and the Lovers are dead, you're coming to Louisiana with me."

"*Louisiana,*" I breathed, the word raising a tumult of emotions.

"If that army wants me to lead them, they're goan to march south at the first opportunity. I told you I'd rebuild Haven for you. Why not settle the area around your farm, establish a new Acadiana? It could be a place of refuge for survivors."

I'd wanted a home! "You really think we could?" The urge to return clamored inside me.

"*Mais yeah*, we've got this. Doan you know? Together we can do anything."

"Even end the game?" My excitement dwindled. "Jack, I need to find my grandmother." Though I had doubts that Gran would help me in my quest (in fact might goad me to play), she was still my last living relative.

"You got to accept that she might be dead."

"I don't believe that." I *felt* that she lived—against all odds. "And I promised my mother that I'd get to her."

"Then let's make a deal. After we ride this route, if you tell me you think we can make it for months out here with no shelter, I'll set out with you. We'll take a contingent from the army."

In a way, agreeing to this would be like making a commitment to him. Again, I glanced toward the door. Aric was out there alone. A memory arose of him staring out into the night, murmuring, "I was called Aric. It means *a ruler, forever alone.*"

"Can we table that for now?" I asked Jack.

After a hesitation, he said, "We'll figure this out, *peekôn*. But in the meantime, I got something for you." He grabbed his pack and dug out an orange from my recent crop. "Tess gave this to me for good luck. I want you and me to share it."

"Like we did the Sprite you gave me."

He slid me that heart-stopping grin of his, still so sexy, though his face was bruised. "*Ouais*. I ain't had fresh fruit since I can remember." He started peeling.

"You should take it all."

"*Merci, non.* I missed your birthday. Consider this a belated party." He handed me half of the succulent fruit.

His lightheartedness began working its magic on me, my tension easing. "Did I miss yours too?" I suspected so.

He shrugged, taking a bite. "God almighty, woman, you're a great cook, you know that? Whipped up this orange from scratch."

I quirked my brows. "You should see what I can do with a pineapple."

We sat in front of the fire, across from each other, eating that orange. It was like we hadn't missed any time, hadn't missed a beat.

"Tell me what's goan on in that head of yours." He tossed the peels away, rubbing his hands on his jeans. "Keep talking to me."

"Why have you never shown me the photos in your bag?"

"You went through my pack? Guess I deserved that, *non?*" When I nodded, he said, "Did you see the book you gave me? The phone with your pictures? I about wore that thing out trying to get my fix of you."

"Answer the question."

"I want to look at those photos, but I never do." Gazing to the right of me, he said, "Doan know if I could hold my emotions."

"My mom once told me that sometimes you just need to be mad or sad. Sometimes you just need to let it happen."

The wind picked up, rain pelting the windows. Where was Aric? Over the last three months, when storms had howled, he and I had sat by the fire, reading together.

"Let's look at them, then," Jack said, probably to distract me from Death. He moved to sit with his back against the hearth.

Reminding myself how invincible Aric was, I settled in beside Jack. He offered me his flask.

Oh, screw it. I could die tomorrow. I was severely confused and doubted that my mental state could actually decline. I accepted the whiskey, taking a long swig. *Burn. Gasp.*

He drew the envelope from his pack, opened it. The first picture was of his mother, sitting with other women around a card table. "*Ma mère*, Hélène. She was at a *boo-ray* hall." *Bourré*, a gambling card game popular with Cajuns. "This was a few years ago, before things got real bad with her."

"She was so beautiful, Jack." With those cheekbones and storm gray eyes, she could've been a model.

"*Ouais. Pauvre défunte Maman.*" That meant *poor late mother*, but Cajuns used the phrase to say *dearly departed*, or *sainted*.

"Did she survive the Flash? You never told me."

He tensed beside me. "That's one of those secrets that goes to the grave."

I parted my lips to press him, but held off. Earlier today he'd confessed he might be about to snap. Now he was sharing these photos, fresh from an argument about Death, after riding for hours with a concussion—and saving me from Baggers.

I would cut Jack some slack.

The next picture was of him, Clotile, his best friend Lionel, and two other Basin kids who'd come to our school. They'd been at some kind of concert, smiling, eyes excited. "We got pickled that night for true."

I remembered hanging out with lifelong friends: the camaraderie, the inside jokes, the easy laughter. My gaze darted toward the door. Had Aric ever experienced that? Surely he'd had friends before his Touch of Death had come online.

Did he even remember friendship after so long?

Jack's voice grew thick. "I miss 'em. Especially Clotile."

I laid my hand on his arm. "Matthew showed me the day when you first met her."

Jack stiffened beneath my palm. "That wasn't a very good one for you to see."

"It only made my feelings for you stronger."

He relaxed. "Then look all you want, *peekôn*. I can handle it better now."

"Why?"

"Before the Flash, I had no control over my life, me. Now, even with all the unknowns and danger, I'm more in charge of my fate than ever before."

"Really?"

"My problems are my own." He pinned me with his gaze. "And it's up to me to figure out solutions."

This close to him, I could spy even darker flecks of gray in his irises. "That's really mature, Jack." He wasn't a boy anymore.

"I got moments, me."

"I think a lot of people used to underestimate you. But I also think those days are over. I know I won't do it again."

The corners of his lips curved. He could make my entire body go soft just from one of those grins—and he knew it: "*Um um um*, would you smell that honeysuckle?"

Clever Jack had figured out that I gave off scents with my moods. Rose? Meant I was about to strike. Sweet olive indicated I was excited. And yes, honeysuckle was the equivalent of me purring.

I flipped to another picture, this one of him and the rest of the group swimming at a spring, all of them tanned and laughing.

There Jack and I sat, reminiscing, swigging whiskey. And for a time, I was able to block out all the misery of the Flash. For a time, I was happy.

He showed me a picture of scenery from that spring. "The camera got knocked sideways, didn't get anybody in frame. I always meant to throw that one away, but now . . . just look at those trees, Evie. That crystal-clear water." He handed me the flask. "I believe we'll have it again."

"You truly do?" I'd been bullish about ending the game, but this interminable nighttime was throwing me. Would the sun never return? Was it better in other parts of the world? Maybe the equator?

"*Ouais*." He tucked the photos back into the envelope. "Your *mère* told me you were special. Your *grand-mère* told you that you would save the world. I believe you will. You got to."

"No pressure," I said with a buzzed smile.

"Get steppin', *fille*. I got an *envie* for things." A craving.

I swigged. "Like what?"

He cast me a wolfish grin. "*Cerises*." Cherries. We'd eaten them before we'd first kissed.

"What else do you crave?" When his wolfish grin deepened, I said, "What other *foods* do you crave? *Contiens-toi*." Behave yourself.

He raised his palms in surrender. "*Je cesse. Pour le moment*." I'll stop. For now. "I miss fried okra and corn on the cob. You?"

"Hush puppies and mashed potatoes."

"I made some mean hush puppies on my old cabin's stove. I'll cook them for you one day." His gaze went distant, his head tipping back. "You remember how warm that breeze from the south could be? Smelling of the sea, of far-off places? I hated where I was so much that I would've gone anywhere else in the world. Now I wish to God I could go back to the Basin."

I'd once regretted that Jack and I never talked. Now, when everything was so up in the air, I realized we'd just needed the *time* to talk. We'd always been on the run, fighting for our lives. And it didn't hurt to get him on the right subject: the home we both missed so badly.

I handed him the flask, our fingers grazing. "I'd do anything to see a field of sugarcane beneath a blue sky. The rasp of the leaves could make my heart swell."

"One day, you and me'll stand together on the front porch of Haven and gaze out at green for miles and miles. We'll swim in springs and go to concerts." He capped the flask, setting it away. "When I look into those eyes of yours . . ."

"What?"

"Not much is still blue in this world. Not the sky, not the water. I look in your eyes and see our future. I *feel* it." He reached into the front pocket of his jeans, pulling out my poppy-red ribbon.

"You still have it!"

"Carry it with me, everywhere I go. *Mon porte-bonheur.*" My good-luck charm. "This tells me we're goan to be together again."

The hope in his expression captivated me—almost completely.

Almost. *I've been dreaming of you, Jack, and I wish I could trust you. Someone else is tugging at my heart. . . .*

"I'm goan to let you borrow this ribbon for now." He tucked it into my front pocket. "You give it back to me when you can't see yourself with any man but me."

Being with Jack was like touching fire. When his fingers lingered on my jeans, I recognized the spark that could turn to an inferno.

My breaths shallowed; his eyes grew intent.

He reached for my hips, lifting me over his lap to straddle him.

"Jack!" I laid my palms on his shoulders.

With his gaze on my mouth, he bit his bottom lip, as if inviting me to do the same to him. "Give my right arm to taste you right now."

A sense of *rightness* bloomed inside me. To be with him like this. To be warmed by our fire. To be on the verge of kissing, of making love. My glyphs glowed, reflecting in his eyes.

He gripped my hips, pressing me down atop his hardness, and I gasped with pleasure. *"Yes."*

Lids heavy, he rocked me over his lap, banking that fire for both of us. *"À moi,* Evangeline," he said, his voice dripping with pent-up lust. "You're mine. And I'm yours. You're goan to find your way back to *us."* He dipped his hands to my ass, the heat of his palms searing me through my jeans.

When he squeezed, I rolled my hips, wrenching a low groan from his chest. His lips parted around ragged breaths. I panted, about to lose control. The chemistry between us was explosive. Combustible. If he ached even half as badly as I did . . .

But if this went any further, I'd only want more and more of him. Already I yearned for his hands cupping me all over, for just one last lick of flames.

Soon I'd reach a point where it was too late to pull back—because I would already be burned.

He must've sensed my hesitation. "But I woan rush you, no." He shuddered as he lifted me off his lap. "I'm in this for the long run."

I was half-dazed when he set me down. He tugged me close to his side, draping his arm over my shoulders to hold me tight. "Just rest your head against me."

I was helpless not to, hypnotized by the drum of his heart.

"I'm goan to tell you about a day we once had in the bayou—when there was no Flash. The day we should've had. Our first date."

Still catching my breath, I said, "What'd we do on this date?"

"We started out early . . ." He switched to French, murmuring in that deep voice, ". . . because I wanted as much time with you as possible. We packed food, beer, and a radio. Then we paddled a pirogue to a cypress stand I knew, one right in the middle of the water. The surface was so still, it mirrored the trees. The cicadas would go quiet whenever we drifted too close." He pressed a kiss against my hair. "We decided it was *our* place. No one else's. Because that was where we became Evie and Jack."

I snuggled in closer, letting his low, rumbling French wash over me.

"You were wearing a red bikini that made me hiss 'mercy' every time I saw you from a new angle. Um, um, *UM*, Evangeline, you about brought me to my knees." I remembered I'd worn one in some of the pictures on Brandon's phone. Apparently Jack had appreciated it. "When the air got spiced with honeysuckle, I felt about ten feet tall."

He described the foods we ate, the sultry rhythm of the blues we listened to, the feel of a southerly breeze—which no longer called to him because he was right where he was supposed to be.

He engaged all of my senses, until I could feel the warm wind playing with locks of my hair, and I swayed to the strains of music. Relaxation stole through me, and my lids grew heavy.

As I drifted off to sleep, he rasped, "*Bébé*, I'll bide my time. Because in the end, it'll always be Evie and Jack."

Through dreams, I relived another one of his memories.

Jack stood in front of a mirror in the courthouse bathroom, about to be arraigned for beating a man who'd attacked his mother. He looked so young, not more than sixteen. His skin was tan and smooth, his eyes storm gray. He tightened his tie, then loosened it, uncomfortable to wear one.

So much rides on today, and nerves are getting to me. I grip the edge of the sink and frown when my hands doan pain me. No new injuries mark my scarred fingers. Somehow Clotile has kept me out of fights until this court date. She and Lionel are the only ones here. Maman is . . . unwell.

My court-appointed lawyer lurches through the bathroom door with bleary eyes. The man drinks like a fish—something for me to say. He's from Sterling and despises "lowlife" Basin folk, made that crystal clear in our sole meeting. "Oh. It's you," he mutters as he makes his way to the urinal.

For Maman's and Clotile's sakes, I force myself to be cordial. "How we looking today, podna?"

He jerks a glance over his shoulder—like I was goan to knife him in the back. The movement and his drunkenness . . .

Oh Christ, my life is in the hands of a man who just pissed on his own shoes.

And didn't notice.

He zips up, then turns to me. "You're in luck." He's almost slurring. "State's got a new cage-the-rage program, for violent offenders with hair-trigger tempers. You're perfect for it."

Hair-trigger? I'd warned the fils de putain who hurt Maman. Told him never to touch her again. Next time I saw him, he was dragging her across the floor by her hair.

"Some are calling it the Rage Cage Program 'cause the inmates are still beating the living tar out of each other—just learning new ways to do it."

I want to show him the ways I've already learned. "Doan do me no goddamned favors."

He squints his bloodshot gaze. "As your lawyer, I'm going to enlighten you on a few matters. I've seen your type over and over, and I can spot a future lifer. When you're old, staring at the bars, you'll remember this talk. You'll remember how right I was. Unless you get shivved before then." He swerves out the door.

I slam my fist into the mirror, fracturing the glass, reopening every scar on my hand.

Over and over, blood-spattered shards reflect the pain in Jack's eyes.

Because part of him believed the man.

26

We heard their agony long before the misty rain allowed us to see it.

For hours today, Jack, Aric, and I had ridden hard, slowing only for this: the plague colony Jack had warned of.

Before us, a valley was filled with the dying, hundreds of men. Blood poured from each one's eyes, nose, and mouth. The disease had contorted their bodies at the joints—as if their bones had been fractured.

Their screams merged into a din as loud as a stadium of fans. Jack had to raise his voice to say, "They're calling it bonebreak fever. Because of how it makes folks look—and because the pain is supposed to be unbearable."

"There are so many of them." The sight dumbfounded me. All day I'd been unsettled by my dream of Jack, but this . . .

"The colony's grown," he said. "It used to be tucked into a corner." Rows of haphazard tents spanned the clearing. "Some say this place'll keep expanding, like a tick, till there are no Flash survivors left."

Along the perimeter, bodies had been discarded in piles. They differed from the corpses we occasionally passed—or rode over. Plague bodies were so misshapen they wouldn't lie flat. "How does it spread?"

"Par le sang." Through the blood. "Maybe the air too. I'd planned for us to ride past this—not through it."

"Have all these men been abandoned here?" I didn't see women or children. "With no one to take care of them?"

Aric lifted his visor. "It's too contagious." Death had no worries about infection. "Once there's a blood show, they're doomed to a harrowing demise. No cure, no survival. I imagine the pain is nearly in league with your poison."

"Or your Touch of Death?" I'd spoken little to Aric today. I vaguely remembered him returning, finding me just waking, rising from Jack's side. He'd scanned my face, then given me a nod of satisfaction. —*You kept your promise.*—

"Just so, Empress."

"If it's spreading, when does it stop?" Would it reach Fort Arcana?

Jack parted his lips to say something, then seemed to think better of it. "We'll figure that out in the future, *bébé*. One thing at a time, *non*?"

"How do we avoid this valley?"

"We doan, or we'll never make it to Dolor in time. We'd have to backtrack a dozen miles to the last mountain pass. The slavers must have figured out a detour, maybe through a mine. But I doan know of it."

Of all the ways to die in this new world, bonebreak fever would rate among the worst. "Let's play it safe and go back."

"Look, I'll wear a bandanna, me." Jack pulled one from his bug-out bag, letting the rain soak the material. "There's a trail skirting the west edge." He pointed out a narrow stretch between the outermost row of tents and a rushing stream. "We haul ass along it, getting through in minutes."

"Only room for one at a time," Aric observed.

I turned to him. "I won't agree to this, not unless Jack rides behind you."

Amusement. "I smooth the way for your squire?"

"You won't get sick, right? Neither will I." I thought. "You go, then Jack, then me. This makes the most sense."

Aric bowed his head in that cocky way. "Then by all means. Let my sacrifice be noted."

"Evie, you doan stop for any reason," Jack said. "This is *not* the time to help a victim or show mercy."

"I actually concur." Aric lowered his visor. "We're closing in on the Lovers. You need to conserve your powers."

"So *doan* do it," Jack added.

"I heard you two loud and clear."

"Good." Aric spurred his horse and descended. Jack reined around right behind him, glancing over his shoulder to make sure I stayed close.

Down in the valley, the yells boomed. For long, tense minutes, we sped along that trail, hooves kicking up dirt.

Almost across!

At the other end of the valley, Jack and Aric ascended the rise. I wasn't far behind —

A man lumbered in front of my horse.

With a cry, I yanked hard on the reins. The mare whipped her head and straightened her legs, skidding to a stop. A few more inches, and I would have run the man over!

Eyes seeping red, jaws stretched open, he yelled in pain, as if trying to communicate like that. More of the sick limped toward me, closing in. Beside me, one man vomited a rush of blood into a small runnel of water. The mare sidestepped with wide eyes, her nose flaring.

Like watching a train wreck in slow motion, I followed the blood's course as it ran and ran. It met the stream, swept away by the current, as if the plague sensed new victims downriver.

How many more humans could we lose?

The sick raised their contorted arms toward me. Wordlessly begging, they offered their hands—fingers splayed wide, bent at odd angles.

Like twigs.

The men made no move to attack, just beseeched with bleeding eyes, yelling between spasms. They wanted me to end their suffering.

Could I? Could I curb the spread? My glyphs stirred—as if my powers had been awaiting a purpose like this.

Tears welled as realization hit me. *Power is your burden.* This was what Matthew had meant.

These men would die in agony, or they would die now. Either way, they were as good as gone. As I had with Tad, I could make them sleep, never to wake.

A peaceful death.

The wind blew in my favor.

Jack and Aric had made the ridge. They'd both asked me not to do this, had agreed it was a bad idea.

"Evie, come on!" Jack called.

Some tiny, vanishing part of me needed to keep the peace with them. To not rock the boat. To fall in line with what the boys wanted and expected of me.

Then I remembered that the Empress of all Arcana wore a crown for a reason.

The red witch whispered, *Demeter withholds viciously—and gives lavishly. GIVE.*

I spurred the mare, forcing my way past this crowd. They wailed when they believed that I couldn't—or wouldn't—help them. Some crawled after my horse. The sound reached a tumult.

I removed a glove. I rolled up my sleeve, uncovering my golden glyphs. The last time I'd pulled from my spore glyph, I'd only intended to make soldiers sleep.

Now I filled my hand with my most lethal poison. Tears spilling, I held up my flat palm and aimed it back.

Pursing my lips, I blew over my hand.

Blowing a kiss.

I turned away when the closest men's lids grew heavy. Staring straight ahead, silently crying, I rode on. Behind me, my poison spread outward like the wave of a detonation.

The din ebbed until I could hear bodies collapse. A last echo of their moans. A stray whimper here and there.

Then silence. In my wake, I'd left a mass of bodies. Power was my burden.

It weighed as much as a crown of stars.

When I reached the ridge, Jack's brows drew together; Aric's gleaming eyes narrowed. But I didn't care if they were angry.

Jack surprised me by saying, "Now that it's done, I'm glad. You cauterized a wound and saved countless more."

I pulled my glove back on. "All right, let's hear it, Aric."

"As the mortal said, it's done. Empress, you delivered many from a short, wretched fate." His tone was full of pride. "Sometimes a reaper is welcome."

Jack frowned at him, as if he couldn't reconcile this man with the indiscriminate murderer he imagined the knight to be.

Aric held his gaze. "Never deny the power of Death."

27

"This doan feel right," Jack said from ahead, his bow at the ready. He was taking point along a rutted track inside another a narrow canyon. Aric rode beside me.

Since the colony yesterday, I'd spoken little to either of them. Last night, we'd sheltered in an old gas station, and I'd passed out the second I put my head down.

Despite the fact that we'd been threading the needle through a cluster of cannibal mines.

Now the three of us surveyed our surroundings. Or tried to. After endless miles on the road, the fog had thickened until we had to slow our pace. Jack rode just a dozen or so feet ahead, but I could barely make him out.

"All right, Reaper, you sensing anything?" Jack waited for us to catch up, then fell in on my other side.

Aric cocked his helmeted head. "A threat around the next corner."

"You want to backtrack, you?"

"Once you've seen me in a real combat, you'll know never to ask me that again."

And the cutthroat competition continued!

"I said I'd sensed a threat, not an army," Aric added, lowering his visor. "But if *you're* anxious . . . "

"Just try to keep up, you."

As we made our way around the corner, I peered into the murk. Something large loomed ahead. Had a tanker toppled over?

Electric spotlights flooded on, spearing the fog, paining my eyes.

When my vision adjusted, I saw a bus parked across the road, sheet metal covering its sides. The words HUMAN TOLL were painted in red along the length of it. Atop it? A homemade gun turret. Someone had taken half of an old satellite dish, then carved out a slot for a really big gun.

Was that what Selena had called a fifty-cal? If one of those could eat into a mountain, it could cut us in two.

"Black hat chokepoint," Jack muttered. "Fuckin' slavers."

A trio of them manned the top, one behind the turret and two more popping up their heads from behind a shield of corrugated steel. I couldn't see the turret guy, but the others resembled each other with their freckled faces and long red hair sticking out from their caps. Had to be brothers.

The bus didn't stretch all the way to the sides of the ravine, so the slavers had strung rows of razor wire, coiled as high as my shoulders. Escape-proofing their chokepoint.

"Hands where we can see 'em, all of you!" Turret Guy called, swiveling that gun. "This here's a toll booth. You wanna live, then you'll do what we say."

I raised my hands, frowning at Jack. When had he ridden so close to the bus?

Aric raised his hands as well. "We want no trouble." He sounded like he was trying not to laugh.

The slavers' attention was focused on him, a stranger dressed in full armor. "Where'd you get that suit?" Turret Guy asked. "Raid a museum?" He peeked over the satellite dish for a better look, revealing his lengthy beard and caterpillar eyebrows.

In a resonant voice, Aric explained, "A death deity sent me a vision, directing me to an ossuary, a bone crypt." Was he stalling for Jack? To do what? "I found this armor on the body of a notorious warrior, the design ages ahead of its time, with the metal already steeped in death. A good sign for one like me."

Turret Guy shared a look with his companions. "'Nother one round the bend. Your horse sick or something?'"

Now might be a good time to *invoke* the red witch. Would the men notice if I pierced my raised hands for blood?

But seeding vines would take too long—

One of those lights shone on me, glaring so brightly I could feel its heat from here.

"You, the boy in the back! Take off your hood."

I shielded my eyes. *What's happening, Aric?* Jack looked like a shadow figure.

—Your mortal's about to attack. Show them something distracting.—

I reached for my hood, easing it back, inch by inch, as they stared rapt.

Turret Guy sucked in a breath. "Christ on a cracker! A girl! Dibs on seconds!"

One of the redheads said, "A *teen*. Fine as the night is long. Call up to the house." Was the other one fumbling for a radio?

In the next instant, Jack was standing on his saddle, bow in hand.

"What the hell?" Turret Guy rotated the gun toward him, but it would only turn so far.

Jack leapt for the bus, the toe of one of his boots meeting the metal siding; he caught the railing above with his free hand, then vaulted onto the roof.

"No, Jack!" There were too many!

Death flung his sword, skewering one of the brothers. Jack fired his bow at the other one.

The redheads dropped, but not before a gunshot sounded.

Why was Jack staggering back? He clutched his chest!

Shot.

"NO!"

"The mortal wears his own armor, Empress," Aric said.

When Jack recovered and charged forward, I choked out a relieved breath. The vest!

Didn't mean I wouldn't kill him for being so reckless. Only one of us could die from a bullet—him!

He aimed the bow at Turret Guy, waving him closer. When Jack motioned down, the man obediently went to his knees.

"How many are up at the house?"

"We never meant no harm, sonny! I wouldn't have hurt her."

"How many? Or I do this real slow, me."

"You'll lemme go if I tell you?"

"We'll see. Four. Three. Two. One—"

"Th-there's our boss and fourteen others."

"Weapons?"

"Armed to the teeth. They're the ones you should go after! *They* would've had their way with your girl," said the man who'd called dibs.

"You got any females for sale?"

Turret Guy smiled, no doubt thinking he'd been handed a lifeline. He had no idea he was digging his grave. If he admitted to hurting women . . .

"Not here, sonny, but we got a batch of young ones coming in." He stroked his beard with a sly look. "Sweetest pieces of ass you ever saw. Trained and everything. Hell, I'd let you sample for free—"

Jack shot the man between the eyes. "Fuckin' *hate* slavers." He collected his arrows.

The radio blared a moment later: "I heard that gunshot earlier, you assholes. I ain't gonna tell you again—no wasting bullets on straggler Bagmen. Do you dipshits copy?"

Jack lifted his gaze. Toward the slaver's house? The one packed with fifteen armed men?

"Jack . . . what are you doing?"

He'd already dropped off the other side of the bus.

"Your mortal's storming the slaver den." Aric's tone was half-amused, half-approving. "I'm hereby inviting myself on his incursion." Eyes lively, he spurred his horse up to the razor wire—and didn't stop.

Like a bulldozer, Thanatos barreled through, catching the wire on its own armor, dragging the snarl free. Barricade destroyed, Aric charged after Jack. I followed.

The slaver boss lived in a sprawling two-story farmhouse that was lit up like a home from before the Flash. Off to the side, gas-guzzling generators hummed. His business must be flourishing.

Aric galloped past Jack to the front entrance. Jack cussed him in French, sprinting on foot to catch up.

In one fluid motion, Aric dismounted his still-moving horse. Never slowing, he strode with superhuman speed toward the front door, right up the freaking porch steps! He *knocked*, as if he were about to drop off a casserole, then raised his hands in surrender.

The men would have no fear of answering, would just see some strange armored guy—who had no gun.

A slaver cracked open the door with a threatening look—and a pistol aimed not a foot from Aric's chest.

Death spoke. Whatever he said made the man pull the trigger. The bullet ricocheted, plugging the slaver in the face.

Jack did a double take, then headed toward the back of the house. Aric drew his sword and breached the room.

Then . . . pandemonium.

Lamps crashed to the floor, dimming the area. Shadowy figures moved. Muzzle flashes blazed. Bullets bounced off mystical metal, a repeated *ping ping ping*.

An amoeba would've learned by now not to shoot at Aric's armor.

Yells came from the backyard. I spurred my mare toward Jack. But he didn't need any help, was firing on any who fled. The hunter had known a sight like Death would drive the men out the back. Then he'd merely waited.

The skirmish concluded in minutes. Aric had slain everyone inside; Jack outside.

The line of bodies stretched from the backyard into the house. Right where the arrow corpses stopped, the headless ones started.

The enemy was done. Neither Jack nor Aric had allowed me to contribute whatsoever. No witch invocation necessary.

With a nod of acknowledgment toward me, Jack retrieved his arrows, his bruised face flushed with aggression—and excitement?

The heat of battle.

At the back doorway, Aric lifted the grille of his helmet, smirking at him. "Eight to seven."

"Only one ahead of me?" Jack snagged a two-way radio from a dead man's belt, clipping it to his own. "And you got body armor from head to toe."

The two of them were acting like such . . . guys. I wanted to strangle them. Neither should have been this reckless going in—or this pleased with himself afterward.

Or maybe I was aggravated that I hadn't gotten to carry my weight.

At the threshold, a man with an arrow in his eye whimpered. Still alive. Jack strode forward to finish the kill, but Death beat him to it, removing his gauntlet on the way.

Aric stared at Jack as he laid his hand over the man's face.

Ghastly black lines branched out over the half-dead slaver. He gulped a lungful to shriek, clawing Aric's hand in a frenzy.

There was no greater pain than Death's touch. It did outstrip even the plague—and my poison.

"Think twice about trying to strike me," Aric told Jack as the man went still. "Oh, and now the score's nine to six." He stood, donning his gauntlet.

Jack snared the arrow, avoiding contact with the dead man's putre-fying skin.

Aric chuckled. "My touch isn't contagious, mortal. The Black Death was a tribute to me; I wasn't a tribute to it."

"All the same . . ." Jack wiped the arrowhead across the bottom of his boot. "If you're done showing off, I'm goan to clear this place."

He kicked the body out of the doorway and motioned me inside so he could lock up that entrance. "We'll stay here for a spell and rest the mounts."

I bit my bottom lip. "Do we have time?" Dolor was only a day's ride away, and I burned to get to Selena.

"We'll make it up with fresh horses. Come on, you."

Claws at the ready, I followed Jack and Aric toward the front of the house. I gaped at Death's destruction: heads and bullet holes everywhere. Sofa tufting clung to the blood splatter on the walls. Guns smoked in clenched hands. The fire in the hearth flickered on, oblivious.

"I'm reluctantly impressed by your take, mortal," Death said. "I thought you were only good at thievery."

With a mean smile, Jack drawled, "Thievery's the *second* thing I'm really good at." He turned to me, all cockiness. "Ain't that right, *bébé*?"

Death gripped the hilt of his sword. Jack had no idea how close the knight was to cutting him down.

"Aric, why don't you go retrieve your other sword?" I mentally added, *You made me a promise.*

—*He courts his own doom.*—

Please?

"Empress," he grated, inclining his head before setting off.

Once Aric was out of earshot, I told Jack, "You don't have to bait him like that."

Jack checked behind a door. Then around a corner. "I bait him to let out steam—or I blow."

"And what if you push him too far?"

"You got this idea of him as invincible. Every man's got a weakness."

Matthew had always said Aric's weakness was me.

"There's a chink somewhere in the Reaper's armor. Just need to find it, me."

Before I could say more, Jack turned toward the stairs.

On the second floor, we investigated nooks and closets. One

bedroom was filled with clothes and packs—stolen from slaves—while three other rooms were furnished and spotless. But then, this boss had enjoyed free domestic labor.

"Oh *ouais*, we're goan to stay here tonight. The windows up here are nailed, with nothing outside to climb. Decent security."

"You don't think more slavers will show up?"

"*Non*. But just in case, we'll drag all the bodies around front." We descended the stairs. "Anybody with a lick of sense will keep goan."

"Why did you take such a risk earlier? Leaping to the bus?" I hadn't had a real moment to process his actions. Right now wasn't the time either, but just like Jack said, I had to let out steam. I stopped on the landing. "When I saw you get shot . . ."

He turned back toward me, curling his forefinger under my chin. "I was fine."

"Don't brush this aside."

"I can take care of myself. And I can protect you just as good as Death can. Provide, too. He only had a head start, *non*?"

Jack had risked his life to prove a point? Was the chip on his shoulder back?

"That bastard knew the Flash was coming and got his ducks in a row. Just give me time."

"Don't risk yourself like that again."

He dropped his hand at my no-bullshit tone. "I can't make that promise. We doan know what we might head into."

"Uh-uh. No. You don't get to take chances like that anymore. People depend on you. If I sign on with you—and that's a big *if*—you promised to earn my trust. You can't do that if you're dead. Maybe you do have a death wish?"

He rolled his eyes. "I doan have a—"

"Promise me you won't take any more unnecessary risks."

He opened his mouth to argue; must've seen I wasn't having it. "Fine. I promise. Satisfied, you?"

At length, I nodded.

"Then come on. Let's finish clearing this place." He led me back downstairs.

Now that we'd closed the exterior doors, the first floor had warmed up, hot air chugging from the vents. In the kitchen, I checked the pantry, found it stocked with canned and boxed goods.

When Aric joined us there, Jack glowered. "Thought you wouldn't darken our door for a longer spell."

"Do recall that I possess superhuman speed. I also had time to move all the bodies outside in order to ward off unwanted visitors." He'd had the same idea as Jack. "After securing the horses, I hastened to get back to my wife."

"You keep calling her that, but if some *fille* tried to murder me on my wedding night, I'd think twice about my nuptials."

Aric's eyes narrowed.

I got between them. "Shouldn't we search the rest of the house? The garage is left."

After a tense moment, Jack started forward. As if by silent agreement, he and Aric kept me in the middle.

When we entered the laundry room, the washing machine was changing cycles. "Why would the boss use so much electricity? With the floodlights and the heater and all these appliances, he'd have to keep generators running full-time."

"The man probably knows his fuel will turn soon," Aric said.

"Turn?"

Jack answered, "Gasoline lasts just a year or two."

"*What?*" I should have savored electricity more at Death's!

"It only lasts that long," Aric said blithely, "unless one had special additives infused into his stores." To me, he added, "Ours will be preserved for well over fifty years."

Jack drew up short, turning to face us. "The military's additives doan extend it more than five years."

"In the U.S.? I bought the technology from overseas."

"How many barrels you got?" Jack eyed him so keenly I figured Aric was due for a break-in soon.

"Barrels? None. I have *tankers*."

Jack scrubbed his hand over his chin with a hungry look. But there was also a hint of something else—surely not a grudging respect?

Aric gazed down at me. "Your dance studio will always be lit, as will your art studio. The libraries, of course. The pool will be heated as long as we live. Who needs the sun, when we have acres of sunlamps?"

My eyes darted to Jack. I could give him all the time in the world, and no matter how hard he worked, he could never match the situation at Aric's. I thought Jack was coming to the same conclusion right at that moment.

"The Empress didn't tell you what her new life was like?" Aric said. "How she was indulged in every way? She enjoyed fresh food daily and a cook to prepare it. She slept in her warm bed in a lavish tower filled with a new wardrobe and every imaginable amenity."

Jack hadn't been a fan of rich people before the Flash. I didn't see that changing just because of the apocalypse.

"She had time to read and draw. In fact"—Aric leaned in, holding Jack's gaze—"she used to dance for me every day."

That muscle ticked in Jack's jaw. He looked as pissed as he had when Aric first called me "wife." But then Jack rallied: "It wasn't like that at first, no. All that came after you got into her head. You think this ain't Stockholm syndrome?"

"The symptoms *are* there."

Jack blinked at Aric's frankness. "Why doan you tell me what you did after you abducted her? Evie refuses to."

"Very well. I made her walk for leagues, barefoot, coatless, and freezing. She was bound, so she couldn't break her falls. All the while she never knew if or when I would kill her." Aric's bearing wasn't proud by any means, but he seemed determined to own up to the wrongs he'd done.

It struck me; this was what forthrightness looked like.

He wasn't finished. "I laughed when she mourned you and insulted her as often as possible. I blunted her powers with a cilice that cut into her arm every hour of every day. To get free of it, she had to persuade Fauna to claw her flesh off."

My glyphs stirred as I remembered that pain.

Jack's eyes had widened. "Part of me wants to punish you for all that. Part of me wants you to keep talking, keep digging your own grave with her."

Aric exhaled wearily. "You've yet to understand what the truth is."

"And what's that?"

"Any harm I do to my pursuit of her is offset by my *honesty*. The Empress can handle anything but deception—because she must always know where she stands. She's been like that since the beginning of time."

He was right. I could handle losing some of my arm better than I could Jack's lies to me: *"No secrets. Except for how bad I want you."*

Jack wasn't deterred. "Truth? Like how you told her about her mother—out of context? Bet you couldn't wait to tell her that."

"He didn't, not for months," I said. "And only when I put pressure on him."

Aric moved in closer to me. "Had I done the same to her mother— and I would have without hesitation—the Empress would've heard of it firsthand." In a tone as old as ages, Death said, "Mortal, if there's one thing I've learned in all my years, it's this: lies are curses you place on yourself."

My lips parted. In that moment, I remembered why I'd started falling in love with Aric.

Inner shake. If only he'd learned in all his years not to coerce women into sex.

As if he'd read my mind (though I hadn't felt his presence there), Aric asked Jack, "Do you know why she left me that night?"

"To rescue me!"

"I told her I could easily free you if she slept with me. I pushed her, and instead of surrendering to me, she drugged me to escape. So if you think I could *ever* get that woman to do something she truly doesn't want to, you're as mistaken about her as I was."

Jack appeared to be grinding his molars. "And you tell me this too?"

"I take no actions that I wouldn't publicly recount. If you can't speak your deeds, then don't *do* them."

If Jack's bravery was like a living thing inside him, Aric's wisdom radiated from him.

Jack clearly didn't know what to make of Death—an uncommon situation for the perceptive Cajun. Since Jack's go-to response tended to be pure anger, with a side of action, I needed to defuse this.

"Look, guys, can we just secure the place? I'm exhausted."

I must've sounded as tired as I was because Jack nodded. *"Ouais.* Come on, *bébé."*

At the back of the laundry room was a door. A ring of keys hung from a wall peg beside it. They looked like old-timey jailor keys.

Jack raised his bow and flipped on all the light switches. "Stay back."

Aric unsheathed one of his swords, tugging me behind him.

When Jack opened the door, fluorescent bulbs sparked to life in the freezing garage, illuminating the space.

I peeked around Aric. "Oh, my God. . . ."

28

"Must be twenty of them." Jack lowered his bow.

Half-dressed men, all shivering.

Aric sheathed his sword. "They're secured." The prisoners had been shackled by the ankles to separate bolts.

"Secured?" I whispered. "Aren't we going to free them?"

Both Jack and Aric shook their heads, then seemed annoyed that they'd agreed with each other.

"Just 'cause they got caught by slavers doan mean they're innocent," Jack said. "They could be rival slavers, murderers, rapists. They doan need to have filed teeth to be cannibals."

Some of the men cast me unsettling stares. One ran his hand over his crotch as he ogled me. Ugh!

I'd so long equated *shackled person* with *good person* that I'd had a misguided impulse to help them.

A younger man among them told Jack, "I'm Rodrigo Vasquez. Franklin sent me a message, said I was supposed to meet you on the road." The guy had dark hair even longer than Gabriel's and deep brown eyes. Cute. And a friendly? "I got trapped instead."

Jack snagged the key ring, then made his way to the prisoner. "You got something else to tell me?"

"Oh. Yeah." Rodrigo rattled off a string of numbers and letters.

They had a code?

Jack unlocked him. "Go scavenge clothes and your gear. Radio your people. Tell them I'm ready to meet." The co-conspirators. His plan was coming online!

That dream of him was still fresh in my mind. I'd wondered why Matthew had given me such a specific vision. Maybe it had something do with Jack becoming a leader, hinting about his future, of things to come.

No man could be more driven to make something of himself.

As Rodrigo eased past me and Aric into the house, he swallowed audibly.

Aric sighed. —*You'd think after two thousand years, I'd be accustomed to looks of fear.*—

To the rest of the men, Jack said, "We woan kill any of you, if you cooperate. Goan to ask you some questions."

"You're the hunter!" an emaciated man exclaimed. "From Cajun country. I've heard of you."

Another guy said, "You killed a thousand Bagmen! With your bare hands."

Jack was turning into a larger-than-life legend. He just needed a blue ox named Babe.

Instead of denying such a wild claim, Jack said, "I was bored that weekend, me." He wasn't a braggart by nature, but feeding this rumor was smart.

"You ride with those Arcana," said another man.

"Got a new pair with me right now," Jack replied. "One'll be staying with me, the other'll be riding on."

Aric gave a humorless laugh. —*It's almost fascinating how confident he is.*— As he'd done yesterday, Death watched him avidly.

"Back to the questions," Jack said. "Any of you a doctor?"

No raised hands.

"An electrician or a mechanic? And doan bullshit me, 'cause I know enough about either to tell if you're lying." Jack had read those trade books so he could determine whether someone had helpful skills. "Do any of you got experience that's valuable today?"

A few raised their hands.

"No attorneys," Jack bit out, and one man lowered his hand. "I ain't looking for auto detailers, hedge-fund managers, or salesmen." With a wink back at me, he said, "And for fuck's sake, no shrinks."

Zero hands were left in the air.

"I'm goan to release you when we head out. Now, some of you are probably thinking about following *ma belle fille* here, 'cause you're just plain stupid." He narrowed his eyes at one guy who was staring at me and licking his lips. "She *is* an Arcana. The Empress of them. Which means she's pretty much a wrathful Mother Nature."

—If the shoe fits.—

Shut it. I was in no mood. Though Aric's honesty had affected me, I was still a little raw from reliving those hardships.

"She's full of poison, and I've seen her tear a man in two with her vines." Jack turned to me. "Show them some of what you got, Empress."

I hesitated. I'd never demonstrated my abilities for anyone except Arcana. But then, Matthew had said remaining secret didn't matter anymore.

So I let my body vine grow, a rose stalk. Creeping out from my collar, it stretched upward like a serpent, then twined around my head in "crown" position, leaves jutting up. I found wearing it like that a comfort.

Jaws dropped.

As the air grew thick with the smell of roses, I raised my purple claws. Reaching for the nearby breaker box, I slashed the metal door like it was paper. Gasps sounded.

With a chuckle, Aric headed back inside, and I followed.

I heard Jack tell the men, "Anybody not a fan of his balls, try something with that one. Anybody else, know that we're goan to be building a haven in Louisiana, a place called New Acadiana, for white hats only. If you fit the bill, you got something mighty fine to look forward to."

By the time Jack locked the garage door and joined me and Aric in the living room, Rodrigo had returned, dressed, armed, and holding a two-way radio.

When Aric strode toward the fire, spurs clinking, Rodrigo stared after him with a blend of awe and fear.

Jack snapped his fingers at the man. "You heard anything?"

"Meeting's tonight. They're sending a truck here." He stepped on one of the new carpet stains, and blood splashed up around his boot. "I'm heading outside to flag them down. ETA fifteen."

Jack told him, "I'm bringing my girl with me."

Aric slowly shook his head. "Do you truly think I'll allow you to take her out of my reach? Straight into a meeting with soldiers? You're deluded in your young age."

Rodrigo said, "Uh, the conditions of the meet are that you come alone and unarmed, with no Arcana."

Once the man had left, I told Jack, "I don't like you going by yourself. Much less with no weapons. Let us follow you."

"Tonight's important, *peekôn*. You got to trust that I know what I'm doing."

"In other words, the Empress should trust that you know who to trust," Aric said. "If your co-conspirators betray you, our element of surprise will be gone. Surely Milovníci put a price on your head."

"He did. I'm the general's most wanted, and he ain't dicking around. The bounty's a woman, free and clear."

My claws sharpened at the threat to Jack—and at the idea of a woman being passed around like that.

"You bade the Empress flaunt her abilities, but not just to frighten those slavers," Aric said. "You're using us to secure power. Once freed, those men will disseminate information—that you shaped."

Jack nodded. "There'll come a time when soldiers are more afraid of us than of the general."

"Wars *are* won by perception." Aric stroked his golden stubble. "Again and again, I've witnessed this."

"I let that rumor grow about me and the Bagmen because people want to believe that something like that can actually happen. They *need* to believe it." A new story to tell. "Like they need to believe there's a girl out there who can seed the ground, if they could just ease her wrath enough."

"You're turning her into a nature deity. With her own fables." Aric's tone wasn't disapproving, more contemplative.

"*Ouais.* Right now I want as many people as possible to think I'm riding the countryside with life and death—"

Aric bit out, "You *are*."

"—and that the two of them demand order."

Headlights glared through the windows. Jack glanced past a curtain then back at me. "It's them. Before I leave out, I'll get you settled in a room." He clasped my hand, leading me up the stairs. Over his shoulder, he enunciated to Aric, "Get her settled upstairs in a room—*to herself.*"

On the second floor, Jack headed toward a back bedroom. Blue walls with race-car wallpaper. "You stay in here with the door locked till I get back. Try to get some rest."

"This is so important that you'll let me stay here with Aric?"

"*J'ai les mains amarrées.*" My hands are tied. "You can't imagine what's on the line. Short of this, I'd never leave you. I trust you, but him? I put nothing past that Reaper."

"I'm nervous about you going alone. "

"*Tracasse-toi pas pour moi.*" Don't worry about me. "Are you goan to be safe here with him?"

I removed my pack and coat, tossing them on the bed. "You saw how he fights."

"No, I mean safe *from* him. He woan try to steal you away?"

"He can't, and he won't. Remember what I did to the plague colony?" How could we ever forget?

Jack exhaled. "Promise me you woan let him guilt you into anything. It's goan to be you and me, Evie. Just . . . just doan give me anything else to hurt on."

In other words, don't get with Aric. "I haven't made any decisions. And until I do, I'm not doing anything—with anybody."

"You mean that bastard's still in the running?" Jack swiped his palm over his face. "I ain't hearing this."

"I can't deny that I have a history with him." And an Arcana connection.

The truck driver laid on the horn. No concern about attracting Bagmen?

"I got to go. But we *will* finish this later." With a wince, Jack shrugged from his bug-out bag. He placed his bow on the bed and removed the guns from his holster. At least he still had his vest on. "Keep this transceiver." He handed me the two-way radio. "I'll take another one, so you can call me for any reason."

I clipped it to my jeans pocket. "*Reviens back sain et sauve. T'entends?*" Come back safe to me. You hear me?

My use of French made his brows draw together. As if he couldn't help himself, he gripped my nape and kissed me. Short. Heated.

He drew back just before I broke away. "Doan want to leave you. After tonight, I doan plan to ever again." As he left the room, he murmured, "Nothing to hurt on, *bébé*."

When Jack reached the first floor, I heard Aric say, "Rest assured, mortal. I'll keep her safeguarded—and warm."

"My gun. Your skull. Think about it." The front door opened. Closed.

I locked myself in, then crossed to the window. An army convoy truck awaited. Two guys with machine guns hung off the sides, outriders ready to blow away anything that neared.

What was Jack heading into? Shoulders back, he strode past the array of bodies. With exaggerated movements, he opened one side of his jacket, then the other. To show them he was weaponless?

As he climbed into the cab, he gazed up at the window, giving me a chin jerk in farewell. I kept the truck in sight until the fog swallowed the taillights.

How could I not worry? Add it to my ongoing apprehension about Selena and Matthew. I fought the urge to reach out to him, to check on him. But if Matthew needed a break from me, I'd respect that.

I unzipped my pack and pulled out my sleeping bag, unrolling it against the wall. I'd just wondered what Aric was up to when he called from downstairs.

"Come to me, Empress." I could hear the grin in his voice. "Why fight temptation?"

Curiosity seized me. But joining him would be a mistake. When he turned on his charm, he was seduction personified. The last time I'd been alone with him, he'd touched me with reverence, murmuring, *This is joy I feel, is it not?*

I called back, "Going to sleep."

"Hmm. Your loss . . ."

I exhaled a huff of breath. Damn it.

29

Aric waited at the foot of the stairs, broad shoulders back, blond hair drying. The golden stubble on his chiseled jawline glinted in the firelight.

Too gorgeous for his own good.

"We're in a house with electricity and food. If you don't take advantage of all its offerings, someone less worthy will." He had his helmet under one arm and a leather saddlebag slung over a shoulder. His version of a bug-out bag. What would a man like him pack?

With my own bag in hand, I joined him. "What do you suggest?"

"You could have a hot meal. Come, *sievā*, unless you eat more, you can't continue to ride as you have been."

The idea of downing another energy bar made me queasy. The pantry here had been stocked.

"Afterward, you could have a long, hot shower." When I faltered, Aric pulled off his gauntlets and reached for me. He laid a bare hand on my lower back, ushering me into the kitchen. Before he released me, his fingertips dug in a little, as if he battled with himself to let me go.

"We should prepare a feast." He placed his helmet, swords, and gauntlets on a counter, his bag on the floor.

He motioned for me to give him my pack, but I wasn't sold on staying. "You expect us to fire up the stove in a slave boss's house and cook?"

"Let's." His amber eyes were playful. "And if we get thirsty from our labors . . ." He opened the refrigerator with the toe of his armor-covered boot, revealing a twelve-pack of bottled beer. "Not as bracing as the vodka we always share, but we'll manage."

"Even with the bodies out there, shouldn't we be anxious about more slavers coming? Or the men in the garage getting free? Or Bagmen? It's A.F., we should be anxious about something."

"If for some reason I don't hear a threat, Thanatos is right out back. He's quite territorial." To put it mildly.

I sidled over to the pantry. Among the offerings was a jar of maraschino cherries, just like Jack and I had found at Selena's.

When I was with Aric, things reminded me of Jack. And the opposite was true as well. Which meant I was forever screwed. If I chose one, I'd never stop thinking about the other.

Pain awaited me, no matter what I did. The idea couldn't be more depressing. . . .

My foraging turned up a family-size lasagna in the freezer. The package didn't even have ice on the edges. The meal wouldn't be gourmet, but it'd be hot and cheesy.

Game. Set. Match. I dropped my bag. "Fine. We'll eat. Just so no one else can have it." I tossed it in the microwave, then hopped up on the counter to sit, my transceiver within reach.

Aric opened two beers—pop-tops with his fist—handing me one.

The same reasons for drinking still applied: *possible imminent demise* plus *severe mental confusion* equaled *to hell with it.*

He leaned one broad shoulder against the kitchen doorway. He was so tall, he barely cleared the frame. *"Uz veselibu."*

"What does that mean?"

"Cheers." We both took a swig. "The mortal's meeting must have been dire for him to leave us together."

"Jack trusts me."

"If only you could return that trust."

I frowned. "Why do you have to taunt him so much?"

"Because he gives me much fodder." Aric took a long draw from his bottle.

"You called him a drunkard, but we're drinking right now. You like your vodka well enough."

"Yet I didn't bring a liter of it in my valise."

"No. But you smoked opium for centuries straight."

Lips curving, he said, "And this is why I should never tell you anything."

"Like who my sworn enemies are?"

His grin deepened. "Am I to get away with nothing, little wife?"

"Jack was a prisoner of the Lovers, just days ago. I still have no idea what they did to him—but it's safe to say he's been through enough without your jabs."

Aric's amusement faded. "I give as good as I get."

"Put yourself in Jack's position. A man with a deadly touch singled out his girlfriend to torment, and she had no clue why. Then the man took her away. Violently. What would you do if someone else treated me like that?"

His expression told me everything.

"In any case, you're so much older, so shouldn't you be more mature?"

"Mature? You know I don't age physically between games, but I probably don't mentally either."

"I don't understand."

"I go into a kind of stasis." Staring past me, he said, "The centuries between feel like one long dream. The games are like briefly waking in the night—to an awareness of threat and peril—only to slip back into slumber once the game ends."

My God, his existence had been horrific. And then I would come along every few hundred years to crash his life. I took a deep drink.

But I couldn't feel guilty any longer for misdeeds committed by another incarnation. I *wouldn't*. "I'm sorry for your past, Aric. I wish it had been different. I wish *I* had been. But I refuse to keep paying for what I did in past games."

He seemed to shake away a haze. "Do you, then?"

"In our first meeting, you skewered me with your sword. In other words: you started it. You didn't ask me to marry you, just ordered it. I played the hand I was dealt."

"I take your point."

Hadn't really expected him to say that.

"Let's begin anew, Empress."

Over the rim of my bottle, I said, "I haven't decided anything."

He made a sound of frustration. "The mortal can't provide for you like I can. I offer you a home. Does he think you'll live in that muddy outpost?"

Defensive, I said, "Jack plans to rebuild Haven House for me."

Anger flashed across Aric's face. He schooled his reactions as quickly as he did everything else, leaving his emotions to seethe beneath the surface. "If you desire something, all you have to do is tell *me*. It will shortly be yours. You'll see soon enough."

I swallowed. Was he referencing the *gift* he'd spoken of? The trick up his sleeve? I almost dreaded learning what it was.

What if Aric could straight-up end the game? Blow up the machine?

"Deveaux will never understand you as I do. As only another Arcana can." Aric replaced my beer. Because I'd finished it.

"Maybe not. But we have other ties." I thought of the ribbon he'd kept all this time, the one now in my pocket. I thought of our mutual longing for our home.

"As do we. We are *wed*." Aric set down his bottle, moving in front of me. "I think of you as mine. You don't see the countless times a day I have to stop myself from touching my wife." His eyes were just on the verge of glowing. Like this, his gaze reminded me less of stars, and more of a sunrise.

In time, would I forget what a sunrise looked like?

I caught his knight's scent: rain, steel, and *man*. My toes curled in my boots. Whenever he was free of his armor, I could detect hints of pine and sandalwood.

He wedged his hips between my knees. With our faces inches apart, he said, "If you had any idea what is going on inside me . . . I'm feeling something I have never experienced, not in my twenty centuries of life."

I swallowed, unsure if I wanted to hear him say the words.

His irises brightened and brightened. Eyes fully aglow, he rasped, "I am in love with you." Irresistible Death. "And you love me in turn."

I gazed at his mouth, recalling how I'd kissed that faint dip in his bottom lip. "Why would you say that?" My voice sounded so far away.

"My fierce Empress protected me before you left our home. Your concern told me much." Pride lit his expression. "What foe did you think might get to me, little wife?"

Flustered, I said, "I didn't know, okay? You said you were always a target."

He pressed a kiss to my forehead, as if in reward. When he drew back, he gave me a real smile, not a smirk, not a grudging half-grin. I'd only seen this a couple of times before.

And it was *devastating*.

Inner shake. "Admit it: after my poison kiss, when you were reaching for your antitoxin, you believed I'd given you a lethal dose."

"I admit it. And I was chastised for my doubt when I woke."

"Chastised? *Chastised?* You broke my heart that night! You didn't notice—or care—how much you were hurting me!"

"When I recognized that you weren't over your infatuation with the mortal, I might have been . . . testing you." He'd tested me the other night as well! "I needed to know if you felt something as strong for me."

"What if I'd surrendered?"

His lips parted as if he was imagining that even now. "I can't believe I'm about to say this, but I'm glad you didn't. You told me that you would grow to hate me. I didn't believe it then, but I do now. I should never have put you in that situation."

"Testing me doesn't excuse what you did. Coercion is not cool."

He backed away, stabbing his fingers through his hair. "Then *teach* me what is! I have no experience with a wife, but you know my capacity for learning. I can learn to be what you need."

"I don't think something like that can be taught. It's part of your makeup, part of who you are."

"My upbringing and history have shaped me, but I do evolve. Going into each game, I've adapted to different epochs."

Epochs? How did he endure it? When he was this close to me, I could *feel* his palpable yearning. I could sense that gut-wrenching loneliness he'd suffered.

I pictured him in his mausoleum of a home, surveying all his lifeless collections. He'd devotedly tended to those treasures, those relics of the past, because they were all he had—all he'd ever hoped to have.

"Aric, selfless acts might be beyond you. And even sex with you would come with strings. What if I hadn't realized you were minus one condom?" The memory stoked my fury. "You were about to trick me—to betray *me*."

He raised his blond brows. "There was no trick, *sievā*. I didn't set out to deceive you."

"You had my entire future mapped out—with me knocked up—and you never mentioned it to me."

He moved in front of me again, gripping the counter on either side of my hips. "It's been this way between husbands and wives for thousands of years. At the time, I thought if we were so blessed, then all the better."

Because his concepts about marriages and families were from a different *epoch*.

He swallowed. "You accuse me of calculation; know that I haven't enough experience in this subject to calculate." A flush covered his high cheekbones. "I was barely capable of speech when I saw you naked in my bed for the first time—much less plotting."

Just like that, my anger deflated. I sighed. "I believe you."

He placed one hand on the wall above me. With his other, he cupped the side of my face. "Then we've already begun. We will learn to trust each other."

Jack had said something similar. My gaze flicked toward the door.

Aric dropped his hand. "I both applaud and curse your sense of loyalty. Without it, you'd be mine. Right now, we'd be in our bed, having just shared our first kiss of the night."

I laid my palms on Aric's armored chest to push him away. My hands looked so pale and fragile against his intimidating armor. How many times had I clawed this metal, desperate to get away from him?

At length, he backed away. "The mortal has another he cares for, would risk his life for." He took a seat at the table.

"Jack doesn't love Selena."

"Maybe he could if you gave him cause to. Let him go, then give them your blessing."

My heart hurt just to think about it. If another of Jack's *opportunities* came up, would he take it? At least, in time?

"Things will be different when you come home with me. I'll teach you about the game. We'll investigate the histories and chronicles I've collected. I'll teach you more about your powers."

"But you won't simply *tell* me about them?"

He pointed to his swords. "I can tell you how to wield a sword, but you won't have built up the strength to hold it yet. You won't have practiced. How much success will you have brandishing it in a conflict?"

"You're not my only resource. I can get help from my grandmother. Not to mention Matthew. And he doesn't require anything in return."

A troubled expression crossed Aric's face. "Empress, let him *rest*." His tone left me with a sense of unease—

The timer went off, startling me.

Before I could blink, Aric was in front of me, reaching for my hand. He expected me to fend off bloodthirsty zombies by myself, yet offered assistance down from a counter?

"What can I do to help?"

"Find some plates and forks."

Once we'd sat down to our meal, I said, "It's not as fancy as you generally like things."

"The company is so exquisite, she makes everything so."

"You can be smooth—I give you that."

"*Labu apetīti.* Good appetite." He took a bite. "This is surprisingly delicious."

"You're just saying that." I sampled mine, my eyes going wide. "It's really good."

Between his slow grins, the hot food, and the cold beer, I started to relax. By the time I'd finished my plate, my belly was full, my mind buzzed.

"I sense questions simmering in you." He appeared as relaxed as I felt. "Ask them."

He'd once told me I'd asked more questions in this life than in the ones before combined.

"Why did Matthew call you Tredici? Is that your last name?" I didn't even know Aric's surname. Of course, it'd taken me three months just to get his first.

"*Tredici* is Italian for thirteen, my card number. I believe the Fool hailed from Italy once."

Matthew had introduced himself as "Matthew Mat Zero Matto." *Il Matto* meant *The Fool* in Italian.

As I turned over this new information, Aric said, "My last name—and yours as well—is Domīnija."

Before I could stop myself, I'd tried it out in my head: Evangeline Greene Domīnija. That'd be a bitch to bubble in on a test.

I didn't bother to argue the point with him. "Will you tell me why Matthew owed you a debt?"

"I kept a secret for him."

Was I finally going to discover this connection between the two? "And that would be. . . ?"

". . . not a secret if I told you."

"But he reneged."

Aric's lips curled. "And yet I do not."

Dead end.

When he rose to get more beers, I asked, "What were my given names in the past?"

He hesitated on his way back. "I've uttered those names ... I felt ..." At length, he said, "I'd rather not discuss this." Still so affected after all this time?

He sat once more, opening the bottles.

I gazed at his right hand, at the four miniature icons that represented his kills: a white star, navy-blue weighing scales, two black horns, and a gold chalice. "Do you ever feel the heat of battle?"

"I did. I learned to control it when I met you." He peered at my own icons: a lantern and a pair of raised fingers. "The Fool told me you consider your Empress nature to be a separate entity. A *red witch*."

"He told you that?" How embarrassing! It made me sound like a psycho. Jack knew about it, but only because he'd listened to my story on tape.

Aric shrugged his armored shoulders. "After the Flash, I saw you restrain your Empress nature again and again. I was curious how."

"Jack helps with that."

Aric's lips thinned. "When you stabbed me with your claws, but withheld your poison, he wasn't near. Did this 'red witch' not whisper for you to end me when I was defenseless before you? Yet you protected me instead."

"That's true," I admitted. "She's icon crazy, but I controlled her. When I told Matthew that, he wanted to know if I could *invoke* her."

"You've reined in your red witch—because you've never truly *unleashed* her. You must learn how."

"Pardon? I didn't hear you correctly. I poisoned a mine full of cannibals. My vines cracked the Alchemist's house like an egg."

"And still you drew on only a fraction of your power."

For so long, I'd feared going full-on Empress—and never turning back to Evie. Just when I was starting to feel more in control, Aric and Matthew wanted to amp up the red witch. "Say I could free her more. What if she wanted to kill you?"

"I wouldn't fight you. So you'd have to figure out how to rein her in at any time."

"It's too dangerous." In my first combat against Death, I'd embraced her. I remembered telling myself, *I am the red witch! . . . I'm going to win the entire game!* Which would mean that all my friends would be dead. "I've been doing okay."

"Some of the remaining Arcana have unspeakable powers. You'll need to invoke your witch to survive—just as those Bagmen summoned their strength to rise."

"Unless I stop the game."

"There are some who'll keep coming, even if they don't have to."

"Like the Emperor."

At the mere mention of that card, Aric's demeanor changed, his irises darkening to cold amber once more.

"What happened with him?"

"It's a matter too wearisome for our night together." He drank deep. "Tell me about your grandmother."

His expression was so stark that I let him change the subject. For now. "Don't you already know as much as I do? Since you trespassed in my thoughts for so long."

"Not constantly. I did have my own life to go about. Such as it was."

My chest squeezed at his words. I drank to cover my dismay. "I don't remember her all that well. Sometimes my memories contradict each other."

"How so?"

"I'll see her as kind and affectionate. In the next instance, I'll recall her wanting me to become 'vicious.'" What if she tried to convince me to take out other cards? My friends?

Aric, even.

Maybe Arcana weren't inherently evil. Maybe our chroniclers or relatives molded us. "In any case, I swore to my mom I'd find her. So I will."

"And I will help you. You know sourcing is a talent of mine—doesn't matter if I'm looking for ballet shoes or my wife's grandmother."

"Yeah, I don't see that working out too well. She was furious at me when I mooned over your card."

"You forget how charming I can be."

Never. "I once asked Matthew if you would prevent me from reaching Gran. He told me the subject bored you, that you don't believe in her as I do. So why would you help me?" I finished my beer.

Like a blur, Aric had another round on the table. "As a Tarasova, she knows a great many things."

"You didn't answer the question."

"I don't have to believe that she holds the key to the game's end. You do—and I believe in you."

Smooth, tricksy knight. "What's the difference between a Tarasova and a chronicler?" How did Gran differ from Gabriel's people?

"Chroniclers are historians and guides. Some say each Tarasova is gifted with the sight. Others say she must be a minor Arcana."

The last time I'd seen Gran, her brown eyes had twinkled as she'd told me, *"You're going to kill them all."*

A chill ran through me.

"Sievā?"

I changed the subject. "Now that you're making the effort to trust me, will you tell me about your childhood?"

He inclined his head. "I told you my father was a warlord, but he was also a noted scholar. He raised me to be both as well. I had martial practice every day, then reading, then debates after dinner." Aric peeled at his beer label, then smoothed it back with his elegant fingers. "I can't imagine what he would think about all that mankind has learned. In his day, everyone believed the world was flat."

Aric had grown up in that age, and yet I'd expected him to act like a modern boyfriend? That he'd come this far was astounding. "What was your mother like?"

"She was merry, quick to laugh. She and my father always wanted another child, blaming it on me: 'If you weren't such a wonderful son . . .' I could ask for no better parents."

"You miss them." After all this time?

"Every single day out of hundreds of thousands."

What could I say to that? Anything I came up with sounded trite. Silence fell over us.

Aric drank, lost in thought. And I knew he was remembering the night he'd killed them. . . .

30

Hot water poured over me in the upstairs bathroom, but it did nothing to shower away my buzz.

Or my confusion.

After dinner, Jack hadn't checked in, and worry preyed on me. So I'd grabbed my bag and told Aric good night.

As I'd left the kitchen, he'd said to my back, "You once told me I was so good at this game because it's all I'll ever have." The sadness in his voice had drawn me up short. "Your words were true, though I didn't wish them to be. Not then. Or now."

I'd heard Aric enraged, playful, fierce, in pain, and in lust. I'd never heard this soft sadness before.

In a murmur, he'd added, "I am ready to defy the will of gods and the dictates of fate to possess you, and yet a mere mortal stands in my way."

My shoulders had stiffened, and I'd hurried away as if chased.

Now as the water sluiced over me, I raised my hand to my mouth, tracing my lips. My emotions might be in total turmoil, but my body wasn't. I equally desired Aric and Jack.

I adored Jack's raw passion; I craved Aric's seething intensity.

Both had given me pleasure—and heartache. . . .

Once I'd finished with the shower, I returned to my room. I locked the door behind me and removed my hoodie to bundle up for a pillow.

Lying back in my sleeping bag, I stared at the ceiling. What was I going to do?

I felt connected to Aric in inexplicable ways. At his castle, he and I had settled in together. We'd read in his firelit study, talking through the night. We'd been happy, his home nearly becoming my own.

Jack and I had never lived together per se, always out on the road—

My bug-out bag! I'd left it in the bathroom, forgetting Jack's harsh lessons. Maybe he should've been harder on me.

I rushed from the room, skidding to a stop in the hallway.

Aric had just exited the steamy bathroom. He wore a towel. Nothing else. His lean face was clean-shaven, his wet hair in disarray, his cheeks tinged with color.

He spied me there, his lips parting. His eyes began to glitter, and I was momentarily blinded by the sight of him. Like staring at the sun.

Glorious man.

When my gaze dipped, his magnificent body tensed, as if I'd struck him. Sinews of muscle contracted, making the black slashing tattoos across his torso appear to move.

I'd wanted to kiss every inch of those runes. I'd never had the chance.

A drop of water trickled down the center of his chest, past defined pecs and rigid abs to his blond goodie trail. . . . My mouth went dry.

He rasped, "You want this?"

I raised my gaze, gasping at the dark hunger in his expression. My mind blanked. Want his body? How could I not? He was pure temptation.

"I meant *this*"—he held up my bag—"but I could easily be persuaded to share anything else my wife might desire."

Say something, Eves. Words would be good here.

He closed in on me, all lethal grace and harnessed power. I realized I'd been backing away from him when I met the wall. He kept coming until we were toe to toe.

The damp heat from his skin was like an embrace. Up this close, I could see the blond tips of his eyelashes.

He tossed my bag past me into the bedroom. Then his gaze dropped to my tank top. It hugged my breasts, outlining them.

"I recognize these clothes. It fills me with satisfaction to see you dressed in them. Not as much satisfaction as when I undress you, of course."

He might be inexperienced, but he was naturally sensual—his every movement, his expressions, even the cadence of his accented words brought to mind promised pleasures.

I was out of my league.

"A week ago, you were naked in my bed for the second time. I kissed you. Petted you." He eased down to say at my ear, "I was about to taste you once more."

My breaths shallowed. "B-but then you broke my heart."

"I'll mend it. I'll repair the damage I've done between us. In these games, I've trusted you when I shouldn't have, and didn't trust when I should have had faith." He cupped my face with both palms. "If you could see your way to forgiveness . . ."

I bit my bottom lip. "I can forgive you. But that doesn't mean I want to put myself in a situation like that again." When he leaned his head in, I said, "Aric, we can't kiss. I'm not doing anything with you. With either of you."

Was he gauging my resolve? "Then we won't kiss. Just let me touch your stunning face." He caressed the backs of his fingers over one of my cheekbones, then along my jawline. "It's a luxury I will always savor."

I had to fight to keep my eyes open, to keep my body from moving against his.

"So beautiful. I won't stop until you're mine. I won't ever rest. *Es tevi mīlu.*"

I breathed, "What does that mean?"

He smoothed his elegant fingers over me the way a sculptor would touch his statue. "I love you."

Answering words bubbled up, but I couldn't be in love with Aric.

"There's a difference between love and desire," I said, reminding him—
and myself.

"If all I wanted was a bedmate, then why do I feel such jealousy?
Why was I racked with misery to be parted from you? For one like me,
a week is a blink of an eye, yet it felt interminable."

He laid his palms over my shoulders, ever so lightly grazing his
thumbs over my throat. His hands shook, as if he was handling the
most priceless treasure in the entire world. "By all the gods, I desire
you, but you must know that you have my love. It's given, *sievā*. Wholly
entrusted to you. Have a care with it."

I struggled to resist him. To remember why I should.

"Our bond goes back over lifetimes; you must feel it."

I shook my head hard, an unspoken lie. I felt endless years between
us, a tie that never died or faded. Something that endured epochs.
Something mysterious and . . . *good*?

I thought, I *feared*, that he was my . . .

Soul mate.

"These days without you have been more miserable for me than
all the centuries before." He brushed his thumb over my bottom lip,
making my heart race. "Tell me you'll be mine. Tell me I'll never have
to know this desolation again."

At that moment, I wanted to tell him anything he needed to hear—

Without warning, he lifted me against the wall, forcing me to wrap
my legs around his waist, my arms around his neck.

"What are you doing?" I inhaled sharply as desire flooded me. His
addictive scent swept me up.

"I need to be closer to you. Why can I never get close enough to you?"
He glanced down. His chest had dampened my tank top, which was now
see-through. His eyes flared bright, his voice roughening as he said, "You
tempt me beyond measure." He pressed harder between my legs.

When my head fell back, he nuzzled my neck, giving me only hints
of kisses. Warm breaths feathered over my throat, making me shiver
with need.

Why had I told him we couldn't kiss?

This closeness was as arousing as the real thing. More so. Knowing he longed to press his lips against me—but was restraining himself—drove me crazy.

He continued his ghost of a kiss until I was panting, my arms tightening around his neck. I could feel his muscles shudder against my body as he held himself in check.

He dragged his head up to face me. Our breaths mingled as I stared into his starry eyes, lost in them. Still he didn't take my mouth. Just made me yearn for more.

Which I couldn't have. Not tonight.

The ribbon I carried in my pocket seemed to burn me. *Just doan give me anything else to hurt on.*

"Aric, you have to let me go."

"Is that what you truly want?" Confusion shone in that glittering gaze.

"Please."

He lowered me to my feet. "I release you. For now. But you will be mine, *sieva.*"

As I pressed him away, the sight of my pale hands against him hit me again. How many times had I clung to his bare chest, desperate to get closer?

When he stepped back, I turned toward my room in a daze. I shut the door, then leaned against it, trembling.

After that, everything seemed to be in slow motion: walking to my sleeping bag, checking the battery light on the transceiver, bedding down.

I stared at the ceiling again, trying to ignore my overheated body. What felt like hours passed before my eyes closed.

Just before I drifted off, I sensed Aric in the room with me.

Was he gazing down at me? He thought I was asleep!

In a soft rasp, he said, "There's so much about the game I could teach you. So much about life you could teach me. Let's begin this, little wife."

—

I dreamed of Death, reliving a memory of his from when he'd been close to my age. Was this one of the visions Matthew had wanted to give me before it was too late?

The scene was night, the wind whipping off the Baltic in a frenzied summer storm. Aric was returning from an errand of some kind.

As I ride past familiar rune stones, my stallion's hooves pound the ground, rivaling the gods' thunder.

The gods that have cursed our settlement with sickness.

Were they angered by the lavish festivities my family held two days ago? Is the House of Domīnija guilty of hubris?

Though I want to follow this line of reasoning, to deduce a cause, my thoughts are too chaotic. Some malady has befallen me as well. Yet instead of suffering like the others in the village, I feel strong.

Stronger than I ever have.

Earlier, I crushed a rock in my palm, crushed it to dust. Each day my power and speed escalate. I am nearing some dark precipice, but I know not what.

When I arrive home, I have to conceal my unnatural swiftness, lest a vassal see. I stride along a stone lane to my father's hall. Just beyond the front doorway, I find him pacing, awaiting my arrival. "Did you employ the physic?" he asks.

Aric's father is a towering blond man with broad shoulders. Though his eyes are ice-blue to Aric's amber, there is a distinct resemblance to his son. I understand their language as if it were my own; Matthew must've bridged this vision for me.

"He is already tending the sick." How can my father look a decade older than he did just yesterday? "I took him directly there."

"Good, good," Father says, his mind distracted. "I'll return anon."

"But you're exhausted. You need to stay strong for Mother. Is she resting?"

He nods. "I insisted upon it."

"This can't be easy on her." Many of those who visited our hall were

stricken, their daughters especially. "I shall return in your stead."

His forehead creases. "But if something happened to you . . . if you were beset . . . I couldn't bear it."

"I've never been sick a day in my life. I've made my decision not to start now."

With that hint of a grin, Father looks more himself. It's been strange not to hear his laughter in our hall, a welcome accompaniment to Mother's.

I put my hand on his shoulder, holding his gaze. "Mark my words, we will get through this."

His blue eyes glint. "Have I told you how proud I am to be your father?"

I cast him a feigned look of grievance. "Daily. Since memory. It's ingrained in me, as if carved into a rune stone."

"But not yet today." Father clasps his hand over mine. "Son, I'm so proud . . ." He trails off with a frown.

"Father?"

His gaze widens, his skin paling. When his expression grows agonized, panic grips my chest. "What's happening?" I lay my palm on his cheek; angry black lines begin to branch out over his face.

Like those of the afflicted villagers.

"S-son?" Suddenly his fists clench, his muscles seizing.

"What is this, Father?" I enfold his convulsing form in my arms, easing him to the ground. "What is happening?" As I gaze down at him, a beatific light spills upon his anguished countenance. It shutters . . . when I blink? "Tell me how to help you!" I beg him, "Please, please tell me!"

He cannot answer me, his body strangled of air. Of life.

He is . . . dead.

Even as grief overwhelms me, a suspicion tries to force its way into my mind—

"Aric!" Across the hall, my mother sees her husband. She screams, her hands covering her rounding belly, instinctively shielding the babe *they've so long wanted. She sways on her feet, her legs buckling.*

I don't think, just run for her. In a fraction of an instant, I've somehow crossed the distance. I reach her in time to catch her as she falls.

She shrieks at my touch.

"Mother? No, no, no!" Black lines fork out along her arm, emanating from my hand.

With a yell, I release my hold. As comprehension dawns, my heartbeat pounds in my ears like the gods' thunder. The sickness is coming . . .

From me.

"Mother, fight this!"

Grueling pain has robbed her of breath, has twisted her lovely face. But I can read her dread. "A-Aric?" She too suspects me.

She writhes in agony—yet I cannot defend her, comfort her. "Please, stay with me!" My tears strike her cheek. That same light shines down on her face. "Fight, Mother. Fight for your babe. F-for me."

She stares up at me, seeming mesmerized by my eyes—as her own grow sightless. Her life is done. She has passed beyond.

My parents gone.

I've wrought my family's destruction. Killed those I loved most, with my very touch.

My dark precipice has been reached. I throw back my head and roar as recognition takes hold.

I am Death. . . .

31

When I woke, muddy boots filled my vision. Jack?

"Get away from her, Reaper." He was pointing a gun! "Or I'll plug you."

"Indeed?" Aric's fingers stroked my cheek, smoothing away . . . tears?

I craned my head around. He sat beside me, and he didn't stop caressing me—despite the threat.

I turned back to Jack. "Please, put that down."

"My gun and your skull, Death. I warned you." He faced me, his gray eyes crazed. "You slept with him?"

"What? No!" Okay, the scene looked bad.

Aric was shirtless, wearing only low-slung leather pants, his armor stacked against the wall. His glowing gaze was hooded with pleasure.

Voice relaxed, he asked, "Can you comprehend what it's like to touch her after so long without? For this bliss, I'll risk the bullet. I'll *take* a bullet."

When I jerked back from Aric, he tsked, as if to say, *More's the pity.*

"Is this what you did at Death's?" Jack demanded. "Let him touch your face, you? After you danced for him?"

"Just put down the gun, please."

Stalemate. "Why didn't you answer the radio?"

"What are you talking about? I didn't hear anything."

"Because I turned off the volume," Aric said with a shrug. "The Empress needed to rest more than she needed to talk to you."

"Jack, you're scaring me. This looks much worse than it is."

Precarious moments eked by before he lowered the pistol. "You're right. I'm sorry, *bébé*." He tucked the gun into his belt. It wasn't one of the pair he'd left here. Had he carried a hidden pistol?

"She refuses both our advances, mortal." Aric leaned his head back against the wall. "Until she sees her way clear to me."

"Advances? You mean you messed with her head some more and reminded her of old games?"

"Not at all. I merely pointed out some of the countless ways I'm better for her than you are. Even you recognize this." Aric rose with that supernatural speed, standing before Jack. "You keep going on about Stockholm syndrome—because you don't want to consider the alternative: that she *wishes* to be with me. That she was genuinely happy with me."

When Jack clenched his hands, I shot to my feet. "Don't touch him!"

"Not goan to poison myself, no. Not when I have a future to look forward to."

"Ah, yes, a new start with Selena. My wife and I extend our felicitations."

Jack turned to me. "Evie, I can't do this anymore! I have to know where we stand."

Aric said, "In this, I agree."

Both of them. Facing me. Expectantly.

For the first time they were juxtaposed with no obscuring armor. Jack had broader shoulders and thicker muscles, while Aric was leaner, tattooed, and a little taller. Both so handsome, I was spellbound just to watch them. Then they started up again.

"You think she's goan to pick you over me? *Imbécile!*"

"I have no doubt in my mind." Where was Aric's unnerving confidence coming from? If his gift would skew my decision, then *was* there even a choice?

At that thought, my headache rebounded. "Maybe I won't pick either of you! Maybe I'll take Matthew, and we'll go find my grandmother. By ourselves!" I rubbed my throbbing temples. "For now, can we just focus on Selena and the Lovers? I guarantee you I won't be deciding anything about my future until I can take a second and *think*."

"When we return the Archer to the outpost," Aric said, "you'll kindly give us your answer. The suitor you pass over will leave you alone." He offered Jack his deadly hand. "Come, let's shake on it."

"Sheathe your goddamned weapons, Reaper, or I'll pull my own again." He asked me, "You agree to this?"

"Yes, I'll give you my answer then. But you should know: my decision isn't just between you two. I have other choices. And when you both act like this, my other options look better and better."

"Noted." Was Aric patronizing me? "Now I find myself particularly motivated to find the Archer."

Finally, he was getting his head in the game! I turned to Jack. "Have the dissenters seen Selena? Is she safe?"

"No one in Azey North has seen her. She's not there."

"The Lovers lied to us." Shocking.

"Milovníci's in camp, with a pair of twins, but I doan know if they're the real deal or not." Jack absently rubbed his bandage. How badly he must want to face them, to make them pay.

"They're not the source twins," Aric said. "Which makes sense. If I had the Lovers' power, I would station myself in some unreachable location and let my carnates do all the work for me."

"How do you know for sure?" I asked.

"I've already heard the carnates' staticky calls."

"Then why did the twins tell me to go to Dolor?"

"A trap," Jack answered. "The camp's surrounded by snipers with dart guns, to take us alive."

For our torture.

"I got no idea where Selena is."

"Hmm. Luckily, I do." Aric leaned a shoulder against the wall. "I can follow her call as long as it continues."

Matthew had once explained that a call never stopped. When an Arcana got close enough to register it, the player could tune it out. "I thought it repeated on a loop. Wait . . . You mean, as long as she lives? You said they wouldn't kill her outright."

"There are other instances in which a call could go silent." Before I could ask, he said, "I estimate she's about two to three days north of here. I can find her, but that doesn't mean we can *reach* her."

Jack narrowed his gaze. "Why not?"

"The Lovers could be surrounded by a moat of flaming oil. They could have troops of carnates with machine guns and rocket launchers. Even *I* would have difficulty against rockets."

"Then what do you suggest, Reaper?"

Aric's smile was chilling. "A hostage of our own."

32

"It's showtime," Jack said.

Dolor was around the next bend. For hours we'd ridden hard to get here, giving me little chance to speak to either him or Aric. We'd followed a rail line, and had just stopped at the outskirts of an old working mine.

Flash-fried machinery—hoists, mine carts, conveyer belts—made for a ghostly junkyard.

Aric removed his helmet. "Where are your rebels?"

Jack shrugged. "In the camp."

"I'm confused, mortal. I thought we were aligning with dissenters for an incursion. You told us we were *taking* this camp."

"*Ouais*. We are."

"Then we need men. We need modern weapons to combat the general's."

"We're goan to ride right in." Jack pulled his jacket collar up when a wet gust howled. "The general and the fake twins will be trussed up for us."

Aric raised his brows at Jack's casual assurance. "That's your plan?" Thanatos hoofed the ground with impatience.

Yes, Jack was becoming an incredible leader, but he was describing a fantasy outcome. I worried my bottom lip. "Say something goes wrong. Maybe we should have a plan B?"

His tone grew cryptic. "That rose crown you wore would look mighty nice when we arrive."

Aric scoffed, "You think we can intimidate them with our gifts? They'll be too busy shooting to pay attention."

Jack ignored him, addressing me, "He's got no reason to have faith in my plans, but you do. You know I got a good head on my shoulders."

I'd told him I wouldn't underestimate him again. If he said he had a plan, and he was this confident . . .

"Call ahead to your people, then," Aric said. "Ascertain the situation."

"*Non.* No radios."

—He tests even my eternal patience. But I make an effort to keep the peace for you.— "Let's pretend you achieve a bloodless rebellion, all it takes is one loyal soldier to signal for reinforcements."

"You think I haven't considered that, Reaper? It's under control."

Aric gazed at me. *—You're buying this?—*

I just stopped myself from nodding. *I am.*

—I find it hard to believe he won't be double-crossed for that bounty.— *You have no idea how good he is at reading people and taking their measure.*

"You two are talking to each other?" Jack scowled.

"Just debating your ability to read people," Aric said, "since we're depending on it, and nothing else."

"You trust me, Evie?" Jack asked, his eyes saying things I couldn't fathom.

"I trust your judgment in this."

"I'll take it." He cast a smirk at Death.

Aric drew on his helmet. "I can't believe I'm going along with this folly."

"You wanted a hostage. I'm taking you to get one." To me, Jack said, "You ready?"

I nodded, crowning myself with my body vine. Blood-red petals and pointed leaves. I let the circlet move and writhe so no one would think it was fake. Plus, it tended to do that anyway whenever I was nervous.

If there were ever a time to be nervous . . .

Aric caught my gaze as we neared the corner. Another gust blew, sending those conveyor belts flapping, ratcheting up my apprehension.

We passed the point of no return, the camp in sight. People were lined up.

Not with guns?

They cheered in welcome! Soldiers—and freed women—waved as if we were an oncoming Mardi Gras float.

I exhaled, hadn't realized I'd been holding my breath. "Holy shit, Jack."

He just slid me a sexy grin.

"A bloodless rebellion." Death lifted his visor. "I'll bite. How did you effect this, mortal?"

"Maybe the answer to a problem ain't always more *Death*." When I looked expectantly at Jack, he explained, "Last night, I gave the soldiers canisters of nerve gas to toss into the Milovnícis' tents."

"Nerve gas," I repeated. "Taken from their own army across the river? That's what was in the duffel bag!"

"*Ouais*. After Rodrigo's men secured the Milovnícis, they told as many people as possible that I was coming, with some of my Arcana allies," he said with a wink at me, a black look at Death. "When everyone found out that we'd liberated the other camp and were gunning for this one, I knew the chain of command would be undermined."

"This is amazing."

As we rode into the crowd, people gawked at Death and me, while they clamored to shake Jack's hand.

All his life, he'd thought he had no reason to be proud. Now he was *different*. Jaw set. Shoulders squared. Eyes flinty with determination.

He had no otherworldly abilities, but look how powerful he was becoming. Look at all the people who admired him.

I turned toward Aric, glancing at him from under my lashes. My dream of him haunted me, a graphic reminder that he had no one. No hope of a partner.

Did I pity him? Yes. But last night had reminded me that there was far more to my attraction than pity.

He met my gaze, and I quickly looked away. Among the crowd, I spied a grinning black-haired boy of about twelve. With his wide-set eyes and the gap in his front teeth, he looked like a miniature Franklin. Had to be his brother. Soon they'd be reunited.

That boy put a face on all that Jack had accomplished here.

Realization sank in: we'd helped *thousands*.

Rodrigo rode to meet us, a huge smile on his face. "The three Milovnícis are this way."

"And the jammers?" Jack said.

"We've had them going nonstop, General. No transmissions could've gone out." He led us deeper into the camp.

Under my breath, I said, "He called you 'General'?"

"I tried to get them to stop," Jack said with a hint of a grin. "Then I realized how intimidating it sounds. Let it stand, me."

"You used jammers to block radio calls." Aric cast him a look—was that the same grudging respect Jack had shown Death last night? "That's why you wouldn't radio ahead."

"I wanted to control any communications from this camp. But now that we've got a hostage and a full army, we doan have to hide your involvement anymore. And we're about to inform the twins of our upcoming trade. Their father for Selena."

Excitement filled me. A hostage exchange sounded workable!

Aric removed his helmet, stowing it on his saddle. "If we allow the carnates to live, they'll transfer all they experience to the source."

"Too risky," Jack said. "We end them."

"Agreed, mortal. Are you going to tell your people the twins are fake?"

Jack seemed to consider it. "*Non*. It'd just be noise, clouding the victory."

Aric nodded. "While you've got Milovníci, we might as well interrogate him for information about the twins, uncover their defenses and carnate numbers."

Now Jack said, "Agreed."

When we stopped and dismounted, Jack and I handed our reins over to a couple of soldiers, but Death just shook his head, leading Thanatos on.

The crowd parted ahead of us, revealing three unconscious forms, bound and gagged on the ground. The infamous Milovníci and his spawn. Or rather, his spawn's spawn.

Finally, I was going to see the man who'd brought so much misery to a world already drowning in it.

The former general's features were sharp, his nose beaklike. Though wiry and thin, he had a florid complexion. I could imagine his face growing even redder whenever he was angry.

His tan jacket read: MILOVNÍCI ELITE SECURITY. His face and clothes had copious amounts of spit on them—and boot prints.

This was the great General Milovníci? He looked harmless. And the twins? They were identical to the ones we'd encountered in the other camp, with the same distorted tableau.

"You should do the honors on the carnates, Reaper," Jack said. "Folks need to see what the two of you are packing."

Low-voiced, Aric said, "We're not circus acts." To me, he added, —*All my life I've cloaked these gifts.*—

"I'm just a figurehead, me. This army can create order, or just the opposite. The more order there is in the world, the safer Evie is. You either want that or you doan."

More people closed in.

Exhaling with irritation, Aric removed his gauntlet. He crouched to place his bared icon hand over each clone's face. Black lines forked out.

Did Aric remember his parents every time his touch killed? I'd heard that he preferred to take out opponents like this. Maybe his Touch of

Death served the same purpose as his tattoos: reminders never to forget tragedies of the past.

Spectators gasped when the carnates' bodies seized.

Jack might be accustomed to attention, but Aric was uncomfortable with the stares. Had the coolly collected knight once been shy around others? The idea made me smile with affection—even as the replicants stopped breathing.

I heard murmurs in the crowd: "Good riddance." "Rot in hell." "They got off too easy. . . ."

Rodrigo cleared his throat. "Uh, sir, what do you want to do with Milovníci?"

"His name's Milo now," Jack announced. "My neighbor had a coonhound named Milo. Went rabid. Got put down." Nervous laughter broke out.

Death stood and slid on his gauntlet. —*That's shrewd. Strip the man of a name that people fear.*—

On our first day out, Aric had studied Jack. Tonight, his attention had redoubled, as if he now found his foe *worthy* of investigation.

Aric had his hunger for knowledge; Jack had his curiosity. Was there really a difference between those two things?

Jack told Rodrigo, "Take ole Milo here and the two bodies back to his tent. He and I are goan to have a chat."

"Yes, sir." Rodrigo could barely hide his glee. He ordered soldiers to carry the three, adding, "You might want to wear gloves."

Jack said, "Death ain't contagious."

Aric looked astonished. —*He does* listen to me on occasion.—

"Oh, of course, sir," Rodrigo said. "If you'll follow me."

As we made our way through the crowd, Jack shook hands, accepting thanks. By the time we reached Milo's tent, the man had been already tied to a chair, prepped for interrogation. The carnates lay on the ground, atop a layer of extravagant sawdust.

Rodrigo said, "Sir, there are about thirty mercenaries who are loyal to him. They fought back before we overpowered them. What do you want to do with them? Firing squad?"

I frowned. "Like Milo used to do?"

"*Non*. But they got to be punished."

Aric leaned against Milo's desk. "And how will you do it, mortal? Will your leadership be callous? Or merciful?" He sounded fascinated with this subject. Of course, his favorite book was *The Prince*. "If you plan to be a leader, then the actions you take now could resonate for your entire life."

"You think I doan know that?" Jack turned to Rodrigo. "Exile them fifty miles from camp with no shoes, shirts, or coats. Give them each a map that leads to five packs filled with gear."

"I'll organize that right away, sir." And off he went.

The corners of Aric's lips curved, his eyes lively. "Most will kill or be killed long before they reach their destination. And I don't suppose there will actually *be* packs."

Jack opened his mouth to answer, then seemed to think better of it. "That's army business, and you ain't army."

I surveyed the tent. The lavish area was spotless, except for around Milovníci's desk. Books, pens, and papers had been swept to the ground. A framed picture of his weird children lay with broken glass. He must've been sitting there when he passed out. "Do you think Milov—I mean, *Milo* will give up information on his kids?"

Jack moved to stand in front of the man, hatred stamped on every line of his body. "He's about to give up everything. I'll make the twins' torture look like love taps."

I blinked at Jack. So ruthless. So unyielding. A million miles away from the drunken boy who'd cared about nothing after the Flash.

Selena had told me that Jack had changed. Yeah. That.

He backhanded Milo. "Wake up, you *fils de putain*." Not a twitch . . .

While we waited, Aric knelt, lifting a weighty black book from the ground. He brushed sawdust from it, then laid it on the desk.

I drew in. "What is it?"

He didn't answer, just turned to the first page. Handwritten text covered the weathered paper. I couldn't determine the language.

Aric's radiant eyes illuminated the page. "Gods in heavens."

"What is it?"

"Chronicles." He turned that brilliant gaze to me. "The Lovers' chronicles."

33

"*What is this?*" Milo demanded, spittle flying into the air. Finally, he'd come to.

Jack stopped mid swing, lowering his hand. "Look who's up."

Milo's pale blue eyes widened with shock. "I know you! The notorious hunter! What do you want from me?"

"Your children," Jack answered. "The real ones. You're goan to give them to us."

When the sounds of the outside celebrations filtered into the tent, Milo's shock deepened. "This isn't possible—my soldiers are loyal!" His lips drew back from stained teeth. "They will retake control." His hands twisted against his bonds, his fingers tipped with long yellow nails. "And when they do—"

"Your loyalists are as good as dead. Just like your twins." Jack nodded to indicate the carnates. "Or their placeholders, anyway."

"That's Death's mark." Milo whipped his head around with confusion, settling on Aric.

He sat at the man's desk, leaning back in the chair, steepling his fingers. The book lay open in front of him.

Milo glanced at it, then studiously away. Did he hope we wouldn't figure out what we possessed?

For once, we'd had a turn of fortune. The book hadn't been in Milo's safe or hidden away.

Because he was the Lovers' chronicler.

At the time a canister rolled into his tent, he'd been recording an entry. The last written word trailed across a page.

The bad news? The language was ancient Romanian.

The good news? Aric said he could translate it in time.

Milo snapped, "Death wasn't part of the deal!"

"The one your kids already welshed on?" I pointed out.

"You!" As I'd suspected, Milo's face grew even redder. I'd never been looked at with such contempt. "All my life I've known who to blame for generations of this family's misfortunes—the Empress. Here she stands."

"I understand your blaming me for the last game. But all the following centuries? That's a stretch."

He gazed at the circlet of roses on my head, making a face of revulsion. "Without your treachery, the Duke and Duchess Most Perverse would have won, becoming royalty. No, becoming immortal gods! They could have watched over and enriched this family eternally. Each generation knows how you robbed us. Our line is forged from vengeance!"

So the Milovnícis had grown more and more bitter about my betrayal? More twisted?

"My children will right this wrong. They are retribution. They will win this, so they can punish you in the next game and the next." He bared yellowed teeth. "Enjoy your final days in this life, you treacherous bitch!"

Jack clocked him for that.

The man grunted in pain, taking long moments to focus his vision.

"Let's talk about those kids, Milo. We're goan to ring them up, inform them of our upcoming hostage swap."

"They won't trade anyone for me."

"For their chronicles, then?" Aric slid the tome into a waterproof sleeve he'd found.

Milo redlined on the crazy meter, spittle flying. "Thief! You have no right to those!"

"Stay on topic." Jack backhanded him again, rocking the man's head to the side. "Your kids. Where are they?"

"I will *never* give them away!"

Jack just smiled. Though I knew Milo had earned the retribution he was about to receive, I didn't want to watch him tortured. Especially not by Jack.

Plus the red witch would probably view it as recreation and crave similar forms of entertainment.

I caught Jack's gaze.

"I got this, Evie. You want to wait outside?"

Aric rose, book in hand. "I'll take you."

As we exited, Milo told Jack, "I remember your pretty sister. Vincent told me she liked to beg in French—"

His scream ripped through the night. Even as I flinched, the red witch found the sound as pleasurable as a petal's caress.

I took a seat on a bench not far from where the petrifying Thanatos waited, giving passersby the willies.

When Milo let loose another strangled scream, Death began to pace, his spurs clinking. "If the mortal can't control himself, this will not work. Torture isn't as simple as one would think." Pacing, pacing. "Does Deveaux know how to torment his victim while leaving the man conscious? Will he avoid major arteries? It's not so easy a feat."

"You want to go back in, don't you?"

"The sooner we retrieve Selena for Deveaux, the sooner you return home with me."

I parted my lips to argue, then decided not to waste my breath. I waved him away. "Just go."

"Don't leave this place, *sievā*, and keep your guard up. There could still be loyalists about." He returned to the tent.

As I waited, Milo screamed intermittently. But I could also hear people talking about Jack, Aric, and me. A group of women gabbed about the hunter's "hot-as-fire" Cajun accent and "steely" gray eyes. They found Aric "eerily gorgeous."

Jealousy flared on *both* counts. I was used to feeling it over Jack and Selena, but not as often for Death. For kicks and giggles, I imagined Aric kissing someone else.

My claws budded.

And what did Azey North think of me? The men found me "unnerving" yet "definitely doable." The women? "She's so creepy." "Did you see that vine snaking around her head?"

Still, whenever people walked by me, I smiled in greeting. They nodded politely, but couldn't hide their nervousness.

I sighed. Just over a year ago, I'd been in high school, making friends with such ease.

Then I caught a fragment of conversation coming from the other side of the tent—about Jack. Was that Rodrigo?

Sidling closer, I eavesdropped as he told another soldier how the hunter had single-handedly ganked dozens of Baggers last night—with nothing but a tire iron.

After Jack had promised me not to take unnecessary risks?

The. Hell.

I strode over to the pair. "Rodrigo, can I talk to you for a second?" Something in my tone made the other guy scurry off.

Rodrigo swallowed. "Sure?"

"You were exaggerating about Jack. Right?"

"No, ma'am," he said, relaxing a touch. "Some of the older guys didn't believe the rumors about Deveaux and Baggers, so they told him to nut up or shut up. I saw him charge into a horde with my own eyes. That guy's fearless."

Jack had broken his promise to me—the same night he'd given it. "Thanks. Uh, carry on, soldier."

When he wandered off with a bemused grin, I pulled that red ribbon out of my pocket.

Why did Jack feel he could risk himself like that? Maybe he did have a death wish.

By the time Aric and Jack emerged, I'd decided not to confront him. For now. We were too close to freeing Selena; nothing could get in the way of that. Not my anger, not his disregard. "Well?"

"That man could dish out the torture, but couldn't take it, no." Jack scrubbed a palm over his chin, his scarred knuckles bloodied. "He told us the twins are in a blast-proof bunker."

"It's over a day north of here," Aric added. "High in the mountains and accessible only by horse. A place they call the Shrine."

Milo could be lying. "Can you trust what he says?"

"*Ouais.* I usually got a good sense about these things, and I think he spilled some truths—in between spitting out teeth like yellow Chiclets. Just to be sure, I can confirm." Jack unclipped a transceiver from his belt. "Got the jammers turned off, me. You ready to ring up the twins' bunker?" I might have been mistaken, but I thought he'd asked me *and* Aric.

"Let's do this." I held my breath as Jack hailed them.

And released it with dread when we received no answer.

34

"I can't remember when I last beheld such a show." In the doorway of
our roadside shelter—an old clapboard church—Aric stood silhouetted
by lightning. Bolts teemed across the black sky.

Inside, Jack was inspecting the explosives he'd requisitioned from
the army. Milo was tied up, fettered to a rough-hewn pew. So I'd joined
Aric to watch the fireworks.

After pushing for miles through a brutal squall, we'd found this
isolated, still-standing church and rewarded ourselves and our horses
with a few hours of rest.

In the nearby graveyard, the tombstones were all crooked and
scorched, as dark and foreboding as Aric's armor. When we'd first
stopped, he'd breathed in deeply amid the crosses, headstones, and
slabs, so at home that I'd raised a brow. "I like churches," he'd said with
a grin. "Graveyards especially."

Even though he'd named his horse Thanatos and he'd discovered
his armor on a corpse in a bone crypt, I'd never thought of Aric as so,
well, death-y.

This wasn't off-putting to me. In fact, I found his fascination with
deathly things attractive, because it was a part of him.

A particularly fearsome bolt spanned the sky. "I could almost swear the Tower called this down upon us," Aric mused. "In past games, he was this powerful."

"I can barely imagine that."

Aric's noble face was relaxed. A hint of blond stubble had regrown over the day. Bolts reflected in his amber eyes until his irises appeared on the verge of starlit.

As I gazed up at him, I realized my feelings for him continued to deepen. I might be . . . falling for him.

Really falling.

"The Tower could throw javelins from both hands, with lightning combusting between them," Aric continued. "The first time I encountered him, I was awestruck by the spectacle. To my detriment. I was new to the game, just sixteen."

Right after he'd left his home. After his parents . . . I shivered.

He straightened at once. "You're freezing. Come back to the fire." He led me inside.

The church's roof had a couple of burnout holes; Jack and Aric had made our fire beneath one. At times today the two had almost appeared to get along.

Without a word between them, they'd dismantled a pew for firewood and secured the horses in an adjoining alcove. Sword and bow raised, they'd cased the immediate area for Bagmen. As if by unspoken agreement, they'd disguised their animosity, presenting a unified front to Milo.

Their dynamic was changing. It had started when they'd stormed the slaver boss's house together. It'd continued evolving with our victory at Azey North. Their mutual scorn of Milo had seemed to blunt their hatred of one another.

Were they still enemies who would murder each other?

Absolutely.

But they might not savor the kill as much as they would've before.

"I didn't mean to take you from the show," I told Aric.

"I'm keen to get to my translating." He ushered me to the fire across from Jack.

I sat cross-legged, raising my waterlogged hands to the flames. I could feel Milo's hateful gaze—two pale eyes surrounded by bruises. He twisted his bound hands, as if he longed to strangle me. Good luck with all those broken fingers.

"Obviously, you don't know this, Empress"—his swollen lips and missing teeth distorted his speech—"but you ride with the very one who *killed* you in the last game! He's played you false!"

"Nope, I knew. He decapitated me. Blah." I sounded blasé. I was anything but about our history.

"Then you're even stupider than I thought."

Like a blur, Aric was in front of him. "Now, Milo, we talked about this. Remember? You do not speak to her unless you'd like to be castrated by horse hoof."

"She's about to know agony as never . . ."

Death slowly shook his head with such menace that the man swallowed. That got Milo to shut up—at least to me. The moment Aric left him, the man turned to Jack. "It doesn't matter how many explosives you stole from me, you'll never breach the Shrine."

"*Non?* You sure sound confident for a man who spent the day hog-tied over a saddle."

Back at the encampment, the Azey had been delighted to see their former leader trussed up in such a humiliating position. Well, except for the bound loyalists who'd been on their way out to endure their own set of difficulties.

The horse Jack had chosen for Milo was one of the finest the army had to offer. He planned for Selena to use it on the way back.

How confident Jack was that we could rescue her—that she'd be able to ride. Whenever my mind turned to what the twins might be doing to her, I had to shut those thoughts down. . . .

Aric took the chronicles from that waterproof sleeve. He sat near me, leaning against a wall. With a look of anticipation, he cracked open the pages.

"Thief!" Milo's beaten face grew an alarming shade of red. "You've stolen what doesn't belong to you! You have no right!"

Milo truly believed he was the innocent party. Aric was a thief; I was a treacherous bitch who'd wronged generations; Jack was an insurrectionist.

When the man got zero response from Aric, he said, "Save yourself the trouble—you'll never read them."

Aric flipped a page without looking up. "Won't I?"

"It's written in ancient Romanian." Somehow Milo's expression was both frenzied and smug.

"I speak ancient Hungarian, which shares roots with that language." Another turned page.

Milo's smugness faltered. "You want to know the contents? It's a revenge contract from one generation to the next. We've renewed our hatred of the Empress over and over."

"I look forward to a little light reading, then," Aric said. "Know that I'll translate every word of this scrawl eventually."

"Eventually? You won't live past tomorrow. My children will reclaim our chronicles off your corpse."

Jack smirked. "So we *are* headed in the right direction then?"

"It doesn't matter that I told you the Lovers' location. You can't breach it."

"Popping open a bunker woan be as easy as, say, stealing your entire army from you. But we'll figure it out. Tomorrow, we're goan to eat good off your stores, and drink too. I already stole the whiskey from your desk." He pulled a bottle from his bug-out bag, keeping it at the ready. "Twenty-five years old? Um, um, um."

"Enjoy it, hunter! Tonight's your last one on this earth." Veins stuck out in the man's forehead as he grew more frustrated. He was used to terrifying people; I think I'd yawned at him a couple of times in the last hour. "Tomorrow you die."

"I've never heard that before," Aric drawled. "And yet . . ."

Jack returned to his explosives inspection, eyeing a serious-looking detonator. "Seems you like to bluster, Milo. The weak ones always do."

Aric glanced up. "I've seen that trait over and over throughout the years. I remember Philip the Second once wrote to the Spartans, saying, 'If I enter Laconia, I will raze Sparta.' Do you know what they wrote back? One word: *If*."

Jack paused at that, cocking his head. I'd bet he was committing that story to memory.

"My children will reign over this world as immortal champions. Unlike you, Reaper!" Milo spat a mouthful of watery blood. "What did you do as champion of the Arcana?"

"Hmm." Amusement. A flipped page. "What should I have done?"

"The entire world could have worshipped death. Cults of it, to pay homage to your deity."

"Historically, Arcana who reveal their secret gifts fare ill. Even so, I haven't done too shabbily. Everyone has heard of the Grim Reaper. And cults of death? People pray before tombs and crypts every day. Cemeteries are hallowed. Look outside these very doors. What's left standing? Monuments to death."

"You could have conquered so much more. Ruled over man as a god. Enriched your relatives' line. You could have sown fear as my twins will sow destruction."

"And in your imaginings, when your spawn win, what would mankind worship?"

"*Love*. It's the most destructive force in the universe."

Really getting sick of hearing that.

"They'll make over the world in their image, populating it with carnates. Eventually my children will control everyone on the face of the earth. They'll win game after game, never dying!"

"No. They won't," Aric said. "Because we're on our way to introduce them to death. But I'll be sure to update your chronicles for you."

Face twisted, Milo sneered, "You've seen how my children love their innocent victims. Imagine what they have planned for the treacherous Empress, who tortured them."

My last nerve said, "He's on me!" I glanced around for a gag.

Milo turned to Jack. "They'll love her far worse than they did your pretty sister, Clotile. The little French beggar."

Jack lunged for Milo; before he could reach the man, Death had used his speed to yank the fiend up, shoving him toward the door.

"You'll pay, Empress!" Milo screamed over his shoulder. "The creature loses its tail but retains its life. You'll see! We are retribution!"

Jack stared after the man, his jaw clenched, his chest heaving.

"You okay?" I asked quietly.

He dragged his gaze from the doorway to me. "I will be." He inhaled deeply. "Tomorrow, I will be."

I parted my lips to ask him if he'd ever tell me what happened to Clotile—and to him—but he turned from me, heading to his bag, to that bottle.

He cracked it open and took a long slug, the wrath in his eyes easing a bit.

When Aric returned alone moments later, I said, "What'd you do with Milo?"

"Tied him beside Thanatos. In proximity to sharpened hooves." He shook out his dampened hair. "I guarantee nothing."

"We could've gagged him."

"This is Milo's first night out in the cold since the Flash. I'd like him to experience it." In a wry tone, Aric added, "Plus, he was setting off your rose scent, which makes it *impossible* for me to relax."

So now we were going to joke about our clashes in the past? Too soon?

When he headed for the chronicles, I asked him, "How long will it take to translate them?"

"I've read some already." Book in hand, he crossed to sit beside me. "They know that your powers are collaborative, that a world without green or sun weakens you."

I gazed out at the night. Endless night. Maybe I *couldn't* fully invoke the red witch, even if I wanted to.

With that bottle in hand, Jack sat on my other side, offering a drink. To hell with it. *Down she goes. Burn. Gasp.* I handed Death the bottle.

Jack grimaced. "Am I goan to die drinking after the Reaper?"

"Sadly"—Aric took a deep pull—"no." With a gauntleted hand, he passed the whiskey back to Jack.

In some small way, it was a measure of trust that Jack drank after Death. And of course, the competitive Cajun had to tip the bottle up longer than Aric had.

"Milo's right, though." Jack handed me the whiskey. "It'll be damn hard to open that bunker. I've got munitions, but a blast door is designed to withstand them. Unless we can wedge the explosive into the metal, it woan work."

"Why not?" I asked over the rim of the bottle.

"It's like throwing a stick of dynamite at a bowling ball. It'll just bounce off. But if you jam the stick into the ball? Boom."

"Maybe the twins will answer tomorrow." All day we'd hailed them by radio and through Aric. Not a blip in response. "They might face us." Though I hoped they actually gave a damn about their father, I doubted it all the same. We'd even dangled the bait of their chronicles. Still, nothing.

"*Ouais, peut-être.*" Yeah, could be. Jack's expression told me he didn't have high hopes either.

I asked both of them, "If we've overridden all the rules to the twins' 'game,' why don't we call up the rest of the Arcana to help us?"

Aric surprised me by setting the chronicles away. He was choosing whiskey around a camp fire over study and contemplation? "Because the Fool's rules still apply, Empress. He said the *three* of us must ride to save Selena."

Strange, I'd forgotten I'd been in fate's crosshairs.

Jack turned to Death. "I like that Spartan story, me. Is it true?"

"That's how I heard it back then."

Back then. Back in the day. He'd been *alive*.

Jack's sense of curiosity was still vibrant in him, forcing him to ask, "What's it like to live for thousands of years?"

Staring straight into the flames, Aric said, "Immortality is the utterest hell."

His words hurt me like a blow to the body. To the heart.

"Are there any others out there?" Jack asked.

"Not that I've ever met."

The bottle made another round. I couldn't believe the two had been talking this long—without fighting. I was hesitant to say anything, didn't want to spook them.

Aric asked him, "How did you come by your talent for reading people?" Though Aric possessed so many gifts, did he wish for that ability? For all these years, he'd been an observer of mortals, but rarely a participant in their interactions.

Jack's gaze clouded. *"Nécessité."* Deep draw. Pass bottle. "That story true about your armor?"

Under my lashes, I gazed from one to the other. They were lowering their guards a bit.

"Very true. I thought I'd been maddened, suffering from hallucinations, until I found the crypt."

"So . . . gods are real?"

Aric nodded. "That's how the game came about. They grew bored."

When he didn't elaborate, I had to speak up. "And? What happened after boredom set in?"

"You wish to hear the origin story?"

"Uh, *yes*." I passed him the bottle.

"Very well." He drank, handing it to Jack, starting another round. "A goddess of magic devised a contest to the death for select mortals. She invited deities of other realms to send a representative from their most prestigious house, all youths. Each one bore their god's emblem upon his or her right hand."

My heart raced . . . *I* had been one of those youths.

"These players would fight inside Tar Ro, a sacred realm as large as a thousand kingdoms, harvesting their victims' emblems; only the player who'd collected them all would leave Tar Ro alive. Naturally, the gods cheated, gifting their own representative with superhuman abilities, making them more than mortal. *Secret* abilities. That's why we're called Arcana."

"Hail Tar Ro," I murmured. "The High Priestess told me that."

"An old-fashioned greeting. She's quite knowledgeable about the games. Very respectful of the old ways."

Probably not who I should be talking to about ending the game. "Why did the gods give us a call?"

"Shortage of heralds?" Arcana humor.

"Saw your hand earlier," Jack said. "You've taken out four cards in this game?"

Death had, but he'd hated doing it. I cast about for a change of subject.

"Four," Aric said, that single word imbued with weariness.

Keen Jack observed, "A Grim Reaper who's sick of reaping?"

Aric schooled his features. "Ending cannibals and slavers is sport. But they're different from most Arcana. All things being equal, I'd rather not."

Jack seemed to be mulling this over as he passed the bottle to me. "You believe this game can be ended?"

"I've failed in the past to do so. But that doesn't mean it's not possible." Then Aric told me alone, —*I'm particularly invested in believing that.*—

Because he wanted to take me back to his isolated castle of lost time. Have kids with me. Live a long life, but not a never-ending one. In answer, I handed Aric the bottle.

After seeing the misery out in the world—the spreading plague, the cannibals, the hobbled women and shackled girls—could I abandon everything?

Our situation *was* becoming larger than the game. We hunted the Lovers, not only because they'd taken Selena, but also because they'd rained down so much terror on innocent people.

After all my evil in past lives, shouldn't I atone in this one?

"Some cards will have to be destroyed regardless of the game." Aric's free hand clenched. Was he thinking about the Emperor? "They will never come to heel. Just as the Lovers refuse to."

"We woan have to worry about those two much longer." Jack absently rubbed his bandage.

"You shouldn't wear their mark, mortal."

Jack scowled. "Ain't like I got a choice, me."

"Burn it with something else. Another shape."

After a moment's hesitation—as Jack clearly weighed and *approved* of this suggestion—he said, "Why you care, anyway?"

Aric drank deep. "If you knew what the Lovers truly want to do to the Empress, you'd ache to annihilate every last vestige of them."

35

I stood on a rise, overlooking the plague valley. Matthew was beside me.

The last thing I remembered was crawling into my sleeping bag after the whiskey had hit me like a two-by-four to the face. Now my friend was here with me. "I've missed you. Are you feeling better?" How much was this vision taking out of him?

"Better." He didn't appear as pale. He wore a heavy coat, open over a space camp T-shirt.

"I'm so relieved to hear that, sweetheart. Why would you bring us here?"

"Power is your burden."

I surveyed all the bodies. "I felt the weight of it when I killed these people."

"Obstacles multiply."

"Which ones?" A breeze soughed over the valley. "Bagmen, slavers, militia, or cannibals?"

He held up the fingers of one hand. "There are now five. The miners watch us. Plotting."

"But miners are the same as cannibals, right?"

He shuffled his boots with irritation. "*Miners*, Empress."

"Okay, okay." I rubbed his arm. "Are you and Finn being safe?"

His brows drew together as he gazed out. "Smite and fall, mad and struck."

I looked with him, like we were viewing a sunset, a beautiful vista. Not plague and death. "You've told me those words before."

"So much for you to learn, Empress. Beware the inactivated card."

One Arcana's powers lay dormant—until he or she killed another player. "Who is it?"

"Don't ask, if you ever want to know."

Naturally, I started to ask, but he cut me off. "Do you believe I see far?" He peered down at me. "Do you believe I see an unbroken line that stretches on through eternity? Centuries ago, I told an Empress that a future incarnation of hers would live in a world of ash where nothing grew. She never believed me."

I could imagine Phyta or the May Queen surveying verdant fields and crops, doubting the Fool.

"Now I tell *you* that dark days are ahead. Will you believe me?"

"I will. I do. Please tell me what will happen. How dark?"

"Darkest. Power is your burden; *knowing* is mine." His expression turned pleading, his soft brown eyes imploring. "Never hate me."

I raised my hands, cradling his face. "Even when I was so mad at you, I never hated you."

"Remember. Matthew knows best." He sounded like his mom—when she'd tried to drown him: *Mother knows best, son.*

I dropped my hands. "It scares me when you say that."

"Do you know what you really want? I see it. I feel it. *Think*, Empress. See *far*."

I was trying! "Help me, then. I'm ready. Help me see far!"

"All is not as it seems. What would you sacrifice? What would you endure?"

"To end the game?"

His voice grew thick as he said, "Things will happen beyond your wildest imaginings."

"Good things?"

His eyes watered. "Good, bad, good, bad, good, good, bad, bad, good-bye. You are my friend."

"Wait!"

But he was gone, leaving me there, in the company of corpses.

I exhaled, gazing out—

My heart lurched; a *girl* lay among them. She was on her front, swords jutting up from her savaged back. Ten of them.

She turned her head, and it was me, crying blood. . . .

I woke from that disturbing vision—to find just as disturbing a sight.

Jack was shirtless, kneeling before the fire, about to press his red-hot bowie knife over the wound on his chest.

Sitting nearby, Aric looked on, as if this was cool or something.

I shot upright. "What are you doing??"

"Prend-lé aisé, bébé." Take it *easy*? Was Jack buzzed? That bottle lay empty beside him. "I'd rather a knife mark than the twins' brand. Can't stand to see it, me. To feel it."

I turned to Aric. "And you think this is a good idea?"

"Your squire entertains." His accent was thick, his words slurred.

Jack flipped him off with his free hand. "Reap. This."

I gaped. They'd gotten drunk together.

Aric shrugged, telling me, "I'd do the same at the earliest opportunity."

I would never, never understand males. These two despised each other. They sniped at each other. Yet they'd worked together.

Then I thought of Selena. Maybe I didn't understand females either.

Because she and I had done the same.

Jack inhaled, holding his breath. His bravery burned as bright as the metal inching closer.

Closer. The fiery red reflected off his sweat-dampened skin, off the beads of his rosary. Closer.

When Aric jerked his chin, Jack pressed the blade down.

Contact. The knife seared his chest. His flesh sizzled, his breath leaving him in a rush.

Jack's head fell back, muscles straining as he silently took the pain.

Years seemed to pass before the blade cooled. He lowered his head, and his glinting eyes met mine. "They got no hold on me."

36

"That is a serious goddamned door," Jack said at the entrance to the bunker.

Aric pounded an armored fist against the damp metal. "Must be three or four feet thick."

Across sheer mountain passes and through winding canyons, Aric had tracked Selena's call, leading us directly here. A couple of hours ago, I'd begun hearing her as well: *Behold the Bringer of Doubt.* The Lovers' call had sounded too. Their real one.

I regarded the mountain enveloping the Shrine. The peak was wreathed in fog, the rock scorched. "Will the explosives work?"

Jack cast a glance at Milo, gagged and tied some distance away. "*Non.* Door's even thicker than I expected. We need some way to worm our way into the metal."

"So what do we do now?" I scouted, searching for an opening, a weakness of some kind—as climbing ivy would. "We can't get in, and we can't get them to answer us." They'd ignored today's attempts.

Suddenly Aric went motionless.

"What's wrong?"

He put his forefinger over his lips and cocked his helmeted head. "The Archer's call just went silent."

My stomach dropped. I couldn't hear her either! "Is she . . . ?"

"I sense she lives still."

"You told me a call could go silent short of death—how?" My glyphs began to glow. "Why?"

Aric's expression was grave. "When an Arcana enters a catatonic state." Jack swore under his breath.

"I don't understand." My gaze darted from one to the other. "She's been with the twins for days. What would bring this about now?"

"She must have reached the tipping point," Aric said.

"Or faced a new horror." Jack stabbed his fingers through his hair. "My mind nearly flipped when I saw that crank."

"So basically her brain is breaking? Oh, screw this! We have to get inside now."

"I'll try the explosives." Jack marched to his horse, retrieving those munitions: a detonation kit and several blocks of plastic explosives.

While he rigged the door, I paced. Aric looked lost in thought.

Minutes later, Jack held up his detonator. "Doan get your hopes up. These explosives couldn't bust open even a foot-thick door."

"Then I'll seed vines." I'd wanted to use my powers to help anyone in need. This was *Selena*. "They'll burrow. Or I'll sand this mountain down with thorns. Somehow we will get in!" I raised my hands to puncture my palms.

"Wait, Empress," Aric said quietly. "I can get us past the door."

Jack looked like he was about to roll his eyes. But then he said, "For true?"

Aric nodded. "I can blow it with something very old. And very strong."

"Then do it!" I clasped his gauntleted hand. "As Selena would say, smash and grab! Let's bring her home."

"Let's? As in let *us*?" Death peeled his hand away "You don't understand. You were never to be risked in this endeavor. Never. We wouldn't be facing mere Bagmen or mortals, and you still haven't learned to invoke the red witch fully."

Jack scowled at me. "You told him about the red witch?"

I breezed past that, facing both of them. "There could be more danger out here. An army of carnates could be lying in wait around the mountain. Besides, the twins don't want to kill me right away. So as long as I'm near, you'll be safer. Not to mention that we have their father. Maybe they'll be protective of him."

"Oh, *ouais*, we'll just use you as a human shield." Jack raised his brows. "Not having it."

"We've come this far, and we will save her. Aric, you're going to blow the door, and Jack, I'm coming with. If you two try to leave me behind, then you better shackle me."

"We would be walking eight icons into their lair," Aric grated. "They will be ruthless."

I pleaded with my eyes, telling him, *Selena's being punished for things I did. You know better than anyone what I was like back then. If we don't save her, I won't be able to live with myself.*

When he still wouldn't relent, I raised my hands again, claws extended. "How much blood do you think it'll take to bore a hole through a mountain?"

He muttered something in Latvian.

"I know that look." Jack shook his head ruefully. "Doan worry; she'll give you your balls back as soon as she's done getting her way."

I lowered my hands and squared my shoulders. "Getting my way— or *leading* the way?"

Jack raised his own hands in surrender. "Lead on, *peekôn*."

To Aric, I said, "What are you packing?"

"It seems I can deny you nothing." With another foreign phrase, he crossed to Thanatos, took a small cloth bundle out of his saddlebag, then returned.

Jack's curiosity was blazing. My own as well.

Aric gingerly unfolded the edges of the black material (because of course it was black). His eyes sparked as he revealed . . . a shimmering silver baton.

I gasped. "That's one of Joules's!" Engraved metal gleamed. "How did you get it?"

"I caught it from the Tower, long before he was Joules." In a dry tone, Aric said, "He shouldn't have minded, since he threw it away."

I found my lips curling. "Why didn't it explode in your hand? You could have lost your entire arm!"

"I took it out of the air, catching it as one would an egg. Loss was possible. But so was gain." Aric gazed down at me. "Without risk, life grows stilted, no?"

Jack watched our interplay keenly.

"You've seen this baton before, Empress, on one of the shelves in my study. Next to the crowns of the many monarchs I have felled," he added, no doubt for Jack's benefit.

Aric had safeguarded all of those treasures in his home for eons. But now he'd taken one off his shelf, out into the world—because *he* was out in the world.

He was no mere observer. The Endless Knight was interacting with us—*living*. Aric was right; he *did* evolve.

"It's priceless, yet you'll still use it for this?"

He inclined his head. "For you."

Was he willing to part with one of his possessions because he thought he would have a life with me? If I didn't choose him, would he go back to stasis? To misery? "Why did you bring it?"

As if a switch had been flipped off, Aric's gaze went cold. "Lest we ran afoul of the Emperor."

Once we'd rescued Selena, I would get to the bottom of Death's animosity toward that card.

"Is that goan to have enough juice?" Jack eyed the baton, then the bunker door, and back.

"From what I understand," Aric said, "the firepower is dependent on how hard it's thrown—and I'm far stronger than Joules."

Jack cast me a look: *I can't even with this guy.*

"In any case, I'll aim for your explosives on the door."

Dragging Milo with us, we took cover behind a rise of rock about a hundred feet away. Aric manipulated the javelin until it extended to its full length.

Milo must've realized what Death held. He went buggy-eyed, yelling into his gag.

"Ready?" Aric surveyed us. "When I throw, I'll cover the Empress. Because—armor."

"Just do it, Reaper!"

He took aim, exhaled a breath. Lips thinned, he launched the javelin, unleashing that harnessed aggression of his.

The spear's trajectory didn't arc, just sped in one line. Like a bullet.

He hunched down, covering me right before it hit. The blast reverberated from the door.

The mountain quaked, the ground rumbling. Gravel rained from the ridge shielding us. As the percussion subsided, smoke billowed.

Had we succeeded?

The air began to clear . . . revealing the warped door. Metal had *melted*, leaving a huge hole.

Aric had done it! I wanted to hug him, but I quashed my excitement. This was only step one.

Besides, he looked anything but celebratory. "Don't make me regret that, Empress."

We approached the entrance with caution. Foreboding red emergency bulbs flashed from the interior, the only source of light.

Jack had his bow at the ready in one hand, Milo's jacket collar in his other. Aric had unsheathed both swords. My claws dripped.

We stepped inside an industrial-looking transition area. Bulky pipes, oversize bolts, welded plates. Orange graffiti covered gray metal walls. In Goth lettering, someone had repeatedly painted:

SMITE   STRUCK   FALL   MAD

In the flashing red lights, those ominous words appeared to move. The same words Matthew had told me.

Jack shoved Milo forward. "Only one way in." The room had no doors, just an elevator.

"This must be a trap." Aric swept his gaze.

"Come on, Reaper? You want to live forever?"

"I don't recommend it." To me, Aric said, "When we face them, you can't hold back."

"I won't." Much. I made my way to the elevator. "The twins wouldn't have expected us to get in so they might not have traps in place. They could be rushing to do something as we speak." I pressed the call button. "We should *hurry*."

The doors yawned wide. Inside, fluorescent lights flicked on and off like those red bulbs.

Aric hastened past me to enter first, sheathing his swords. "Let me look around." After a few moments, he motioned for me to join him. Behind us, Jack booted Milo inside.

Lit buttons showed thirteen floors. The numbering was reversed; the second floor was below us.

So many levels? This place was like a subterranean hive.

"Should we torture Milo for their floor?" Aric yanked the man's gag away. "Do you have something to tell us?"

We didn't have time. "Aric, look at the buttons. Hard." With his superhuman sight . . . "Can you see which one's been used most?"

He scanned them. "The six button has the most wear. Fitting, since it's the Lovers' card number." He pressed it.

Milo went ballistic. "You trespass—you have no right! We're the just defenders, the righteous in this game. We are love's destruction!"

As the doors slid shut, Aric moved closer to me. Under the crackling lights, Jack and I shared an uneasy glance.

My heart thudded when we began to descend, seeming to inch to the next floor. "I am the lizard's tail. I am the tail." Milo kept blathering that. "I'm shed when we're caught." He'd said the same thing last night.

What could he mean? Sometimes when a tomcat caught a lizard, the creature would shed its tail, allowing it to escape.

My eyes widened. "Push the emergency stop!" The twins were going to sacrifice their father. We *had* entered some kind of trap. They would bet on me surviving, regenerating for their torture. "We have to get out of here!"

But Aric was looking up—at the access hatch that had just opened.

A girl peered down, a replicated tableau glimmering over her.

With a giggle, the Violet clone dropped a grenade into the cab—and slammed the hatch shut.

37

Jack had told me about grenades. *Once you pull the pin, a grenade is not your friend.*

And most exploded within five seconds.

One thousand one . . .

Aric dove for it, just as Jack did. Collision. Cursing. I couldn't see what was happening in the wavering lights.

One thousand two . . .

Milo kicked at their faces, so I slashed him with my claws. Aric caught the grenade.

One thousand three . . .

He vaulted upward, punching that hatch so hard it flew off the hinges. The Violet clone shrieked. Jack snatched me in his arms, pressing me against the wall. "Brace yourself."

One thousand four . . .

With a yell, Aric lobbed the grenade straight up through the opening. The only place he could.

Where the cables were. The *brakes*.

One thousand five—

BOOM!

We . . . dropped. Free fall. That feeling of weightlessness wrenched a scream from my lungs.

"I got you, *bébé*! We'll get through this. We'll get through—"

Landing.

Bone-jarring impact. Grinding metal. Stabbing pain?

The force pitched Jack from one side of the half-crumpled cab to the other. I was held fast. With a swallow, I peered down. A piece of metal had skewered my waist, just over my hip.

Stone and debris plummeted onto the top. The clone gave a cry. More rocks bounced, then spilled through the opening, blood-smeared from the girl above.

I needed to *move*. Stifling a scream, I stepped forward, nearly collapsing.

"Evangeline!" Jack's hands searched me for injuries. "Christ, you bleeding?"

"I-I'll be okay. Are you hurt?"

"*Non.*"

"Aric?" I asked.

"I'm fine. Milo's been better."

He was rolling on the floor, moaning in pain. Stones continued to fall.

Jack gazed up. "We got to go before we get buried."

Aric unsheathed a sword to pry open the mangled cab doors. "Or before another carnate drops more explosives." He wrenched one of the doors from its track; it clattered to the floor.

Holding my side, I gazed out into a dimly-lit warehouse. Were those pallets of canned food?

Over the falling rocks, I heard snarling.

Jack snapped a glow stick from his coat pocket, tossing it. The tube skipped across the floor.

When it stopped, I lost my breath.

Bagmen. What must be hundreds of them. All branded.

Milo laughed. "The tail. The tail. Now the cunning lizard gets away."

With crazed snarls, the horde charged.

Jack shoved me at Aric. "Get her out!"

As Aric lifted me to the hatch, Jack hauled Milo up and tossed him to the oncoming Baggers.

Ignoring the pain in my side, I scrambled to the roof, past the dying clone. A boulder rested on her crushed torso, like she'd caught it.

She smiled at me serenely, as if she were on a train, heading off on an adventure.

As if we'd be sure to meet again. Then her lids slid shut.

More rocks fell, pinging me on the head. A big one connected. I staggered, seeing four of the dead clone.

"They're goan to overrun us." Jack drew his pistols, picking the Baggers off.

"Climb up here!" I'd thought he and Aric would be right behind me. The snarling grew louder and louder.

"If we don't stop them"—Aric's swords flashed out—"they'll power their way through the top of the cab."

I raised my gaze. "There's another floor, maybe thirty feet up." The doors at the elevator stop had been blown wide from the grenade. Red lights pulsed from that landing.

Jack snapped, "Get her out of here, Reaper. NOW!"

Before I could argue, Aric leapt up to join me, grabbing my bloody waist. He drew back to the opposite side of the shaft. "You can do this."

"Do *what?*"

He tossed me. I flew upward, arcing toward the opening.

Oomph. The edge gouged my wound as I landed, half of me inside, half clambering.

"Climb, Empress!"

My boots scrabbled against the uneven shaft. Before I could hoist myself in, pain shot through my head.

Another rock? Cracked skull? Blood poured down one temple. My glyphs flickered. With the last of my strength, I hauled myself up into some kind of storage room.

Louder snarling below. No more gunshots. *Jack?*

I couldn't release my thorn tornado without risking him. Poison wouldn't work on them. I had no ground to grow vines, no plants to revive.

I flopped onto my front and shimmied to the edge. "Aric!" I saw him through a frame of dripping blood. A crimson slick gathered around me, pooling over the lip of the floor. "Don't leave him!"

After a heartbeat's hesitation, he seized the coil of severed elevator cables, ripping them free. "Deveaux!" He threaded the length through the hatch. "Grab hold!"

"Got it! Go, go! Fuck—they're in!"

In one motion, Aric heaved on the cable and vaulted toward me. Midway, he lost momentum, snagging the edge of the floor with the tips of four fingers. "The mortal's caught on something."

Jack dangled halfway out of the hatch; Baggers scrabbled to drag him back down, clinging to his feet.

Cable in one hand, crossbow in the other, he fired. For every Bagman he killed, two more took its place.

Hanging by his fingertips, Aric grappled to heft Jack—and the chains of Bagmen suspended from each of Jack's legs. A Bagger tug of war. "Can't hold this for much longer. The mortal's probably been bitten."

A rock the size of a soccer ball struck the back of Aric's head, knocking his helmet off.

It fell. . . .

Snagged by a small jut of stone—right above the rising tide of Baggers.

"Must have that." Aric's gaze darted from where it balanced to Jack and back. How long before he dropped the "mortal" to save his all-important armor? What if he *didn't* drop Jack?

If I lost them both . . .

Never again to see Jack's clear gray gaze.

Aric's unguarded smile.

The Empress didn't get collared or caged—and she didn't lose those she loved. Despite my injuries, the heat of battle welled inside me. My heart thundered as I wobbled to my knees. Aric wanted me to unleash the red witch? I was ready!

But how to fight Bagmen? My eyes darted. *How?*

Dig deep, the witch whispered. *As you would in earth.*

Could my arsenal come from . . . within me?

"Goddamn it," Jack bellowed. "Out of arrows too!"

"*Sievā*, I can't hold this."

My body began to thrum in unknown ways. As an almost electrical pleasure spread inside me, my breaths shallowed until I panted.

I was familiar with the feel of roots churning beneath the ground. Now they seemed to churn within me.

And it was *sublime*.

The red witch rose—*watch out Death, here she comes*—and I let her free. Light exploded from my glyphs, radiating from my face, through my clothes.

The Baggers screeched, shielding their sensitive eyes.

My body vine shot upward from the back of my neck, dividing into a mix of ivy and rose. Writhing green ropes fanned out behind me like a giant aura.

I snatched the base of the vine, ripping the wriggling mass from my skin. With a scream, I hurled it into the shaft.

A grenade of my own.

I envisioned spears of green shooting out, branching like arteries, *invading*—growing not from earth, but from my own power.

My lips curled with bliss as I let myself go adrift—until I could perceive vines as they punched through slimy chests and impaled skulls. As they opened up Bagmen from the inside out.

Yes, sublime.

Baggers wailed as ravenous ivy suckers burrowed into their skin, prying hands from Jack.

"That's it, Evie! I'm loose!"

Before my eyes, rose stalks and ivy slithered up the sides of the shaft, blanketing the rock. Shimmery green painted everything. Vines wove a net above me to catch falling debris.

Aric released his hold on the stone lip and dropped down a few feet to grasp one of the strong stalks. He reeled in that cable, hauling Jack up.

Then Death and Jack ascended—like mysteries brought to light.

Once they'd reached my floor, Aric demanded, "Were you bitten, mortal?"

Jack inspected his legs, yanking up the slime-covered material of his jeans. No blood. No broken skin. "*Non.* It was close, but no." We'd saved him in time.

I commanded that net to drop, trapping the swarm of Baggers below. They tore at it, clawing to rise up—just as the red witch continued to clamor within. My outside battle mirrored the one inside me.

With the scent of roses flooding the air, my gaze slid to Death. Five icons from him alone. He had no helmet to protect him.

"Rein this in, Empress." Death's face was tense, his brows drawn. "Remember: I will not fight you."

I turned to Jack for help. Yet as I met his eyes, I realized he wasn't my *anchor*.

He was my *reminder*—that I wanted to keep my humanity.

Wasn't Aric a reminder as well? Of my vow never to hurt him again?

Inhaling deeply, I grappled to contain the witch. Anxious heartbeats passed before my claws retracted, my glyphs fading.

I'd used my powers as never before. A handful of icons had been there for the taking. But I'd muzzled my witch!

Eerily carried by my vines, Death's fearsome black helmet floated upward. I retrieved it, handing it to him. "How'd you like that?" I said between breaths. "Unleashed enough for you?"

He shook his head.

"Come on! It gets worse than that?"

Slow nod. "That wasn't even a fraction, Empress."

"Seriously?" As quickly as the heat of battle had risen, it dissipated.

Light-headedness overwhelmed me. "My glyphs could've lit up a small Midwestern town. And I went all *Little Shop of Horrors* with those vines." Selena's nickname for me.

"Indeed. Still not more than a fraction."

Jack swiped his hand over his face. "Where'd you learn how to do that, *peekôn*? Baggers thought they were in the sun! How many vines can you make at a time?"

At least he was impressed. "I don't know. It's a new bag of tricks."

Jack turned to Aric. "At every second I thought you'd drop my Cajun ass. But you didn't."

"I suppose it wasn't your time yet." Aric donned his helmet.

"In any case, thanks for not *making* it my time."

Seeming uneasy with the gratitude, Aric knelt beside me. "You cut your scalp?"

My surge of adrenaline dwindled, making way for the excruciating pain in my body and an onslaught of nausea.

Aric parted my hair. "Not just a cut. You cracked your very skull. And your side was pierced through."

"I'll heal."

Jack watched us with narrowed eyes.

I narrowed mine in turn. "What were you thinking? It made no sense for you to face off against Bagmen, with limited weapons—and no armor." My worry morphed into anger. "Just like it made no sense to rush into a horde of them the other night! Even though you'd promised me."

Jack's expression: *busted.*

"Another time for this, perhaps," Aric said. "There's movement in the stairwell." A green EXIT sign gleamed not far away, below it an open door.

"Out of ammo, me." Jack ran his sleeve over his sweating brow. "More Baggers?"

"We won't be so fortunate."

A chorus of voices sounded from that doorway: *"We will love you ever so much."*

38

Carnates spilled into the room, so many that my woozy mind couldn't reconcile what I was seeing.

Faultless duplicates. Paper cutout dolls stretched side by side forever, except these carried swords.

Death unsheathed his own and marched into the fray. Right beside him, Jack snagged a fire extinguisher as his only weapon.

When I tried to rise, I heaved. Turning to one side, I vomited into that pool of my blood.

"Just stay back, Empress!" Aric's swords sliced out.

"We got this!" Jack bashed in a Vincent head.

I tottered to my feet, propping myself up against a wall. Once my strength returned, I'd call for a flood of green from the elevator shaft—

A hand covered my mouth!

The ground seemed to move under my feet—no, *we* were moving. A false wall rotated us into a hidden area. Would Jack and Aric even know I'd been taken?

"If you want to see Selena alive," a male whispered, "you'll be a good girl."

Vincent. I sensed he was the *real* one.

His idea of a good girl was something I'd *never* be. When he looped an arm around my neck, I grew my thorns, about to inject him with poison. One half of an icon was about to be mine!

"Recognize this?" He raised a pressure sensor in front of my face. "Selena wears the collar now."

But . . . but the Lovers' icon . . .

No, no, Selena was my friend. She'd lost the Archer's arrow meant for me.

I inhaled for calm. Vincent might take me to her—and to Violet— guiding me through the Shrine. I raised my hands in surrender.

"I'm amazed, Empress. You *do* care for another card." He dragged me into a smaller secreted elevator, not much larger than a dumbwaiter. "Vi and I debated if this threat would curb your bloodlust."

He and I ascended—couldn't tell how many floors before we stopped. He hauled me out into a hallway with that same industrial look, those same orange words spray painted.

SMITE STRUCK FALL MAD

His tableau appeared over him, upside down, but crystal clear.

At last, I faced one of the source twins.

Vincent was a far cry from his tall, flawless carnates. His real body was somehow both scrawny and pudgy, his skin jaundiced and slicked with oil. His black hair was matted, his sleeveless T-shirt and jeans bloodstained. Scars and new slices covered his arms—from his blood-letting.

He'd created carnates with his *idealized* appearance. Vain? Oh yeah.

I couldn't wait to see the real Violet. "Admit it: you Photoshopped your carnates."

"Do you really want to go there about appearances?" Even his voice was higher pitched than his carnates'. "You're covered in blood. Surprisingly it's your own this time."

That was fair. "Where are your sister and Selena?"

"I'm taking you to them." He motioned for me to walk with him.

I did, deciding to play along while I recharged and healed. I would come up with a plan to get that sensor, take out the twins, and get back to Aric and Jack.

Vincent and I strolled side by side down the hall, like we were heading to class. As if I wouldn't kill him at the first opportunity. As if he wasn't imagining how he'd first make me scream.

As if Baggers hadn't just eaten his father.

The calm before the storm. Both Vincent and I knew it.

"Why paint those particular words?" My voice was thick from throwing up and screaming.

"So Violet and I never forget the power we wield."

"And that is?"

"We control the most destructive force in the universe."

I was *done* hearing that. "I was wrong when I said that about love."

He scowled. "Of course it's the most destructive force—it's *our* power. Love begets violence, murder, and war. Why else would mortals equate it with such horrible things?"

"What are you talking about?"

"Sunstruck, moonstruck, and lovestruck all mean maddened. We fear storm breaks and heart breaks. We fall blind, fall into a trap, fall sick, fall *madly* in love. Why not rise in love?"

I had no answer for that. I didn't know exactly how to describe love—just knew his idea of it was perverse.

"If shot through the heart with an arrow, you get lovesick. Sounds painful, doesn't it?" With his free hand, he pulled the collar of his shirt higher, rolling his head on his neck. "And *smitten*? One touch of the dart, and an invisible affliction smites you down."

"Love hurts. I get it."

He grinned; I grimaced. His yellowed teeth resembled his father's. "You hurt right now, Empress. Your love isn't diluted anymore. It's divided—between the hunter and Death."

Somewhere in this lair, Aric fought tirelessly for me. I *did* love him. As I loved Jack.

"It's complicated." My answer of the month.

"You broke our rules by bringing Death here. But I'm glad you did. Now we have two beloved to use against you. Perhaps we should take them alive." Vincent's gaze went blank, his irises turning black.

"You're seeing through your carnates' eyes right now."

"We are."

—*Sievā, open your mind to me!*

Aric! I'm okay for now. Are you and Jack?

—*Engaged at present.—*

I'm with Vincent. Can't find Selena or Violet.

—*I'm coming for you soon. Hold tight.—*

I can stall.

No answer.

Vincent's eyes had cleared. "Have you remembered our history?"

I shook my aching head. "But when Death translates your chronicles, I'll read all about it."

"Our carnates are retrieving our stolen property from your horses as we speak."

"From the Reaper's armored mount?" I had to laugh. "All the best with that." They had better hope they *couldn't* catch that stallion. Thanatos bench pressed three eighty and made Bagger Spam with his hooves. "Why are those chronicles so important to you?"

"Our earliest memories are of Father reading them to us, each night before we went to sleep." Blood-drenched bedtime stories. "We're sentimental."

Sentimental? "Because of you and your sister, your dad is being *digested* right now."

He nodded. "Today we loved our father. We loved our mother as we began these new incarnations." Had she died in childbirth?

A suspicion arose. "Vincent, have you ever left this place?"

He blinked. "Why *would* we?"

At my disbelieving expression, he explained, "Our father bought the Shrine when our mother was pregnant with us—just in case his children would ring in a new game, and a new catastrophe. As soon as he found out we were twins, he knew the game was starting. We've been safe within here since before we were born."

The twins had never felt the sun on their own skin?

He pointed toward a doorway. "In there."

Again, I made the decision to go along with him.

Once we'd crossed the raised threshold, he shut the door behind him. Never taking his finger from the sensor, he locked us in with a combination I didn't see. I was trapped with him?

He was trapped with *me*.

Come, Lover, touch . . .

He'd taken me to a sizable game room. Against one wall stood a fridge, a microwave station and sink beside it. A trashcan overflowed with frozen food packages and empty potato chip bags. Clothes were wadded up around it.

A hi-tech desk ran the length of another wall, covered with keyboards and video game controllers. Monitors hung above. Different video games had been paused mid-action.

In front of a cushy gamer's chair sat a plate with a half-eaten Hot Pocket beside a can of Coke.

"So this is your dukedom. You sit in here and play?" While everyone else in the world was fighting for survival? How did the least deserving assholes on the planet score these digs?

"We play when we're not practicing our craft. Or being interrupted," he said with an annoyed look at me. Sensor in hand, he dropped into that chair. "In a way, our lives are video games. We send our avatars into the world, and the Shrine is the big boss cave."

Vincent was a monster—and yet he sounded like an excited teenager when he said, "We've turned it into a house of horrors! We've got carnates patrolling every floor and Baggers in the basement to guard our treasure. Congratulations, Empress, you survived our little prank explosion, so you got to this secret bonus level. But you only have one life left." He cast me that vile grin.

Vincent Milovníci had microwave snacks galore but had apparently never seen a toothbrush. I turned from his smile, frowning at those clothes near the trashcan.

Were those Selena's?

Yes, that was her shirt, coat, and boots—to be discarded with the food packaging. Because the twins believed she'd never need them? "Where is Selena? What have you done to her?"

In a perplexed tone, he said, "We loved her."

Fury erupted inside me. "You raped her?"

"Me? Cheat on Vi? Are you crazy?" He was so aghast I believed him.

I never thought I'd be relieved to learn that Vincent was faithful to Violet. "You said you'd take me to see Selena."

He pulled on his collar again. "What's your rush? We have *all the time* in the world."

"Are you embarrassed for me to see her? To see your sick kicks?"

He grinned again. "Our *lovesick* kicks."

I cast him my best Selena impression. *Really?*

His black brows drew together. "We're proud of our work, Empress. We always have been."

Work?

"If you're so eager to be enlightened . . ." He pressed a button on the desk. A wall panel folded back, revealing a torture chamber. The air from within wafted over me like a foul breath, and I nearly threw up again.

This area made the Azey South tent look like amateur night. All the devices from before were here, with new ones too. A pillory, a rack, and a real-live guillotine.

Shackles hung from beams. Gore-covered mallets and cleavers lay atop a work bench. A pegboard displayed various metal masks, crank contraptions, hacksaws, and pruning shears.

A large fire burned within a vented pit, a rack of pincers and pokers at the ready.

One corpse rotted on a chair with spikes; a second decomposed in a suspended cage.

"My supply of victims has gotten smaller and smaller." Vincent sighed, as if embarrassed by the lackluster amount of carnage. "But now that you're here, with your regeneration, you'll be like a video game that never ends."

There was a bed with twisted sheets. The twins slept in here, amid the bodies and stench. "Where is Violet?"

"She's always *close*."

"If you and your sister have Wonder Twin powers, why would you not go everywhere together?"

"Our talents are . . . evolving." He seemed to think that was hilarious.

All the way to my right, I saw a bloody wood stump with an ax embedded. Someone knelt in front of it.

"Selena?"

39

She was motionless, her dark eyes staring blankly.

Her long hair tangled around her face. She wore only her jeans and a bra, and she looked like she'd lost twenty pounds in just days. Every inch of her bared skin was covered in bruises.

"Your arrival interrupted us." Vincent's tone was peevish. "We were just about to take the Archer's hand—"

I ran for her, dropping to my knees beside her. "Selena!" Behind a wicked looking ax blade, her arm stretched across the surface of the stump.

Oh dear God, they'd hammered a rusty nail through her hand to hold her in place. Was that what sent her over the edge?

I tugged her hair from her face, pulling it over her shoulder. A crusted brand marked her chest, two overlapping triangles, bisected with arrows.

Rage boiled up inside me. Another body vine grew from my neck and split behind me. Not a green aura this time; it felt like a cobra's hood.

Vincent shuddered with disgust. "You can't comprehend how repulsive you are to us." He raised the sensor. "Easy, Empress. Now that we have you, we don't need the Archer as much."

Damn that sensor! I could control my rage. I gritted my teeth, forcing the vine to collapse onto itself.

Gradually it retracted. Once it'd slipped beneath the surface of my skin, I turned back to Selena. "Please say something." She didn't react. "Selena, answer me!" Nothing.

I leveled my gaze on Vincent. "What the hell did you do?"

He sat on a trunk at the foot of the bed. "While we waited for the Archer's arm to heal, we kept her in a standing sweat box with a noose around her neck, forcing her to balance on her toes atop a heating plate." His attitude was as la-di-da as his carnate's had been. "Mortals break after just a couple of hours, but she endured for days, without food or water. She emerged, a blank canvas for us to work with."

If they'd done that to her, what had they done to Jack?

"Today we planned to lop off her fingers one by one, tormenting her with the knowledge that she'd never let sail another arrow. But Vi decided she wanted the Archer's hand in one chop. So naturally, I secured our prisoner and started sharpening my ax." With an exhalation, he said, "Anything for love."

My claws dripped. I ached to plant them into his greasy jowls.

"Right before you arrived here, I hiked the ax above my head, pausing for effect. I expected her to weep and beg—you know, as prisoners *do*. But the hardhearted Archer couldn't cry, as if the tears had been trained right out of her. She just broke. Vi thinks she was conditioned to turn off her senses in the face of torture. I think the Archer snapped because she beheld my sister for the first time."

Chills skittered up my spine. "Why would that make Selena go catatonic?" Would it make me?

Another grin. "You'll see."

I swallowed.

"With you here, we held off from making the chop, hoping you could snap the Archer out of this daze. She should experience our practice fully. . . ." He trailed off, gazing at something past Selena. "Just a second. We're at a critical period." He rose and shuffled to her other side, to a large pool of blood.

"Is that Selena's?"

In answer, he rolled his pale eyes. With his free hand, he drew a folded straight razor from his jeans pocket, flicking it open. He sliced his arm, groaning with . . . pleasure? Then he stretched the wound—and the sensor—over the pool.

When the first crimson drop hit, the air over the surface blurred, as if with heat. I sensed power, like when Finn spun an illusion. "You're creating a carnate."

Vincent folded the razor, pocketing it. "We hatch them beside prisoners so our children understand the ways of love without delay."

I needed to give Aric and Jack enough time to get to us—which meant engaging this freak in conversation. "Don't you and Violet have to share blood to clone yourselves?"

"Hers is mixed in there."

"How many have you made?"

He puffed out his chest. "Legions. We send them out exploring, all the way to what used to be the Pacific and down to the equator even."

He would've seen everything they'd beheld. "And? What's out there?"

"It's all exactly like it is here, ash and waste over every mile. Oblivion. The world was loved, and now it's destroyed."

He was talking like we'd already come to the end. There had to be something more! A point to all this. A lesson. We just had to discover it. Otherwise, we were simply *enduring* our remaining years, till the bitter end.

Enduring shit like *this*.

He tugged on his shirt collar again. "Survivors chase whispers of sanctuary, roaming the ash. But the joke's on them. There's nothing out there."

There could be a Haven.

Maybe the point was to hope against hope—and stay decent. "You and your family could've done so much good in the world. But you chose to become nightmares instead."

"As opposed to you? Face it, Empress, you're evil. All the cards are."

"That's not true. Death isn't evil."

"If you believe that, then you don't know him very well."

"I've known him over lifetimes," I said vaguely, that blood pool calling my attention. Firelight reflected off it, triggering glimmers of a memory.

A summer dawn.

The overwhelming scent of roses.

I'd asked someone, "How fares my flower?"

The memory faded as fingers broke the surface of the blood. I sucked in a breath at the ghastly sight. A carnate was arising!

As if from a grave.

A hand emerged, but blood didn't stick to its porcelain skin. A tattoo appeared, black lettering in that same Goth script. Was it a number? Like a serial number? That couldn't be the accurate tally.

Selena didn't respond even to this . . . birth.

The carnate continued to float up, another hand budding. When I could yank my gaze away, I noticed that Vincent's deadened eyes had grown darker again. Watching the fight? Did that mean he was blind to his own surroundings?

Aric hadn't checked in for a while.

"This battle should be very interesting. Now that Death has realized you're gone, he'll take out the hunter, thinking you won't see."

"Death wouldn't do that to Jack. He has honor. Face it, Vincent, you're going to have to accept that some cards are good. . . ." My gaze slid back to the blood pool. To the Violet creature emerging.

The memory of my past with the Lovers fluttered so close to the surface. I recalled hills of roses, with thorns as big as daggers, and Violet's blood dripping from a height. I'd caught it in my cupped hands like rain.

Why had she been raised above me?

I gasped as the full scene hit me. The room seemed to shrink down on me, my lungs contracting. I'd bound Violet in vine, trapping her to . . . the blade of a windmill, the fabric-covered sail. Her blood had saturated the white material, dripping down for me to catch.

The structure had groaned under the weight of rose stalks, the Lovers' lands invaded by them. By me.

I'd ordered vines to burrow under her skin—while keeping her alive. As she'd spun round and round, her agonized screams had carried.

She'd looked younger than I was now. My stomach pitched.

The Army grinds on, a windmill spins. I'd believed Matthew had been warning me of the Azey's approach.

Oh, he had been—just not in the way I'd thought.

I'd kept Violet trapped like that for days. Until Vincent had come for her, sacrificing himself.

Come, join her, pay the price. There is no shame in surrender, Lover. I'd parted those thorns, calling him closer. *How artfully we beckon. How perfectly we punish.*

I'd sliced him to ribbons. I'd choked them both in vine. I'd clawed out their eyes and seeded sprouts in the sockets.

The twins hadn't necessarily been monsters in that life, but I had been, as evil as an invoked red witch.

And Aric wanted me to give her free rein? How could I say I knew Death—when I didn't even know myself?

"You're remembering!" Vincent blinked to clear his eyes. "At least you kept your promise to dispatch us together. But then you desecrated our remains. When my line's chroniclers found us, your hideous roses were flourishing inside our bodies!"

My breaths shallowed until I was on the verge of hyperventilating. Once I got us free of this place, I would take my memories like penance. For now, I had to help Selena.

Vincent said, "In this life, Vi and I will never be parted—never again."

Then where in this hellhole was she?

His eyes flared once more. "We've decided one of your lovers should die today. And it should be *your* choice. The Reaper? Or the hunter?"

I shook my head hard. "You can't make me choose."

"Then we'll decide for you." He tapped his chin. "The hunter will fall. Our carnates turn on him now."

Aric! Help Jack, please!

—A merry chase, wife.—

Had Selena stiffened? The desperate need to protect Jack filled me; was she feeling it too? Enough to shake this daze?

If anything could break through to her . . .

For Jack, Selena Lua could do *anything*.

In a taunting tone, Vincent said, "My children never make clean kills. The thieving hunter is about to die—badly."

Okay, Selena had definitely twitched.

When Vincent grew distracted—between creating a clone and communing with the ones fighting—I whispered to her, "J.D. is in danger, Selena. Do you think he knows why you don't have his six?" My God, I was sick. "All your strength and speed, just sitting on the bench while he's under attack."

Beneath that collar, her pulse point fluttered faster.

"What are you saying to her?" Vincent blinked rapidly.

"Um, your carnate needs you." I pointed at the pool beside Selena. Both of the clone's arms had risen, the top of a head crowning. Like a toddler, the creature repeatedly grasped at air, as if wanting to be picked up.

"Follow my voice," he crooned to the thing as he knelt at the edge of the pool—

WHAM.

In a spray of blood, Selena had snatched her nailed hand free then whipped her straightened arm out at Vincent. The line of her tensed limb connected with his throat.

His head snapped back. Lolled at an odd angle. His body collapsed backward.

Selena had awakened to break Vincent's neck—with one strike.

"The sensor!" I dove for it, but he'd dropped it into the blood beside the now sinking carnate. "Selena!" I twisted around to claw her collar off.

"It's okay," she murmured.

"NOT okay!" I wrenched the piece off her neck, throwing it away.

She turned toward me. "I saw . . . his thumb slip . . . nothing happened. The sensor for the collar is broken, has been broken." Without warning, she lunged at me.

"Selena, wait!"

"Evie!" she cried, hugging me tight. "You came for me."

"Oh! Um, you're going to be all right," I assured her as I stroked her tangled hair. "But we have to take Violet out too."

Selena pointed at Vincent. "Look at him."

He sprawled on his back, his pale glazed eyes fixed on the ceiling. His shirt had shifted to reveal a weird tattoo on his chest.

"He has his own brand," she added.

"I don't understand. Let me go look." I pried myself free from her, then took a step closer to him—

"*AH!*" I scrambled back, slipping in the blood, arms pinwheeling as I busted my ass. Below Vincent's collarbone, right over his heart, a wide-open eye stared at me.

Pale blue. Like a dead fish's.

"Oh, my God! What *is* that?" Never taking my gaze off it, I managed to turn over on my knees. When the eye blinked, I stifled a shriek. Real? Unreal?

"*That* is Violet," Selena bit out. "He told me he loved her so much, he took her into him before they were ever born. So the Empress could never separate them again."

Vincent had absorbed his twin in the womb. His sister had never been a . . . person.

Matthew's words: *The twins—inseparable. Never parted.* "B-but Vincent talked like she existed. The general did."

"Because they were crazy!"

No wonder Matthew had been confused. No wonder the twins had never used their most potent powers. They couldn't whisper together or clasp hands and swing arms.

The eye darted. Right. Left. Then it stilled, wide open, as glazed as her brother's.

Violet was dead.

I couldn't breathe, was ready to lose it, but as Matthew had told me, we weren't out of the woods yet. "Selena, I'll be right back. Getting your clothes. Okay?" I stumbled to the outer door. Combination-locked. Could Death break it down?

Aric? What's happening?

—The remaining carnates collapsed.—

Vincent's dead. The Lovers are gone. Are you and Jack all right?

—We will be if we can find you. Are you safe?—

We're okay. Just stuck in here.

—Help me find you.— I heard him yell, "Empress!"

You sound far away!

—And now?— He yelled, Jack joining him.

Closer.

While I waited for them to call out again, I went to the sink, hastily washing off the worst of the blood. Then I grabbed Selena's clothes and a roll of paper towels, returning to her. "Let's do a temporary bandage for your hand." I couldn't tell for sure, but I thought the nail had missed the bones. I folded paper towels, fashioning a wraparound covering. "Okay, time to get you dressed."

"Wh-where's J.D.?"

"He's coming. He's good. All the carnates dropped dead."

She nodded, kept nodding. Still nodding as her face crumpled. "Evie, he branded me." I didn't know what rattled me the most in this room: Violet's location or Selena's reaction.

She needed to cry. But the tears *had* been trained out of her.

I grabbed her good hand. "We're here. We're going to get through this."

I heard Aric's yell. *You're getting closer.*

"That's not J.D."

"Uh, let's get your shirt on." I helped her pull it on. "Boots, next."

Once I'd gotten her dressed, I said, "Hey, you should know, Aric is here with us. He's the reason we were able to get to you."

She jolted back. "Death?"

"He and Jack took on the carnates together. Baggers and slavers before them. They've been fighting side by side for days."

Pounding footfalls sounded as they closed in. *There's a combination lock on the door. Can you break it down?*

—What can't I do to reach you, Empress?—

At the revelation that Death was here, Selena started looking spacey. "No, no, stay with me, girl! He's not going to hurt you. He's helped us every step of the way. They're busting us free, okay?"

Seconds later, Aric's armored boot pounded the metal door. And again.

Send in Jack first. Selena's not good. You might freak her out even more.

Suddenly she loosed a scream that echoed off the walls. She was staring in horror at her hand, the uninjured one.

An icon was appearing, one that matched her brand. The Archer had been marked by the Lovers . . .

Twice.

40

Selena's gaze remained fixed on that icon even when we heard the door give way.

"Evie?" Jack called. "Selena?"

"In here."

He rushed inside, his gaze sweeping the area, showing no emotion at all the blood, the torture contraptions, Selena's condition.

Not yet.

"Where's the sister?"

"Look on his chest," I said.

Jack frowned at Vincent, then squinted. "Is that . . ."

"Yep. Vincent absorbed his twin."

"*Mère de Dieu.*" Collecting himself, he said, "It's over, then. You two all right?"

"I think so. *Define "all right."*

"Any of that blood yours, Evie?"

I shook my head. "And you?" He had a shallow slice down his neck, and a deeper slash over his arm.

"I'm fine. How you doing, Selena?" A muscle ticked in his jaw as he surveyed the Archer. "Come on, *fille*, answer me."

"J.D.?" Selena roused from her daze. "It's you!"

"You're goan to be okay. We're taking you home."

When Death entered, Selena scrambled back. "I-I can't do this!"

"He woan hurt you," Jack assured her, making both Aric and me do a double take. Going to one knee, Jack clasped her uninjured hand. "Trust me in this, *cher*." His position looked romantic.

I flushed with guilt that my thoughts had gone there.

"You gotta get me out of here," Selena pleaded. "I have to get out."

He reached for her, lifting her against his chest, her long hair spilling over his arm. "We're goan."

I told him, "Death and I will do a search for survivors."

With a nod, Jack carried Selena out of the room, murmuring soothing French words to her.

"And so the day is won, another card trumped." Aric's gaze roamed over me. "I'm surprised the Archer took their icon. Your witch didn't want it?"

I shook my head. "Let's search this place—then get out." I wanted to stand in the rain, taking another car wash/shower.

"Of course."

As Aric and I walked down that spray-painted hall, I said, "I remembered what I did to the Lovers in the past." To those kids.

I'd wondered if Arcana turned evil because of nature or nurture. I'd debated if evil was innate in us or manufactured by chroniclers. What if we made *each other* evil? Perhaps we traded torments from one game to the next, spreading a contagion.

Like the plague.

I wrapped my arms around myself. "I never want to be like that again. It's selfish, but I didn't want that icon. Aric, I'm done killing. I am *done*."

He shouldn't look so troubled by that statement. "The game begins in earnest. You have to be prepared, *sievā*. There might come a time when your ruthlessness would be rewarded."

I gazed up at him. "You weren't ruthless tonight. You could've let Jack die twice."

He stopped in the middle of the hall. "I wanted to prove to you that

I can be selfless." He slid off his gauntlet to press his bare hand against my face. "I can be what you need."

Those red lights illuminated his spellbinding face. When we were alone together, I felt like I was *supposed* to be with him. He would understand me better than Jack ever could. Aric knew my real history, what I'd really been like. And still, he wanted me.

But was I already too far gone for Jack?

"Release the mortal, Empress," seductive Death said. "Deveaux will help the Archer heal. She'll continue to be his perfect partner. Let them have each other with your blessing."

Jack had murmured to Selena in French. I'd thought that had been our thing. And, God, could I be any more petty?

"Your eyes are green," Aric observed. "Jealousy rules you."

I glanced away. "I can't control it."

"If you could, I'd demand to know how. I've experienced jealousy all my life. Of men whose skin doesn't kill. Of men who can cherish a wife and start a family with her. I have never known it like I do when I think of you and Deveaux together."

"If it's any consolation, I pictured you kissing someone else and felt just as jealous."

Though my words seemed to please him, he said, "But there will be no one else."

"By some quirk of fate it's me you can touch. It could just as easily have been Selena or even Tess."

"You think that's all I see in you? I told you I was raised to be a warrior scholar; my match must be one as well. Quintessence might read alongside me, but she's no warrior. Selena is all warrior, but no scholar." His thumb stroked my cheekbone. "I didn't *want* to fall in love with you, equating it to my own doom. I resisted with everything in me but was no match for your fierce courage and keen mind."

"Fierce? I'm the one who doesn't want to fight anymore."

"But when forced to, you fight to win. When I captured you, you devised a brilliant impromptu plan to destroy me and my allies."

"I lost."

"*Three* Arcana narrowly won. I admired you then. Perhaps more than admired. Still I resisted, until one night in our study."

I found myself leaning my face into his palm. So warm. Comforting. "What happened then?"

His amber irises lightened. "You were entranced with knowledge. You've a greedy intellect that must be fed. It called to my own, and I conceded defeat." He gave a humorless laugh. "Can you truly imagine Selena reading with me? Or Quintessence taking off her thumb so she could take my head?"

Sweet, good-natured Tess would've bawled in that conflict. The Archer would've chafed in Death's study, tossing her book away, demanding to go *do shit*.

Maybe Aric and I *were* perfect together.

Wait . . . "What's this about my intellect?" I stepped back, narrowing my eyes up at him. "I thought you found my musings 'banal and tedious.'"

He continued on, muttering, "Only when they were about Deveaux."

"Do it *now*," Selena bit out.

Jack glanced from her to the bowie knife he heated in a fire. Earlier, as they'd ridden together, he'd told her what he'd done to his own brand, and she would not be put off.

So we'd made camp in the same church, building a fire out of another pew.

Death and I sat on the other side of the flames. Selena had refused to look at him, acting as if he didn't exist. With a shrug, he'd taken out those chronicles again.

All night, he'd remained close to me. In our search of the Shrine, we'd found medical supplies, more food stores, fuel, weapons and ammo. A Prepper's wet dream. But no survivors.

Afterward he'd helped me wash in the rain, rinsing the blood from my hair and checking my healing injuries.

My body had mended, but my mind raced. And my emotions were going haywire.

Jealousy and guilt warred inside me. . . .

"The pain's even worse than the first time," Jack warned Selena, but I knew she'd still go through with it.

She'd been like a blank-eyed zombie—until she'd learned of a way to get rid of that brand. "I don't give a shit. I might have to wear their icon"—she'd used her injured hand to claw at it—"but I don't ever have to see this brand again." She tugged down her shirt for Jack, baring her ravaged skin with her typical stoicism.

"All right, then." He withdrew the blade from the flames, then knelt before her. Again, his position looked romantic. Again, I flushed with guilt that my thoughts had gone there.

Death paused his reading. —*They've been through tortures that we will never know and can never understand.*—

Jack and Selena had already been ideal for each other. Now they'd bonded in this. Both had survived the Lovers; both would wear matching scars.

With one hand, Jack brought the red-hot blade closer. He clamped his other hand over her shoulder. She never took her dark gaze from his as he scalded her, marking her forever. Binding the two of them for life.

Under his voice, Aric said, "*Look* at them, Empress."

As if I could look at anything else.

In the three months I'd been away, Jack had changed so much. His heart could change. He wasn't twenty yet! With me out of the picture, he could love the Archer.

By choosing Jack, I would doom not only Aric, but Selena as well.

41

"This is blowing my ever-loving mind," Selena muttered as we watched Death and Jack riding point together.

The four of us were heading south on horseback, along the slavers' alternate route, a shortcut recently discovered and mapped by the Azey.

The "day" was cold and black, with spates of drizzle. Every now and then, I thought I spied a snowflake—like the sole one I'd seen at Aric's—but it always turned out to be a bit of ash.

"If someone had told me a week ago that I'd be riding with Death," Selena continued, "I would've shoved his head up his ass."

The four of us could've taken a truck, trailering the horses, but we all had reasons to ride instead.

Selena wanted to heal more before she faced everyone at Fort Arcana. Her accelerated regeneration was erasing her bruises, mending her new burn wound and her hand. She thought she'd be able to draw her cherished bow soon. She'd been stuffing herself, already gaining weight. But she scratched at that icon so much, she'd taken to wearing gloves at all times.

Jack had voted for horseback because he burned to roust out any other slavers that had set up in Azey territory. No takers so far.

I'd been desperate for time to come to a decision. We were due back at the outpost tonight, and I still hadn't made my choice.

Death had laughed at the idea of trailering his horse. Which was understandable, considering what that stallion had done to those chronicle-seeking clones.

Thanatos bench pressed three eighty and left us a pile of carnate chum. . . .

Selena steered her mount closer to mine. "You didn't hear—because your senses are like a rock's—but those two were talking earlier."

"About what?" Deepening my voice, I imitated a guy, "You fought well, worthy foe."

"I know, right? So J.D. goes, 'I'm Jackson Deveaux. We've been in battle together. You goan to give me your real name, or what?' The Reaper was all stumped, like he's not used to being asked that."

He wasn't. And he was even less used to answering that question. Aric would never tell Jack.

Selena continued, "But then the Reaper says, 'My name is Aric Domīnija.'"

My eyes went wide. Just like everything else about Aric, his name had come out into the world. I found my lips curving. Until I thought of my looming decision. Pain awaited me either way.

Selena cocked her head. "If J.D. can tolerate Domīnija, then I guess I can too. It's easier when the Reaper isn't raising a sword or wearing that creepy helmet."

Aric had kept it stowed on his saddle more often than not. To some degree, he must trust Selena and Jack not to strike. And maybe he felt our strength in numbers against an outside threat.

Perhaps he'd realized all these fascinating new interactions were easier with his face unconcealed.

Jack received a transceiver call from Rodrigo then, answering with important-sounding military lingo.

"Didn't I tell you he was a leader?" Selena all but sighed. "Isn't he amazing?"

I got the weirdest impression that she was *selling* me on him. Or was she just bragging?

278

"I'm glad you got to see J.D. with the army last night."

Jack had given an inspiring speech about being a force for good—providing protection for survivors. And he'd outlined a game plan.

Azey South was marching to Louisiana to start work on a new settlement. Azey North would descend upon the Shrine, eliminating the Bagger infestation to secure all the supplies.

Then the two armies would unify again to form New Acadiana.

Jack had been magnetic, giving folks a new story to tell. Hope had been palpable. Even as the temperature dropped—and night endured.

I gazed up at the murky sky. "Selena, you ever think the sun will come out?" The question reminded me of Jack's words: *You ever think we deserve better than the Basin?* If he'd had the courage to hope, shouldn't I as well?

Selena rolled her eyes. "If the sun can *dis*appear, it can *re*appear. Really, Evie. *Duh.*" She took out her canteen, trying to open it, about to take the top off with her teeth.

I leaned over and yanked it from her. What was I going to do with this girl? "Here." I handed it back, opened for her.

She chugged, swiping her coat sleeve over her chin. "Hey, drop back a little. Want to talk to you."

Was she finally going to confide in me about her ordeal? I'd asked her a few times, but she always refused. "Anything you want to discuss, Selena. I'm here."

"Not about . . . that. I've put that time out of my head." The circles under her eyes belied her nonchalance.

"You can't just ignore it."

Her signature *the hell* expression firmly in place, she said, "Do you think about the cannibals you laid out? Or the time you almost ate raw human? Or the plague victims you offed? Yeah, I heard about that. You don't dwell on painful stuff. Neither will I."

I hadn't given up on getting her to confide in me, but I backed off for now. "Then what's on your mind?"

"What's going on with you and Jack?"

Excellent question from the Archer. "Well, we talked after his speech, about the past few days and such." Without a word, he'd led me behind a tent. . . .

"How you leaning, peekôn?"

"I wish you hadn't broken your promise to me." He kept risking his life, going above and beyond, and I wasn't having it.

"These Azey soldiers respond to courage, and they needed to see it in someone they might back. Can you understand my thinking?"

I could. At so many points in this journey, I'd marveled at Jack's bravery. Though he was vulnerable, he put himself out there. Death was impervious, yet he only wanted to return to his sanctuary.

However . . . *"And in the Shrine, Jack? What was that?"*

Color tinged his cheeks. *"I've probably done smarter things, me."*

"If I picture us together, I see us working as a team, making decisions together. Not this Jack-runs-off-to-save-the-day shit." Otherwise, I should be with Death. Who at least was doing better—not worse. . . .

Now I batted away a wisp of ash, telling Selena, "He and I discussed my grandmother. I still want to find her, but Azey South's marching tomorrow."

Jack had grinned at my concern. "I can give them damn directions, Evie. Me and you'll take some men and head to the Outer Banks. After we find her, we'll meet up with the others in Louisiana." He sounded so confident. *"You want to end the game, Evangeline? Then we will. Remember, together we can do anything. . . ."*

"Then Jack and I touched on other stuff." Such as him finding something meaningful with the babe beside me.

He pinned my gaze with his own. "Selena's an ally and a friend, but she'll never be more than that. Because it's you for me, peekôn." He curled his finger under my chin. *"When she's nearby, she doan make everything in me light up like goddamned fireworks. You think I can give her my heart? After I already gave it to you? I can't offer what I doan have."*

I cleared my throat, face flushing under Selena's scrutiny. "And, uh, we discussed Death."

"*If you choose the Reaper because you feel more for him, then I got to accept that, me. But doan choose him because you got sympathy for someone with a shit fate.*" He leaned in closer, resting his forehead against mine. "*I got one too.*"

"*What does that mean?*"

"*I told you I couldn't keep doing life after the Flash, not without you. That's changed. I will go on—'cause I got a job to do now—but I will never be right. I've got to feel you with my every step, Evangeline.*"

I managed a casual shrug for the Archer. "We didn't get to talk long. Rodrigo needed him for that Shrine incursion meeting." Jack had pressed a kiss to the top of my head, then reluctantly left me.

"Uh-huh. And did you talk to Death?"

"Briefly. He was scarce for most of the night." At every opportunity, he read those chronicles, looking more engrossed than I'd ever seen him. Translating them must be critical, because his campaign to win me had taken a backseat.

When I caught up with him, I'd pressed him to tell me about his history with the Emperor.

"*I can deny you nothing,*" Aric said with a defeated exhalation. "*In the game before last, he killed you. I hadn't found you yet, hadn't had a chance to determine what you were like. Or if we could be together.*" He clenched his fists, his eyes gone starry. "*The Emperor murdered my wife.*"

"*Who took him out?*"

"*I did. To avenge you and punish him for separating us. In that game, I harvested your icon from him.*" Aric's voice went hoarse as he gazed down at his hand. "*I stared at it as centuries passed me by.*"

So what would Aric do now if I chose to be with Jack?

"You've got a decision to make." Selena handed me back the canteen to close. "And frankly, I don't see what the issue is."

With all honesty, I told her, "The issue is that I don't know what's going on in my head right now."

"Well, figure it the hell out."

I waved airily. "There! Done. *Voilà*."

"Seriously, if you can figure out how to get Domīnija and J.D. to ride together and be civil, this should be cake."

I sighed, about to tell her it was complicated, brushing her off. But how could I expect her to confide in me when I wouldn't do the same in return? "I love Jack. But I have a connection to Aric." One forged over millennia, like an endless wave along a shore.

Today, he'd gazed at me, but not with his usual confidence. He'd looked shaken—as if he suspected I was drawing away. But I wasn't. My heart remained divided. "I . . . I think I've fallen for him as well." He'd come so far, had made such strides. I believed he could be a good partner for me.

If he didn't turn to coercion again. I dreaded the trick up his sleeve.

"Shit, girl. What'd you go and do that for?"

I glared. "Like I could help it?" My dreams of both of them had given me glimpses into how they'd become the men they were today. But those dreams hadn't helped me come to a decision.

She tugged a silvery blond tress from her cheek. "Granted, Death's different from what I thought, but would you really choose him over J.D.?"

"Aric told me I should give my blessing to you and Jack."

She snorted. "You can bless us all you want, but it's not happening."

I frowned at her. "You told me things had changed between you two."

"Yeah. As in, I made peace with the fact that I'll never be with him. It was a done thing between you two before I ever came into the picture."

"Why are you so sure?"

"After he heard you didn't want to have anything to do with him, J.D. took it bad—like head in his hands, pulling out his hair. So we got wasted together. I told him how I felt about him, and I tried to kiss him."

Jealousy scored me.

"And do you know what he did?"

I held my breath.

"He pushed me away, telling me that the people of his mother's blood fall in love once. They pray they get it right—because it can't be changed. He told me his mother loved his father, unrequited, and nineteen years of misery couldn't shake it."

The root of his mother's pain.

Selena gazed at him. "That's why you and J.D. have to get back together." The Archer's eyes could be so dark and cutting, but for Jack alone, they went soft. "I can't stand for him to hurt like that."

"You and he never . . . ?"

"Never. He doesn't even see me when you're around."

I felt guilty for doubting him in this. Maybe I could give him my trust again?

"Besides, I'm not settling for someone who can't love me totally. I mean, check me out—do I look like a girl who needs to settle?" She squared her shoulders. "A make-do runner-up? I've been number one at everything I've ever done."

Normally I would have groaned to hear her talk like that. Now a bit of my worry lifted. She would recover from the Lovers; I believed that.

"I'm not going to stop being number one just for a guy."

"What if the guy's perfect for you in every other way?"

"Not in the way that counts most." She admitted, "I even fooled around with Finn—in the form of Finn, mind you—to distract me. But the Magician's still hung up on Lark."

"What about Gabriel? You don't remember this, but before we went back in time, we got chased by the soldiers. The first person he evacuated was you. The Archangel has fallen for the Archer."

"Whoa, I was talking about *hooking up* with another card. But to fall for an Arcana?" She met my gaze. "Only an idiot would do that."

I didn't argue. I'd fallen for Aric, despite loving Jack. *Idiot* seemed fair.

42

FORT ARCANA

"You bagged the Lovers!" Finn hobbled into the courtyard to meet us, Cyclops at his heels.

When Selena paled, Jack stepped in to say, "They're done, podna." He dismounted, then helped her down. "I'll tell you about it once we've rested up."

Rest. All I wanted was to drop facedown and starfish my cot. But I was itching to check on Matthew.

Plus, my decision. I gazed at Jack, then Death.

After the Flash, life was so precarious that time seemed to pass differently. A day, much less a week, was an eternity. I couldn't string this along. In any case, the army was leaving tomorrow a.m.

Jack would need to know if he was setting out with them—or heading to North Carolina with me.

Aric had waited long enough.

He alighted from his saddle to help me from mine. On the ground, I turned from him, from the question burning in his amber eyes.

Yes, I needed to give them an answer. I just wished I had one.

I faced Finn. "Where is everyone? Where's Matthew?" I hadn't heard any calls. But then, I'd been asleep in the saddle all the way up to the minefield.

"Joules and company vamoosed a couple of mornings ago. They

smoked out the remaining traitors and exiled them. According to Joules, they were 'big feckers.'"

"Gabriel was okay with leaving?" He'd been so worried about Selena.

Finn sliced a glance at Death. "With you guys all heading home, and the Priestess hanging around, Matthew warned about convergence, was kinda stern about it."

Circe remained? On the way back here, whenever I'd passed a stream, memories of the High Priestess arose. In one, she and I had laughed so hard we'd cried. We would finally stop, look at each other, only to burst out laughing again. . . .

"Joules & Crew told me they'd check back in over the winter," Finn said. "Maybe spend the holidays with us."

Did holidays still exist? Okay, sure. "Is Matthew in bed?"

Finn's excited demeanor dimmed. "Uh. He kind of . . . split, too. Rode out the other day. I don't know where to."

"What do you mean by *split*?" My glyphs began to glow.

"Hold it, blondie, Matto's a grown dude, and there was no stopping him."

I shoved my hair from my face, my gaze darting. "He's got a huge head start." He'd already been on the road when he'd visited me in that vision! Had he been telling me good-bye, for *good*? "I have no idea how to find him."

"Don't," Aric said quietly.

"Excuse me?"

"The Fool knows this game and this world better than anyone. He can take care of himself."

"But he can't see his own future! And he was so sick." I glanced at Jack and Selena. Both looked torn.

"Matto was doing tons better than before," Finn assured me.

"*Sievā*, he'll travel with another person, reading his companion's future to safeguard his own. You know his weaknesses, but you ignore his strengths."

"What does that mean?"

His blond brows drew together. "Again, Empress, let him *rest*."

Could I? I ached to make sure he was okay. But I didn't want to be part of the problem. "Wh-when will he come back? Will I ever see him again?"

Aric's eyes were grave. "He'll find you when you least expect it. . . ."

In Finn and Selena's tent, I dropped onto a spare cot, still numb over Matthew's disappearance.

Jack and Aric followed me inside. They both stood so tall and built, seeming to soak up all the oxygen in the area.

"*Coo-yôn* will be okay," Jack said. "He sometimes went off by himself."

Even if I accepted that Matthew wasn't in danger, I couldn't accept that he'd gone out on the road alone. Months ago, I'd left Finn's by myself, and I had never known such loneliness. For the first time in my life, I'd had no friends or family to talk to, no one expecting me.

Kind of like Aric Domīnija's life for the last two millennia.

My couple of days versus his eons.

Too much to process. "Can we please talk in the morning?" I fell back on my old argument: no one could make me choose before I was ready. "Is there an extra tent where Aric can stay?"

"*Ouais*." Jack rubbed his hand over his black stubble. "But, Evie, before you make a decision, you need to consider something."

"What?"

He turned to Aric with an almost guilty expression on his face. "You saved my life, Domīnija. You've done me right. But I can't lose my girl again."

Aric clenched his fists—as if he knew what Jack was going to say.

Jack faced me. "What if you can't stop the game? It spools on as long as more than one player lives, all the Arcana aging. Which means the Reaper's got to have a patsy."

"What are you talking about?"

"He's goan to kill every Arcana that's a threat. If you're the last two left, one of you *will* die first, leaving the 'winner' to walk the earth as an immortal. What if you get to be eighty by the time he dies? It doan matter if you're Arcana—at that age, you'll hurt, you might be sick—and you'll stay like that for centuries. How're you goan to fight in the next game?"

I swallowed. I'd been horrified by the idea of living so long—more so if I was forever cursed to be sick, to be in pain.

I gazed at Aric; he stared back at me as if his world was crumbling around him—and he could do nothing but *let it*.

"He's smart enough to have figured out all of the angles," Jack continued. "He woan condemn either of you to that, so he'll keep one other Arcana alive to take that fall, to be the winner."

I'd never thought of this. Jack with his tricky mind. "Aric, how had you planned to get around this?"

"We intend to end the game. But if we can't, the odds are exceedingly slim that we'll live to be eighty in this world."

"Answer the question."

His shoulders rose and fell. "Lark volunteered. She doesn't need youth or strength as long as she has her creatures. She wants to repopulate their numbers."

My jaw slackened. "You should've told me. Once again, you mapped out my existence without mentioning your plans to me."

Brows drawn, he admitted, "Yes."

My head started to pound again. I rubbed my temples, wondering how I'd gotten myself into this situation. No answers came to me; my mind limped along. "W-we'll talk in the morning. Just, both of you, give me time to think."

Jack opened his mouth to say more, then closed it. At the tent flap, he murmured, "*Peekôn*, it'll always be Evie and Jack." Then he was gone.

Aric crossed the tent, kneeling before me. In a low tone, he said, "I had something I was going to offer you that would guarantee you chose me. But you would accuse me of strategizing, of coercion."

This explained the recent doubt in his expression. "The trick up your sleeve. Your 'gift.' I've dreaded this."

"You see me in such a harsh light." He exhaled wearily. "And it's all my own doing. Fear not, I won't play it."

"Tell me what you were going to give me."

He shook his head. "I'm doomed either way. If I win you like that, it would be as good as losing." He removed a gauntlet. Eyes aglow, he laid his hand against my face, savoring the touch as if it would be his last. "Empress, I *have* learned about you in these days. I've realized that I can't compel you to go with me—or it's meaningless. And that I should tell you everything that affects your future. I've learned, *sievā*, but have I learned too late?"

I didn't reply, refusing to commit to anything.

"If you choose me, I want it to be because you love me in turn," he rasped, "so I offer you nothing this night. Just my hope."

Even in the face of my anger and confusion, Aric pulled at my heart. "It means a lot for you to say this."

"But does it mean *enough*?"

This man was a part of me, had been for epochs. I felt our soul-deep bond, could almost hear that endless wave along the shore. Still I had to whisper, "I don't know."

43

I'd been dozing on my borrowed cot when the Magician returned with Cyclops.

Finn maneuvered himself on his own cot, propping his leg up. "Can't sleep, blondie?" The wolf lolled on the floor beside him. *Thump, thump, thump* went his massive tail.

I shook my head. "Where's Selena?"

"Talking to Jack. Pep talking him, if I had to guess. You got a choice to make, huh? Whole fort's speculating about it. Seems like you'll be getting scarce tomorrow either way."

"Yep." I sat up, rubbing my eyes.

"So which bachelor will it be?"

"I know who you would pick for me."

He nodded. "The Cajun's a class act. Death allied with Ogen, who flattened a mountain—while I was inside it. Ergo . . ."

"Death also helped us rescue Selena, and he saved Jack's life."

Finn scratched behind one of the wolf's scarred ears. "I get it. Things change. People change. We just have to keep up with the program."

"Like with Lark?"

"You think I should give it a shot with her?"

"I do. I know that she's got a good heart, and she cared for you."

Cyclops's tail thumped harder. So Lark was listening in?

"Yeah, I figure my chickie's worth some couple's therapy. Hey, I hope it's cool, but the wolf is staying here with me. As soon as I can ride, Cyclops will guide me to Lark."

"It's cool. I feel better knowing you have a plan."

If I chose Jack, I'd never see Finn or Lark again.

Aric.

Matthew? "Finn, what was Matthew like before he left? Did he bring supplies with him? Food?" He was always hungry.

"A metric shit ton of food."

"Did he tell you good-bye before leaving?"

"Kinda. You know Matto. He said a bunch of weird stuff."

"Like what?" Weird stuff from him could be critical.

Finn peered at the tent roof. "He told me, 'I see far' and 'the gods mark us all.' And something like 'All is not what it seems.' I thought he was kind of joking around, but he didn't laugh."

"Anything else?"

Finn snapped his fingers. "Oh, oh, and right before he rode out, he caught my eye and said, 'I've made peace with it.'"

With *what*?

Long after Finn had passed out, I remained awake, listening to the rhythm of his breathing, his sleepy murmurs.

Sometimes he talked about surfing. "Sickest curl ever." Most times, he talked about his parents. "They coulda made it. Cali would be safe. Cali's always the best."

Strangely, Selena never returned to the tent. Where would she be this late?

I was still concerned about her, and I'd gotten used to having her around. As these hours crawled by, I wouldn't have minded some company. I was half tempted to go call on Circe.

Instead, I mused over my choices, readying to make the most important decision of my life.

I called to mind Aric's face. He was connected to me, a soul mate.

Leaving him to wallow in misery went against everything in me. He did have a shit fate. But it didn't have to be.

When I imagined him pacing the lonely halls of his home, forever alone, my eyes pricked with tears. But a future with him would be filled with difficulties.

Immortality. Intrigues. Plotting.

I did believe he was learning how to treat me and would change even more—because he was *trying* to be a better man for me, a trait I'd always admired in Jack.

How hard Aric had fought to save his rival's life. For me. . . .

I pictured Jack's face. He was my first love, and we'd claimed each other in more ways than one. But he had so much going for him, so many things to distract him from me. He'd taken control of armies and had become a respected man—as he'd obviously craved since boyhood.

If I chose him, I'd have to find a way to trust him. I'd have to accept that he would never share his secrets. I'd have to throw all in and hope that he didn't disappoint me.

Mistrust. Fear. Vulnerability.

Both would help me find my grandmother. Aric could do it faster, but Gran might be out for blood if she saw him. . . .

At what should have been dawn, the roosters crowed, demanding my answer.

At what should have been dawn, it came to me.

I imagined myself on a road, my life as a journey. On one side of the road was Aric. On the other side was Jack. Who would I beckon to join me?

I knew what I had to do.

44

As I hurried across the fort, the air was colder than I'd felt it A.F. My breath smoked. Whenever I had to step off the plankway, frozen mud crunched beneath my boots.

I stopped outside Aric's borrowed tent. I could hear him pacing, his spurs clinking. I knew he hadn't slept. "Can I come in?"

He opened the flap, ushering me inside. He scanned my face. Flashed me a look of disbelief. "You've chosen the mortal."

I might feel like I was supposed to be with Aric, but . . . "I fell for Jack before you changed toward me. It was a done thing."

Aric's eyes slid closed, but not before I saw the anguish in them.

I'd chosen Jack for more reasons than one. I'd decided what I wanted to do with my life: blow up the machine—and remain a decent person. I would repurpose myself, return to Haven, and rebuild a life—with Jack, Gran, and one day Matthew.

I would fight to make life better for people, which meant being out in the world. Instead of barricading myself inside Death's castle of lost time.

Aric's eyes opened. "By his actions, I wonder if Deveaux still feels the same way? I had a conversation with him, explaining some realities—"

"Stop, please. I'm going to trust him, just as he trusts me."

"And so it's . . . done?" Aric looked as if he couldn't reconcile this, like he might double over—or crush something. "I felt so strongly about you, I thought . . . I had no doubt that you must feel the same." His expression was baffled. He'd never been in love before, didn't understand what had befallen him.

Like an affliction? I shook that thought away. "Aric, I do love you. But I loved Jack first."

"How much of your decision rested on what he told you yesterday?"

"I could never expect Lark to play patsy for us." And how would that program work with Finn in the picture? "If that's the only way to be with you . . . can't you see why it'd be wrong?"

"It was a backup plan. In case we're unable to end the game."

"But you don't believe we can?"

Curt shake of his head. Honest as ever.

"You want me to turn into that horrifying witch, unleashing a power in me that should never be brought to light. I can't do it. I can't live like that."

His pupils were blown, as if he were in shock. Gritting his teeth, he reached forward to clutch my nape. His other fist clenched so hard, metal groaned. Voice a harsh rasp, he said, "Do you remember when the Fool sent you a vision of me, one with nothing but blackness and ruins?"

I nodded up at him. "You told me that's what it's like in your head. You asked me if I thought Death should dream in color."

"*Sievā*, when we were together, I *began to*. Will you banish me back to that place of nothingness?"

My heart stuttered, my eyes watering.

"Even now, your tears gut me." He dropped his hand, turning from me. "I can't . . . I can't be here."

"Wait, can't we please just talk? Are we never going to see each other again?"

He twisted around. "You think I can be near you? Knowing I have no hope of you? You'd curse me to that? My immortal lifetime wasn't enough time spent coveting you?"

Tears fell. "I don't want to hurt you." For strength, I slipped my hand into my pocket, rubbing that ribbon. I'd made up my mind to give it back to Jack. Totally decided.

So why did I feel this unbearable grief to part from Aric? This *wrongness*? Why was I wrecked to the core? "I'm just having a hard time accepting that this is good-bye. Forever."

"Oh no, not forever," he grated, his eyes dazzling with pain. "You'll win this game, wife, I'll make sure of it. Then *you* will wait an eternity for *me* to return." With a last consuming look, he said, "After so much killing, it comes back to me, Empress. Something dies in me today." He strode away.

For long moments, I stared at nothing, my body trembling. Had I just made the worst mistake of my life?

Aric Domīnija was a magnificent, brilliant man who wanted me above all things. And I loved him. I knew I always would.

One love fated. One love endless.

I stumbled out into the dark morning. Dazed, I made my way to Jack. I needed him to enfold me in his arms, to murmur in French that everything would be okay.

And I wanted to find out what Aric had told him. What *realities*?

I entered his tent

My breath hitched. Empty? His bag was gone, his books. I dropped to my knees to look under his cot. He'd taken his stash of whiskey bottles.

Jack had left me.

45

I was hyperventilating by the time I found a letter next to a two-way radio on his desk. Tears hit the paper as I read:

> *Evangeline,*
> *I'm riding out early with the army.*
> *I know who you're going to choose, know it won't be me. Now that I'm more familiar with that bastard, I've got to face facts. You weren't with him because he messed with your head—you were with him because you wanted him over me. You and Death have something that I don't understand, and I've got to start trying to get over you.*
> *To pull your thorn from my skin.*
> *Doesn't mean I won't be looking over my shoulder, praying you'll come running after me. Or pick up that radio and tell me to rush back to you.*
> *Selena's riding out with us, says that'll make you jealous and up my chances. I'm not above that, peekôn.*
> *But I don't expect it. You're going to head east toward the last of your family. And once you find your grandmother,*

you'll need to keep her safe. She doesn't belong out on the road any more than you do. Both of you will be protected at the Reaper's home. Hole up and plant your roots there.

Sunlamps and food and safety. Sounds mighty nice. I want that for you.

Because I love you.

This might be the most noble thing I've ever done. Noble, for the record, hurts like a blade to the heart.

Je t'aimerai toujours,

Jack

Je t'aimerai toujours. I will love you forever.

I snatched up the radio, pressing the talk button. "Jack!"

Static.

"Can you hear me? I'm coming to you!"

Nothing.

Radio in hand, I stuffed the note into my jacket and hurried back to Finn's tent for my bug-out bag. He still slept.

I whispered, "Good-bye, Magician." Cyclops raised his head and sighed. I bent to scratch his frizzy head. "Thank you for everything, boy. I hope I get to see you and Lark again some day." I grabbed my bag, then sprinted for my horse.

How much of a head start did Jack have? Surely I could reach the army in a couple of hours. The convoy would be hauling trailers, and the roads sucked. I could follow the wheel ruts.

Jack had no idea how much I loved him. I'd never even said the words, "I love you" to him. The urgency I felt to reach him, to tell him, strangled me.

When I careened into the stable, my poor mare's expression: *Oh, for fuck's sake.*

I saddled her in record time, then tore out of the gate. Shit, the mines! How to get around them? I knew *about* where they were.

I spotted tracks in the frozen mud. Thanatos's hoofprints. Using them to reach Jack didn't seem fair; I still did.

Past the mines and rock forest, I followed the river toward the bridge.

In the distance, I saw Death atop a rise, his shoulders back, his helmet off, his pale hair blowing in the wind.

Even from here, even amidst my panic, I felt his longing. In another lifetime, I could have been happy with him. In another lifetime, perhaps I would be.

With tears threatening once more, I turned from him. *Don't look back, Evie, don't look back.* He'd see it as some kind of sign. As encouragement. I knew this.

But I wanted one last glimpse of the man who'd turned my existence inside out. We locked gazes, his eyes like stars.

Time seemed to slow. I thought of the tattoos on his chest and his centuries of longing. Now he knew what he was missing. He'd told me the week we'd been apart had been gut-wrenching; I was leaving him for the rest of this lifetime. Banishing him to a place of nothingness.

How could he endure it?

Doubt filled me. No, I loved Jack. I was going to be with Jack. I would focus on the road ahead, on the future. Instead of the past.

When I dragged my gaze from Aric, his blood-curdling roar echoed across the countryside.

I pressed the back of my hand against my mouth, stifling a sob as I reached the bridge. Speeding across Circe's abyss, I gave her tears in toll. . . .

For over an hour, I rode, checking the radio's reception at every rise. Uninterrupted static.

I thought I spied a snowflake, wafting down like a petal. Probably just more ash—

No, there was another. And another. Real snow! This had to be a good sign. If the world couldn't yet improve, at least it could *change*.

If the sun could *dis*appear, it could *re*appear.

I tried the radio again. Nothing.

The flakes grew into a flurry. Soon a layer of snow stuck to the ground, painting it white. Did the air feel fresher? Fluffy down blanketed soot, and I welcomed it, even as riding became precarious.

Was Aric seeing the snow? Did it remind him of his childhood home in the north? I could scarcely comprehend that I would never see him again.

Every other minute, a snowflake would hit one of my eyes directly, the sting blurring my vision. I would blink to clear my eyes, and a detail from one of my last encounters with Death would blossom in my mind.

His hooded gaze as he'd said, "Can you comprehend what it's like to touch her after so long without? For this bliss, I'll risk the bullet. I'll *take* a bullet."

Blink.

The way his hands had shaken when he'd held me, as if I was the most delicate and precious thing in the entire world. ". . . you must know that you have my love. It's given, *sievā*. Wholly entrusted to you. Have a care with it."

Blink.

His murmurs late in the night: "There's so much about the game I could teach you. So much about life you could teach me. Let's begin this, little wife."

Blink. Blink. Blink. My tears mingled with crystalline snow. . . .

Time passed, the landscape becoming rockier, icier, white fluff obscuring the trail.

I passed an abandoned mine entrance—never welcome—and increased my speed even more. How long had I gone without checking the radio? I urged the mare up a steep grade. "Go, go!" At the top, I pressed the talk button. "Jack? Please answer me!"

"Evie? . . . can't . . . you."

"I'm coming for you!" Down the slippery hill I went, the mare's hooves skidding on ice. Spurring the horse, I crested a higher rise. "Can you hear me?"

From this vantage, I could see the army in the far distance! They'd descended into a valley. The lights of the slow-moving convoy looked like a glowworm wending through the snowy dark. But I didn't see a trail down.

"*Bébé?* Where are you?"

"I can see the Azey trucks! I'm on the rise looking over the valley!"

"You coming with me, *peekôn?*" he rasped. "For true, you chose Ole Jack?"

"Like you could get rid of me that easily, Cajun." I grinned madly, convinced I'd made the right decision. "I don't ever want to be apart again."

I heard Selena in the background saying, "Told you it would work, dumbass." She sounded like her eye-rolling self. As ever, she was by his side, watching his six. "We should go get her before she breaks her stupid neck."

I'd better get used to the Archer, because apparently, she'd be living in New Acadiana with me and Jack, Matthew and Gran. "I *can* ride to you." I held my hand over my eyes, squinting against the snow. "Just tell me the best way down."

"*Non*, you stay put!" Jack quickly said. "The way's icy. I know where you are; we're coming to you!"

"Okay, I'll be here." I couldn't stop smiling. *This* was why we fought to survive. For love.

Vincent had it all wrong. *I'd* had it wrong. Love wasn't the most destructive force in the universe.

Love is *the universe.* That *is the point.*

Between breaths, Jack said, "So this is snow, huh?" He'd never seen it before.

Excitement bubbled up, and I started laughing. I pressed the radio button. "Isn't it amazing? Everything looks clean."

Over his mount's pounding hoofbeats, he said, "Still can't believe you're coming with me. I'm goan to take you home, Evangeline Greene!" The joy in his voice sent my heart soaring. "Goddamn, I love you, woman."

I parted my lips to finally say those three words—

—*QUAKE BEFORE ME.*—

I jerked in the saddle. Arcana call?

Dread spiked inside me. "Jack!" I cried into the radio. "The Emperor's here! You've got to get away!"

BOOM! BOOM!

Explosions, one after another, rocked that snowy valley. A split second later . . .

The white ground turned black in an outward surge. A blast of heat.

A scorching shockwave slammed me, seared my face. Flung me off the horse. I hurtled through the air. Landed on the back of the rise.

I plummeted down the slope, clutching the radio, screaming for Jack.

How far had he ridden? A rock sliced my head. Was he outside the blast? The air turned to sulfur. How far?

I crashed face-first into a boulder. Bone snapped. The radio shattered. Quakes hammered the ground.

Blood sprayed from my mouth as I screamed, *"Jack!"* I struggled to my hands and knees. I crawled up the shuddering hill.

My vision was blurred . . . sight couldn't be right. Smoke rose in a mushroom plume, as if from a nuclear bomb.

Had he escaped? I shrieked, *"JACK!"*

I made the rise. Sheer will to stand. I gazed into the valley.

At hell.

Flumes of lava spewed from the ground. Flames so hot they consumed rock. From the two mountain peaks, more lava poured, filling that valley. A seething red pool where the army used to be.

Fighting realization: Jack was down there. "No, *NO!*" Vines sprang from the ground, following me as I ran toward the firestorm. The heat blistered me even from this distance.

Just before I reached a curtain of red, an arm seized me around my waist.

Death stood behind me? He'd ridden after me?

Between heaving breaths, Aric said, "You can't . . . save the mortal. The Emperor . . . advances. We leave—*now*."

"NO! I have to get to Jack!" I fought, but Aric snatched me against his chest. I clawed at his armor, at the scalding metal. "Let me go to him! Let me GO!" Nothing would keep me from Jack. My vines coiled around Death, trying to pry loose his viselike hold on me.

"Flames will kill you!"

"I don't care, don't care! You want Jack dead! You want me not to save him! I can find him!"

Death gripped my shoulders, shaking me till my head rolled. He twisted me around toward the valley. "Do you see any signs of life? No human could've survived this!"

"Don't ever underestimate him! Everyone does and he ALWAYS surprises them. He's alive!"

"Look upon this sight, Empress!" The valley floor was blanketed in lava, had to be thirty feet deep. Waves of it lapped at this rise. "Mark this image. *Where* will you search for him?"

I didn't know, just knew I wanted to be with Jack. As Aric dragged me away, I fought him even harder.

The Arcana clamored.

—*The Emperor struck.*—

—*Took out the Archer.*—

—*The Moon sets. The Moon rises . . . no more.*—

Was that last one *Matthew*'s voice?

MATTHEW, I NEED YOU! Where is Jack?

Silence.

ANSWER ME!

Selena had been riding directly beside Jack, watching his six. If she were dead . . .

"AHHHHHHH!" I screamed my pain, my fury. The earth trembled again—from me.

"You'll share a grave with him!"

"*Good!* Let me go!" Death kept taking me farther from Jack. I stretched my arms out, fingers splayed toward the heat. "He can't be dead." I sobbed. "Can't. *NO, NO, NOOOO!*"

"You want to follow the mortal? Get your revenge first. The Emperor mocks your pain."

I could hear that fiend in my head—laughing.

The red witch exploded inside me, a force that could *never* be contained. I shrieked, "You will *PAY!*"

As the Emperor laughed and laughed, Death murmured in my ear, "I have your grandmother, *sieva*. That was the gift I spoke of. We'll teach you how to kill the Emperor. You'll avenge Deveaux."

"Don't you understand? Jack's not *DEAD!*" I screamed that over and over. "He's alive!"

With my mind teetering on the brink, I spied something in the skies above us. I gaped, disbelieving.

Real? *Un*real? Just before oblivion took me down, a mountain of water curled over our heads, racing toward that hell of flames. . . .